TH EDGE CHRONICLES

'Stunningly original' *GUARDIAN*

'Beautifully illustrated' *THE TIMES*

'Entertaining fantasy as its finest' *TES*

www.randomhousechildrens.co.uk

THE
EDGE
IN
THE THIRD AGE OF FLIGHT

NEW HI

THE FARROW
RIDGES

DEE

HIVE

THE MIDWOOD
DECKS

GREAT GLADE

THE EASTERN
WOODS
THE TWILIGHT
WOODS

THE
GORGES

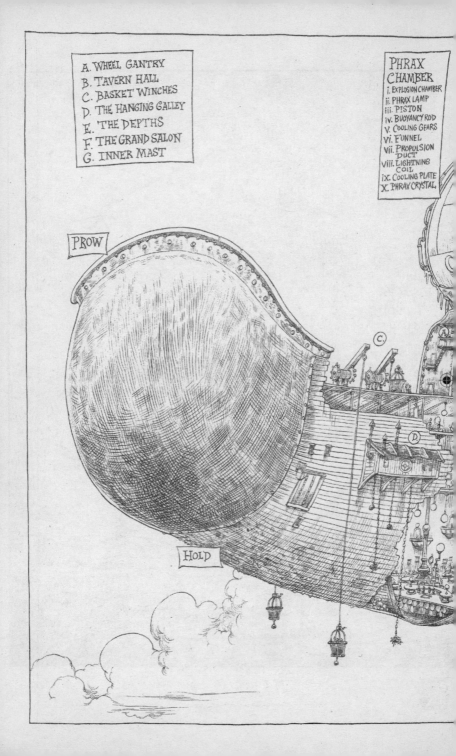

STERN

MIDSHIPS

CABINS

RUDDER

HULL WEIGHTS

THE
XANTH
FILATINE

THE EDGE CHRONICLES

DOOMBRINGER
⊷BOOK 2 OF THE CADE SAGA⊷

STEWART & RIDDELL

CORGI

DOOMBRINGER

A CORGI BOOK 978 0 552 56758 9

First published in Great Britain by Corgi,
an imprint of Random House Children's Publishers UK
A Penguin Random House Company

Corgi edition published 2015

1 3 5 7 9 10 8 6 4 2

Penguin Random House is committed to a sustainable future for our business,
our readers and our planet. This book is made from Forest Stewardship Council®
certified paper.

Set in Palatino

Corgi Books are published by Random House Children's Publishers UK,
61–63 Uxbridge Road, London W5 5SA

www.**randomhousechildrens**.co.uk
www.**totallyrandombooks**.co.uk
www.**randomhouse**.co.uk

Addresses for companies within The Random House Group Limited
can be found at: www.randomhouse.co.uk/offices.htm

THE RANDOM HOUSE GROUP Limited Reg. No. 954009

A CIP catalogue record for this book is available from the British Library.

Printed and bound in the UK by CPI Group (UK) Ltd, Croydon, CR0 4YY

Paul: For Julie
Chris: For Jo

· INTRODUCTION ·

Far far away, jutting out into the emptiness beyond, like the figurehead of a mighty stone ship, is the Edge. A torrent of water pours endlessly over the lip of rock at its overhanging point. This is the Edgewater, a mighty river that crosses from one end of the Edge to the other.

At its source, far to the west, lies Riverrise, the city of night. While to the east, at the very tip of the Edge cliff, where the thunderous waters plunge down into the void, is the mysterious floating city of Sanctaphrax; now a pale shadow of its former glory.

Between Sanctaphrax and Riverrise lies a vast, sprawling landscape, from the muddy wetlands of the Mire to the mist-wreathed barrenness of the Edgeland Pavement; from the eternal golden glow of the Twilight Woods to the inky darkness of the Thorn Forests.

Along with Riverrise, there are two other great cities

that have prospered in this, the Third Age of Flight – Great Glade and Hive. There are smaller towns too: Thorn Harbour and the Midwood Decks, Four Lakes and the Northern Reaches. And then there are the smallest outposts of all – trading stations and mining camps, and isolated supply posts that exist only because they are on the routes of the great skytaverns that crisscross the Edge.

One such a place is the sky-platform at the Farrow Ridges. Passing skytaverns dock there briefly, taking fresh water on board and trading supplies for local produce with its solitary platform-keeper. They don't stay long, for this is a wild, untamed area, with savage hammerhead goblin tribes roaming the forests, and fearsome white trogs said to infest the caverns beneath the ridges.

Yet a few intrepid pioneers have made the Farrow Ridges their home. Individuals who want to put their past behind them and carve out a new life in this beautiful, unspoiled corner of the Edge, with its lake and waterfalls, its untouched forest and rich, fertile land.

In the First Age of Flight, when buoyant rocks kept mighty sky galleons airborne, sky pirates and leaguesmen established the first trade routes across the vastness of the Deepwoods. But then stone-sickness struck and put an end to this age, and tiny skycraft of buoyant sumpwood and spidersilk sails ushered in the Second Age of Flight. Brave librarian knights and other adventurous explorers mapped and gathered information on the many wonders of the Edge.

Then one such academic managed to harness the explosive energy of phrax crystals. It was a discovery that led to the invention of phraxchambers: the artificial flight rocks which power the mighty skytaverns in the Third Age of Flight. Now the skies over the Deepwoods are traversed by such vessels, carrying passengers between the great cities and linking isolated communities like never before.

But with such links come new dangers . . .

The Deepwoods, the Eastern Woods, the Mire and the Edgewater River. Sanctaphrax and Undertown. Great Glade, Riverrise and Hive. The Farrow Ridges. Names on a map.

Yet behind each name lie a thousand tales – tales that have been recorded in ancient scrolls, tales that have been passed down the generations by word of mouth – tales which even now are being told.

What follows is but one of those tales.

· CHAPTER ONE ·

The fishing line looked fine. Untangled. Still weighted deep in the water. All Cade needed now was a bite.

After a hot and cloudless day, the sun was low in the sky. Far off at the southern end of the Farrow Lake, the Five Falls looked like five ribbons of gold fluttering in the late afternoon glow. On either side of the falls, the forest pines were black and jagged against the pale sky.

Cade rested a hand on the side of the coracle, then traced his fingers idly backwards and forwards along its upper edge. The leather pleats beneath his fingertips were satisfyingly smooth and flat.

The little vessel was holding up well. The plaited framework, with its curved strips of water-soaked will-oak, had kept its shape. The black pitch he'd applied to the tilder hide had rendered the little craft both waterproof and buoyant. Now, as he sat out here in the middle of the lake, fishing pole in hand and the early evening

sun warm on his face, the hard work he'd put into making the coracle all seemed worth it.

He peered over the side. The water beneath was still and dark and deep, and full of fish. If only one of them . . . Just one. He wasn't greedy. If only one fish would bite.

Cade sniffed the air. It smelled of lufwood smoke and grilling fish. Over on the east shore, he could just make out the pointed roof of his friend Thorne Lammergyre's hive-hut poking up through the trees. He smiled as he pictured Thorne's wood-burning stove blazing purple, with the flat skillet perched on its top, lakefish sizzling inside it.

Cade owed the fisher goblin so much. Thorne had designed and helped

Cade build a lakeside cabin; he had taught him how to pickle and salt and cure provisions to stock the storeroom beneath it, and he had taken the time to teach him the fine art of coracle construction so that Cade could venture out onto the Farrow Lake on his own to fish.

He glanced at the fishing line. It was motionless. Limp. Unfortunately, not even the fisher goblin could make the lakefish take Cade's hook . . .

Turning away, he looked over his shoulder at the north shore, where his own cabin, with its stone jetty leading down to the lakeside, nestled below a low bluff. A great hulking figure was shambling about at the water's edge, stooping and stamping and waving his arms. It was Tug, a nameless one from the far distant Nightwoods who Cade had adopted – or who had adopted him; he was never sure which. He was playing with a frisky young prowlgrin, Rumblix, the pedigree grey that Cade had raised from a hatchling and that was now almost fully grown. The two of them would be expecting a supper of lakefish.

Cade turned back to his line with a sigh.

A little way off, a pair of lakefowl dabbled. Glitterwings droned from the reed beds. A skein of grey and white plattergeese flew overhead in V-formation, their honking cries, half cough, half yodel, fading into the distance as they passed over the Five Falls – only to be replaced by the far-off boom of a steam klaxon.

Cade looked across the lake to the east, where Gart Ironside's sky-platform towered above the treeline.

Gart must have heard the steam klaxon too, for as Cade peered up, he could just make out the tiny figure of the platform-keeper scurrying here and there, preparing for the imminent arrival of the *Xanth Filatine*, a mighty sky-tavern on its way from Cade's home city of Great Glade. When it arrived, laden with cargo and teeming with passengers, its great funnel billowing ice-cold steam, the skyship would dock briefly at Gart's sky-platform to refill its water tanks and take on supplies before moving on to its destination in the great city of Hive.

The skytavern passed by once every four months, and each time Cade heard its booming klaxon call his stomach churned. For he had enemies aboard the *Xanth Filatine*, and one enemy in particular he hoped he would never run into again . . .

Cade shuddered. The fishing would have to wait. He needed to get off the lake and out of sight before the mighty vessel came into view. He was about to wind in his line when the pole in his hand shuddered, then bowed, and the fishing line went taut.

He'd hooked something. Something big. But before he could begin reeling it in, the pole was torn from his grasp and disappeared into the lake. The coracle pitched and lurched and started bobbing wildly about. Cade gripped the sides of the little boat tightly, breath held. All around him, the water swirled. Large bubbles wobbled up and burst at the surface as a dark shape rose from the depths.

It was huge. Cade caught a glimpse of dark scales, the flash of savage-looking teeth and the glint of a silver eye as the creature neared the surface. It glided underneath the coracle, then circled back round, Cade's fishing pole and line trailing behind it.

It was a snagtooth. It had to be. Cade had never seen one before, but Thorne had warned him about them. Usually they kept to the deepest, darkest places of the lake, lying in wait for plump, unsuspecting lakefish to swim by. But in the early evening, as the light began to fade, snagtooths were liable to stir . . .

In the distance, the boom of the steam klaxon sounded once more. Cade grabbed his oar and started paddling furiously for the shore.

All at once, the great creature broke the surface of the water and reared up. A long snout, fringed with fangs, gaped open as a row of undulating flippers that ran the length of a gnarled and leathery body flexed and thrashed at the air. It spat out the rod and line and lunged at the boat, its fangs glinting and eyes ablaze.

Cade fell back, the oar gripped in his hands.

The snagtooth plunged back down into the water, sending a wave crashing against the side of the tiny coracle, which bucked and rolled precariously.

I've learned my lesson, Cade told himself, gulping mouthfuls of air as he leaned forward and stabbed his oar down into the water. Never again would he go fishing so far out in the lake, not at this time of day. He strained at the oar, pushing the coracle on.

The stone jetty was coming closer. Tug and Rumblix had stopped their game and were looking back at him.

Not much further to go.

But the snagtooth had not given up. It had sensed Cade's fear. Now it wanted blood.

Cade glanced down to see a ridged back, nubbed and pitted, rising up beneath his boat. The next moment, the coracle gave a sickening lurch and tipped right over, throwing him into the roiling water.

Arms flailing, he sank down into the green depths.

This is it, Cade thought. *This is the end . . .*

Suddenly he was grabbed by the shoulder. Cade lashed out wildly, trying to hit the snagtooth that had him in its jaws, but succeeding only in taking in a lungful of lake water as he was pulled up towards the rippling light. At the surface, Cade coughed and spluttered, and found himself being propelled across the lake, away from the bobbing hull of his capsized coracle.

Fighting to catch his breath, he looked back to see the creature, far behind him now, leap up out of the lake. As it crashed back down again, it seized the coracle in its jaws and disappeared beneath the water.

Whatever had hold of him, it wasn't the snagtooth.

His speed began to slow and beneath him Cade saw the glimmer of pebbles. He was in the shallows, not far from the stone jetty of his cabin. His shoulder was released and he fell back, the lake water lapping at his chin.

'Please accept my apologies,' came a soft voice close by his ear. 'That was all my fault.'

· CHAPTER TWO ·

Cade turned. There, sitting back on his haunches in the shallow water, was a webfoot goblin.

'*Your* fault?' said Cade.

The goblin nodded. 'I'm afraid so.' Tall, rangy, with scaly, pale green skin, he had a long face, large triangular ears, droop-lid eyes and a scallop-shaped crest at the top of his head which, as Cade watched, changed colour from bluey-green to a deep pulsating crimson.

'Phineal Glyfphith,' he said, and thrust out a scaly hand.

Cade shook the webfoot goblin's hand and, expecting it to feel like the fish it resembled, was surprised by how warm and soft it was.

'Cade,' he said. 'Cade Quarter.'

The goblin climbed to his feet and splashed over to the shore. Cade followed, noticing the goblin's large flat feet with the webbed skin between the splayed toes, and the

long curved spikes that protruded from the backs of his ankles. He took note of the snailskin tunic and patched breeches the goblin wore, and the various tools and decorations that adorned his body. There was a string of shells around his neck. Hooks, jag-blade knives and a barbed spear hung at his belt, along with a heavy-looking stone with a hole at its centre that was attached to a length of coiled rope tied around his waist. On his back was a forage-sack that bulged with contents Cade couldn't even guess at . . .

'That's where you live?' Phineal was saying.

Cade looked up. Phineal was staring at his cabin, a little way along the shore.

'I built it myself,' said Cade, a note of pride creeping into his voice. 'With a little help,' he added.

Phineal nodded. 'We webfoots also construct our buildings on stilts,' he said approvingly. 'In case of flooding.'

The crest on his head shifted through colours from orange to yellow to green. His scaly brow furrowed into a frown.

'I owe you an explanation, Cade Quarter,' the webfoot said seriously. 'You see, I was down on the lake bed doing some fishing myself, when I saw your line. So I did what I always do for fellow fisherfolk – I placed one of my catch on your hook . . .'

The goblin's crest turned from green to blue.

'Unfortunately, I only spotted the snagtooth when it was too late. It appeared out of nowhere and swallowed

the fish whole, taking your hook with it. And that must
have whetted its appetite, because when it spotted your
coracle, it went wild. There was no stopping it.'

The webfoot goblin paused, his crest flashing from
blue to purple. He was staring at something back along
the shore, and Cade turned to see Rumblix and Tug
coming towards them.
The prowlgrin was
bounding   ahead
with Tug lumbering
behind him.

'It's all right,'
Cade reassured
Phineal, whose
crest was now
shimmering errati-
cally. 'They're harmless.
Rumblix   is   my
prowlgrin. And
the other one is
called Tug.'

Even   as   he
spoke, though, Cade found himself seeing Tug the
way the webfoot must be seeing him – the way *he*
himself had first seen him when Tug had emerged
from the forest on the night of the great storm. The
powerfully built body, with those long arms, and fists
like boulders that looked capable of crushing you with a
single blow. The misshapen head. The jutting brows and

skull ridge. The tiny deep-set eyes. The crooked fang-studded jaw . . .

And yet that wasn't how Cade saw him now. Tug was kind and hard-working and loyal. Tug was his friend.

'I've seen such creatures before,' Phineal said, his voice a low sibilant whisper. 'They live in the Nightwoods, where they're enslaved by the red and black dwarves. They call them nameless ones.'

Rumblix reached them and, after giving Cade a slob-bery lick on the hand, began sniffing tentatively around the goblin's ankles. Phineal stroked the prowlgrin's back, but his eyes remained fixed on the nameless one plodding towards him.

'Well, I gave this nameless one a name,' said Cade, stepping forward and resting a hand on Tug's arm as he stopped beside him.

'Tug, Phineal,' said Cade. 'Phineal, Tug.'

Phineal nodded. He didn't offer a hand in greeting, but his crest flashed a pale crimson colour. Tug shuffled from foot to foot, his small dark eyes flashing from Cade to the webfoot goblin and back again. Phineal slipped the forage-sack from his shoulders and reached inside, and for a moment, Cade feared that he might be going for a weapon of some kind. But instead, when he withdrew his hands, Phineal was holding two large, plump lakefish.

'I can't replace your coracle,' he said, turning to Cade, his crest a soft shade of orange, 'but I can provide us all with supper. If you provide a cooking fire.'

Cade happily agreed and the two of them headed

along the shore towards the cabin.

Tug and Rumblix remained behind at the water's edge, the nameless one hunkered down eating feather-reeds while Rumblix scampered about, giving playful chase to the lakefowl. The sun had slipped down behind the horizon and lumines-cent flameflies flickered and danced against the orange sky.

'Welcome to my home, Phineal,' Cade said.

He lifted the latch, pushed open the door and ushered the webfoot inside. As he followed him in, Cade noticed how different the *slip-slap* of Phineal's bare feet was to the echoing *clomp-clomp* of his own boots. It was dark inside and he lit the table lamp, bathing

the cabin with soft, golden light – the sleeping-quarters to their left, with his buoyant sumpwood bed swaying gently next to an open window; the living area, with its rough-hewn table, stools and bench, and the kitchen to the right, complete with fireplace, stove and washbowl.

'Make yourself at home,' said Cade. 'I shan't be a moment.'

Lighting a second lamp, he ducked through the door next to the fireplace, went down the stairs on the other side and into the storeroom. Cade had been working hard, and the place was satisfyingly well stocked with provisions that he'd gathered over the preceding months – and that he hoped would last him for several months to come.

Shelves bowed under the weight of boxes of oak-apples, crates of woodpears, earthenware pots of jugged woodfowl and barrels of saltroot, pickled blue-cabbage and rock-whelks in brine – as well as a series of pitchers of winesap in various stages of fermentation. Burlap sacks stood in a line along the base of the far wall. Each one was bulging. There were dried herbs, barley-rice, and beck-lentils; tagberries and peppercorns, and flour that Cade had ground himself. Above them, suspended from a row of hooks, were tied-up bunches of nibblick and glimmer-onions, dried pipefish and tanglecarp, and a gleaming flitch of smoked tilder.

Cade gathered up some herbs, glimmer-onions and beck-lentils, and a pitcher of the winesap that his nose told him was ready to drink. Arms full, he returned upstairs to find Phineal busy gutting and cleaning the lakefish on the table.

Just then, the echoing boom of the skytavern echoed across the lake. Cade had forgotten all about it. He hurried to the window to see the *Xanth Filatine* docking at Gart Ironside's platform-tower, and shivered.

Phineal followed his gaze. 'A skytavern,' he said, and Cade could hear the bitterness in his voice. 'My home in the Four Lakes changed for ever the day skytaverns started to arrive.'

· CHAPTER THREE ·

As the jet of white flame shut off at the propulsion duct, the *Xanth Filatine* came to a standstill. With a slight tremor, the skytavern hovered some twenty or so strides above the trees, the vast hull and phraxchamber dwarfing the towering ironwood pines beneath, and making even the distant Five Falls look small and insignificant. The steam that poured from its funnel, stained purple by the remnants of sunset, billowed like storm clouds.

Dazzling hull-lamps came on, lighting up the vessel. Crew members were busy on the decks, while passengers were spectating, draped over deck-rails, clustered at viewing-platforms, or with their heads poking out of the rows of portholes. Then the lamps were realigned until they were shining down on the treetops and the wooden sky-platform that rose above them, illuminating a modest cabin, a tethered phraxlighter, a stack of crates and an

20

over-sized water tank, beside which the tall, thick-set figure of the platform-keeper was standing.

In a rising swirl of glittering steam, the skytavern began to descend. It came lower, slowly, then ground to a halt when the hull-weights grazed the uppermost leaves. Tolley-ropes appeared at jutting lower-deck gantries at the prow, midships and stern, and uncurled as they dropped. Crew members slid down them, secured the ends to the upper branches of the trees then scrambled back on board.

The platform-keeper, Gart Ironside, was waiting. One hand was pressed against the side of the water tank, the other raised to his forehead, shielding his eyes from the glare of the hull-lamps as he peered up at the sky-tavern. Nets appeared over the side, bulging with sacks and boxes and, raking his fingers through his thick black hair, Gart strode across to the stack of crates beside the phraxlighter.

The net swung close. Gart grabbed hold, eased it down onto the wooden boards, then opened it up and removed the contents, stacking the sacks and boxes of provisions next to the wall of the cabin. In return, he took two of his own crates and loaded them into the net. Then he reached up and tugged the rope twice. The net lifted off the platform and was winched up to the skytavern.

With the words *Trade Goods – G. Ironside* scrawled on the wooden sides in red leadwood pencil, the crates contained the fruits of Gart's labour for the past four months. Lemkin pelts. Pinewood resin. Fire crystals . . .

Small items of high value that Gart had managed to col-
lect without ever having to leave his phraxlighter
and set foot on the ground – items that ensured
that the platform-keeper was provided with
more than just the basics.
After all, it was a harsh
and solitary existence
he led up on the sky-
platform – one that
was made more
bearable by the
occasional
crate of

winesap or sack of strong, aromatic oakwood tea.

When the last of the cargo had been exchanged and
the nets withdrawn, Gart opened the top of the water
tank, then stood back. He looked up expectantly, wincing
into the bright light that turned his sallow skin to burnished silver.

Moments later, a long flexible pipe was lowered

towards him from a hatch in the midships. Swaying like the trunk of a giant fromp sniffing out barkbugs, the pipe spiralled down through the air. Gart seized it in both hands and thrust the end down into the water tank. From above, a plume of vapour rose from a short funnel that jutted out from the hull as a steam-pump juddered into action, followed by a tremor that ran the length of the pipe as water was sucked up from the tank and into the reservoirs in the bowels of the skytavern.

Further along the ship, some of the wealthier passengers of the *Xanth Filatine* were taking advantage of the stop at this distant outpost of the Deepwoods. There were mine-owners and merchants in heavy leather longcoats, together with their wives, dressed in quilted satin jackets and fur mufflers, and weaving excitedly in and out of them were numerous children, all bundled up in clothes that kept out the evening chill. In groups of eight, they were taking turns to step into the viewing baskets. As their gloved hands gripped the sides of the plaited wicker, they were winched down to the tops of the trees – then plunged deeper still into the forest itself.

Fingers pointed and arms waved in excitement as the folk from the big cities experienced the Deepwoods for the first time in their lives. Guides in sky-blue top-coats and conical hats consulted their notebooks as they explained to the passengers where they were and what dangers lurked in the surrounding forest, the pages fluttering in the gathering wind.

Back on the sky-platform, Gart Ironside attended to his work. He had heard the litany many times before – about how bleak and inhospitable the area was; how the woods were rife with savage hammerhead goblin tribes and the caverns behind the Five Falls were infested by terrifying white trogs. Only the most desperate or fool-hardy would risk setting foot in such a place . . .

The sudden slackening of the water pipe announced that the tank had been drained. Gart pulled the pipe free and watched it being hauled back up to the hovering skyship and disappear inside.

The basket winches were raised, and the groups of sightseeing passengers climbed back on deck, chattering excitedly to one another. The steam-klaxon boomed – once, twice, three times – and the vessel rose slowly into the air, leaving the sky-platform behind. Then, when even the lowest hull-weight was at least twelve strides clear of the highest trees, there was a flash and a loud roaring, a jet of white-hot air exploded from the propulsion duct at the back of the phraxchamber – and the *Xanth Filatine* sailed off into the dark night.

Cade stood rooted to the spot, the spyglass raised to his eye. He watched the skytavern until it was no more than a fuzzy ball of light, then returned the spyglass to the top pocket of his jacket. He felt uneasy. With skytaverns constantly crisscrossing the Edgelands, it was difficult these days to hide yourself away, no matter how isolated a place you chose to make your home.

And the beautiful Farrow Lake certainly was isolated. Its only connection with the world Cade had left behind was the sky-platform before him, one of hundreds of lonely outposts that existed only to supply the passing skytaverns on their flights between the great cities.

Cade had been a city boy once, growing up in the brash, bustling melting-pot that was Great Glade. But no longer. He'd fled the city in fear for his life, stowing away on the *Xanth Filatine* to escape his father's murderers, henchmen of the powerful Professor of Flight, Quove Lentis. Cade had intended to start a new life in the mighty city of Hive, far away from the professor's clutches, but it hadn't turned out that way.

He shuddered as he remembered the sinister figure

he'd run into on board the skytavern, a gangmaster by the name of Drax Adereth. He could picture him now, the white skin, the spiked hair in needle-like points, the large pale eyes staring from behind tinted goggles; and the breath, tainted with the smell of fish and sour milk.

The gangmaster had got his claws into Cade and forced him to do his bidding. There had been no choice – not if Cade wanted to keep his fingers from joining the severed ones that Adereth kept in a bowl in his lair in the depths of the skytavern.

Then, to his horror, Cade had learned that the gangmaster was yet another of the high professor's cronies. There had seemed to be no escape. Up at the ship's prow, Cade had seen Adereth casually murder two of Quove Lentis's enemies, and Cade himself would have been just as casually murdered if he hadn't leaped from the tavern, not a moment too soon . . .

Now, here he was, on the shores of the beautiful Farrow Lake, far away from the murderous machinations of the High Professor of Flight. And that, he thought, was the way he wanted it to stay.

· CHAPTER FOUR ·

Cade turned from the window. Phineal was standing at the stove, the lamplight playing on his scaly features as he prodded the four pieces of sizzling fish turning golden brown in the skillet, then stirred the pot of bubbling lentils and glimmer-onions.

'It smells good,' Cade said.

Phineal stepped over to the table, the top of his crest almost touching the ceiling. He picked up a knife and began scraping the mess of guts, skin and fish heads left over from the filleting of the two lakefish into a wooden bowl. He held the bowl up to Cade.

'At the four lakes, we feed these to the lake-eels we cultivate in the eel-corrals,' Phineal said, his crest rippling green then yellow. 'I don't suppose . . . ?'

Cade smiled. 'I've got a better idea,' he said, taking the bowl and walking out onto the veranda.

Standing at the top of the steps that led down to the

jetty, he saw Tug and Rumblix. The pair of them were still both down by the shoreline.

'Over here, you two!' Cade called.

They looked up and sniffed the air. Cade held up the bowl, then descended the steps as they came running. Rumblix got there first.

'Here we are, boy,' said Cade, scooping the innards out onto the stone of the jetty.

Purring loudly, Rumblix began slurping at the slimy fish guts with his tongue. The purring grew louder as Cade continued to scoop, until only the two large fish heads and tail fins were left in the bowl.

'And for you,' said Cade, as Tug loped up towards him.

He handed him the

bowl. Tug sniffed at its contents carefully. His small eyes widened.

'Tug like,' he grunted in that gruff guttural way he had. 'Good. Taste good.'

Cade reached out and patted the creature's massive forearm.

Tug was certainly primitive, one of the strange and nameless life-forms that inhabited the Nightwoods – and yet, it seemed to Cade, his friend was developing and learning new skills almost daily. Tug's language had grown richer, his use of tools had become more sophisticated as he helped Cade tend their garden, and his tastes had widened. At first, Tug had grazed only on sweet meadowgrass; then on the woodbeets, glimmer-onions and other vegetables that Cade had introduced him to. And now, for the last month or so, fish. Or their heads at least, which had become his favourite delicacy.

Head down, Tug shuffled underneath the veranda. He sat down heavily in his bed of meadowgrass and began nibbling on the

lakefish tails with unlikely delicacy, before pushing the fish heads into his mouth and crunching down on them with obvious relish.

Cade left the two of them to their meals and returned to the cabin. The smell of the frying fish was mouth-watering.

Phineal turned to him. 'Nearly ready,' he said.

'Excellent,' said Cade. 'I'm famished.' He picked up the pitcher and filled two wooden goblets to the brim, then carried one across to Phineal.

Phineal raised the goblet to his nose and sniffed. His crest flashed dark purple. 'What is it?' he said.

'Winesap,' said Cade. 'I made it myself,' he added proudly. 'Picked the sapgrapes from wild vines, pressed them, set the juice to ferment . . .'

'If it's all the same to you, I'll just have water,' said Phineal.

'Oh,' said Cade, disappointed.

'We webfoots drink little else,' Phineal added, sensing that disappointment.

Setting the pitcher aside, Cade took a jug from the cupboard and filled it with rainwater from the water butt outside. He poured the winesap back into the pitcher and refilled the goblets from the jug. Then he drained the lentils and ladled steaming portions into two bowls. Beside him, Phineal had removed the skillet from the heat, and was sliding two pieces of the golden-brown fish onto each of the two waiting platters. The pair of them carried the food over to the table and sat down opposite one another.

'To fine food and better company,' said Cade, echoing something his friend, Thorne Lammergyre, would always say when they had supper together.

Phineal raised his goblet of rainwater and smiled, the scales at the corners of his mouth forming tiny corrugations as he did so. 'I'll drink to that,' he said.

Cade picked up his fork, speared a chunk of the golden fish and ate it. Opposite him, Phineal's fork remained untouched. Instead, the webfoot broke off a little piece of fish with his hands, added a small portion of lentils and onions, then, using the tips of his fingers, rolled the whole lot together into a ball, which he flicked into his mouth with his thumb.

He caught Cade looking at him and smiled. 'Not bad, eh?' he said.

Cade nodded, chewing slowly. He frowned. 'What *is* that taste?' he said. 'Sort of peppery . . .'

'That's the lake moss,' said Phineal. 'It grows in deep water,' he explained, resting an elbow on the table. 'I picked it myself in that beautiful lake of yours. Back home we webfoots chop it up and use it to season our food.' He paused, his crest flickering pale green. 'You like it?'

'It's delicious,' said Cade, taking another chunk of fish along with a spoonful of the beck-lentils. 'I've never tasted anything quite like it.'

'There are great carpets of lake moss in your lake,' Phineal said. 'As well as glistening forests of rock-sage, water fennel, sweet-root kelp – all delicious to eat. Not to mention the lakefish . . .' The webfoot's crest glowed orange with excitement. 'I've never seen such a variety. Sticklefronts, sideswimmers, lantern-eyes . . . Just like the four lakes before . . .' Phineal's eyes glazed over and his crest dimmed to a dull grey colour.

Cade leaned forward. 'Before what?' he said softly, then remembered the webfoot's words at the window earlier. 'Before the skytaverns came?'

Phineal nodded, small ripples of blue and green pulsing across his crest.

Cade hesitated, his loaded fork poised close to his mouth.

Phineal sat back on the stool, his large hands resting on his thighs. 'Where to begin?' he said. 'One skytavern came. Then another, and another. More and more of them, more and more often. They brought traders who sold us things we didn't need; that we had done without for hundreds of years, but that our young'uns began to crave. Velvet topcoats, crushed funnel hats, floating sumpwood furniture, hive-ware pots and glade-enamel vases . . .' He reached up and tugged at one of his large triangular ears. 'The old ways began to be lost. After all, why learn how to weave eel-corrals; why learn the skills of clam-tending, or snailskin-curing, or stilt-hut construction – or any of the other traditions that make us webfoots webfoots? Why learn any of this when you can get everything from a passing skyship in exchange for a lake pearl?'

The webfoot's crest was shifting colour, from indigo to purple and back again, flashes of white and yellow splashing against the quill-like membrane.

'That's all the young webfoots cared about. Harvesting lake-pearls and selling them to the skytavern traders, to build and furnish ever more lavish lakeside mansions. The four lakes – the Silent One, the Shimmerer, the Lake of Cloud, and my own home lake, the Mirror of the Sky; one by one, they began to change. The shores became crowded with new buildings. The eel-corrals silted up and the lake fish grew fewer in number as the vegetation died back.'

He shook his head.

'Finally, even the most short-sighted of us knew this had to stop. So the council of the webfoot tribes decided to ban the skytaverns and to end the trade in lake-pearls, in order to allow the lakes to be tended properly once more. And to recover.'

'And did they?' asked Cade, putting down his fork. 'Did the four lakes recover?'

Phineal stared down at his feet, the enormous toes splayed wide, the web between each one pulled taut, then creasing as they twitched. For a long time, he didn't speak, and as Cade watched the webfoot's emotions registering on his crest – dark, brooding purples and blues – he began to realize the answer to his question.

'The skytaverns left and didn't come back, and the four lakes did begin to recover,' said Phineal at last. His voice was hushed but hard. 'But . . . but then they *did* return – and with mire-pearlers on board. Gangs of armed toughs, recruited from the dregs of the great cities by rich and

powerful merchants to do their bidding. They ransacked and pillaged our settlements to get their hands on the pearls we had nurtured and harvested. And not content with that, they attacked the clam beds themselves.'

Phineal was sitting forward now, his elbows on his knees and his crest flashing. His fists clenched and his expression darkened.

'We tried to fight back. But the mire-pearlers had phraxmuskets and phraxcannon. With our throwing nets and harpoons, we didn't stand a chance.' He banged a fist down hard on the table. 'Our finest warriors were defeated and the council had no choice but to sue for peace.'

He fell still, but his body was taut. And as for his crest, it was flashing so fast and furious now that the colours were a blur. Cade swallowed, uncertain what to say.

'The mire-pearlers had brought phraxengineers with them,' Phineal continued. 'Professors from the Cloud Quarter of Great Glade.'

Cade reddened. His own father had been a professor at the Great Glade Academy – a phraxengineer. Cade had his father's scrolls of working drawings pinned to the wall above the mantelpiece. They were all he had left to remember him by.

'These engineers,' Phineal went on. 'They dammed our lakes, drained them of half their water, then used phrax-explosives to blast their way into the clam beds.' Phineal's voice choked. 'Only when they had extracted every last pearl, and the Great Blueshell Clam was dead, did they finally leave for good.'

The webfoot breathed in. He surveyed Cade calmly, his anger seemingly spent.

'Those were dark, dark days. Eventually, with work and care, we managed to repair the worst of the damage. But the clams have never returned,' he added bleakly. 'Nor will they. Instead of traders and mire-pearlers, the skytaverns now bring settlers. To Four Lakes. A name on a map. These days its shores are home to goblins, waifs, trogs and fourthlings from all over the Edge. It has become a bustling city in its own right.' He sighed. 'And yet . . . And yet . . . Without phrax and the so-called Third Age of Flight, the four lakes would still be . . .' His crest trembled and turned a pulsating rosy-orange. 'A paradise.'

He climbed to his feet and crossed to the door. He opened it and stood there, feet splayed and hands gripping the doorframe, as he looked out.

'Just like here.'

Cade pushed back his chair and joined him. The pair of them stepped outside onto the veranda.

The wind had dropped, the clouds had cleared and the stars in the sky were like sparkling marsh-gems on a blanket of black satin. There was the whoop and chitter of night creatures, the gentle roar of the distant Five Falls, and the sound of soft snoring as Rumblix and Tug slept beneath the cabin in their nest of meadowgrass.

Phineal was right, Cade thought, as the pair of them

stared out across the dark waters of the lake. The Farrow Ridges *was* a paradise.

Of course, with the wild hammerhead tribes in the surrounding forest, and the bloodthirsty white trogs in the caverns behind the falls, the Farrow Ridges had earned the reputation of being a dangerous and barbaric backwater – a reputation his friend, Gart Ironside, was only too happy to play up, embellishing the gruesome tales each time the *Xanth Filatine* docked at his sky-platform.

'You love Farrow Lake, don't you, Cade Quarter?' said Phineal quietly.

As Cade looked across the still water, out of the corner of his eye, he saw the webfoot's crest glowing a warm reddish-orange.

'I do,' said Cade.

'Then tomorrow,' said Phineal, 'there is something I must show you.'

· CHAPTER FIVE ·

Cade sat up in his sumpwood bed. Beyond the window the new day was dawning. The stars were gone, and to the east the horizon was stained pink and orange with the first feathery blush of the coming sun.

Phineal was sitting at the end of the jetty, his webbed feet dangling in the water as he stared out across the lake. His conical snailskin tent was pitched at the water's edge a little way off. Rumblix was sniffing at its hem, his tail trembling, while Tug, knee-deep in lakegrass, looked on.

Cade pulled on his homespun breeches and padded out onto the veranda. The ironwood planks were cold beneath his feet.

'Morning, Phineal,' he greeted the webfoot goblin. 'Would you care for some breakfast?'

'That sounds good,' said Phineal, climbing to his feet and motioning to Cade to follow him to his tent. 'But first, I propose we go for an early morning swim. As I said last

night, there's something I want to show you.'

The sun had risen above the jagged treeline of the Farrow Ridges and was glinting on the still waters of the lake. Yet as Cade went down the wooden steps and along the stone jetty, he shivered.

A swim? Yesterday he had almost been devoured by a snagtooth, and Phineal was proposing they go for a swim?

Cade jumped down from the end of the jetty onto the lakeshore. The sand was soft between his toes. Rumblix trotted over to him, whiplash tail a blur, and licked his outstretched hands. Tug lumbered over, his hands full of lakegrass, which he was stuffing into his mouth and slowly chewing. Phineal ducked inside his tent and, a few moments later, emerged with a forage-sack, which he emptied onto the ground.

'A swim?' said Cade. 'I'm not sure . . .'

He looked at the items Phineal had spread out at his feet. Fish-hooks, barbed harpoons, a long rope, a small net, a stoppered copperwood pot, a leather gourd with a flexible tube attached to a mask that had glass eye-panels set into it; and a pair of mats that were triangular, made of plaited glade-grass, and had looped raffia straps attached to them. Then, almost as an afterthought, the webfoot untied the ring-shaped stone from his waist and laid it down next to the rest.

'What are all these things?' Cade asked.

'Well, these are for you, Cade Quarter,' said Phineal, picking up the copperwood pot and unscrewing the lid.

'So you can accompany me on a swim to the bottom of the lake . . .'

'The bottom of the lake!' exclaimed Cade. 'But how?'

Phineal tipped up the pot, counted out half a dozen shrivelled brown mushrooms into the palm of his hand and dropped them into the gourd.

'We webfoots call these fenniths,' said Phineal. 'They're a type of water mushroom that live in the shallows of the Shimmerer – the lake of the tusked webfoots, who harvest and trade them. They taste delicious.' He smiled. 'But they also have this strange property that makes them invaluable for any visiting outlakers who wish to swim with us. Watch this.'

Wading into the lake, Phineal scooped up a single handful of water and poured it into the gourd. From inside, there came a soft fizzing noise. Phineal rammed a cork stopper down the neck of the gourd and shook the whole lot vigorously.

Slowly, the creased leather began to smooth and go taut. The gourd was being inflated from inside. After a couple of moments, Phineal flicked it with a finger. The sound was hard and hollow, like a drum.

'Trust me,' the webfoot told Cade, who was looking at the gourd with a mixture of fascination and unease. He picked up the two glade-grass mats. 'These go on your feet.'

Cade slipped his feet through the looped straps.

'This goes on your back,' Phineal continued and, adjusting the straps of the gourd, helped Cade slip it

into place. Next, he picked up the heavy stone and used
the tether line to secure it round Cade's waist. 'This is
my anchor stone,' he said. 'Every webfoot has one. We
use them to help us keep our bearings when lakes are
muddy and visibility is low. But in your case . . . well,
you'll see.' Then he took hold of the mask which, Cade
saw, was attached to the end of the long thin pipe that
stuck out of the front of the gourd. 'And this,' he said,
giving it to Cade, 'goes on your face.'

As Phineal secured the mask
tightly to Cade's head, Cade was
astonished to find his mouth fill
with cool, mint-scented air.
He sucked it deep down into
his lungs. It was the sweetest,
freshest air he thought he'd ever
breathed.

'All right?' said Phineal.

'Think so,' said Cade, his voice
muffled inside the mask. 'But
what about the snagtooths?'

Phineal's crest glowed
a cool blue as he smiled.
'Don't worry about them,
Cade Quarter,' he
said. 'The sun's up.
They'll be fast asleep.
Now, follow me.' He waded out into the lake. 'And just
keep breathing normally.'

Leaving Rumblix and Tug watching from the shore, Cade followed the webfoot goblin. And when, with the water up around his chest, the webfoot kicked off and disappeared down below the surface of the water, so did he.

For a moment, Cade felt disorientated. It didn't feel right being under the water. He should be spluttering, gasping for breath, and he had to remind himself to do what the webfoot had told him. Keep breathing normally.

Breathe in . . . Breathe out . . . In. Out. Simple as that.

Phineal turned towards him and raised the palms of his hands questioningly. And Cade nodded back.

He was fine.

Phineal swam off again. Able to breathe water like air, the webfoot swam effortlessly, his body rippling up and down as his huge flat webbed feet propelled him forward. His arms trailed at his sides, hands acting as rudders.

Cade tried his best to keep up, but it wasn't easy – and it certainly wasn't effortless. The glade-grass flippers worked well enough, but compared to Phineal's flipper-like feet, they were ungainly. Unlike the webfoot, Cade had to make use of his arms, pushing back the water with cupped hands as best he could. And as for Phineal's rippling body motion, Cade was incapable of copying it.

Despite all this, as he followed the webfoot down deeper still, Cade began to enjoy the sensation of swimming underwater. Beneath him, the gentle incline dropped away and he found himself swimming over a great chasm. It was like flying. Kicking his legs and sweeping back his arms, he swooped down after Phineal through the crystal-clear water, the heavy stone around his middle helping to counter the buoyancy of the air-gourd on his back.

A cloud of tiny silver fish, thousands in number, swam from left to right, then, as one, switched direction, then switched direction again, like sheets of silk flapping in the wind. Gelatinous mushroom-shaped creatures with long, trailing tentacles glided past. A column of blotch-red henchpike with backspines and jutting lower jaws approached, then swerved away, their mouths opening and closing.

The deeper they went, the darker it became. The water was clear still, but it was as though it had been dyed blue-green, the colour growing more intense as they approached the lake bed. When Cade breathed out, tiny bubbles escaped from a valve in the mask and rose through the water like constellations of shimmering stars.

It was eerily silent down in the shadowy depths. The floor was covered with a jumble of rocks and boulders, their surfaces encrusted with lake-coral, feather-anemones and fire-crustacea that turned the drab stone into a riot of colour. Clumps of waterweed, from sleek tongue-like ribbons to iridescent turquoise fronds, swayed in the water's ebb and flow.

Cade was spellbound. So many times he'd sat at the end of his jetty looking out across the lake, never for a moment imagining the splendour of what lay below. It was as though he'd entered a different world.

Just then, out of the corner of his eye, he caught sight of two large sleek creatures with long snouts and leathery ridged backs, fringed with undulating paddle-like fins, lurking in among the watergrass on the lake bed. Cade's heart missed a beat.

Snagtooths.

Terrified, he looked wildly around, only for Phineal to place a reassuring hand on his arm. The webfoot pointed at the snagtooths, and Cade saw that they were motion-less, their heavy-lidded eyes closed.

Phineal beckoned, then turned and swam away, kicking out with his feet in slow, steady strokes. Cade followed him, not daring to look back. The water became colder and currents grew strong. They plucked at his legs and buffeted his side. And when Phineal, arms and legs splayed, came to a halt again, it was all Cade could do to remain hovering in the same spot beside him.

The webfoot pointed downwards with a scaly green finger. Cade frowned. He seemed to be drawing his attention to a shell.

Greyish blue, rooted to the rocks and the size of a two-glader coin, it didn't look particularly impressive. Was this what Phineal had brought him down here to see? Cade looked more closely. The shell was deep ridged, he noted, and pitted, and in the slight gap between the two halves of the shell he could see the rippling orange frill of the creature inside.

He looked round at Phineal, who smiled and nodded,

then pointed to a second shell. And a third. And then to a cluster of ten or twelve a little further on.

Cade peered through the glass panels of his facemask as he and Phineal swam forward. Ahead of them, he saw that the shells grew both in number and in size, until the entire floor of the lake was covered. And between the shells, joining all of them together, was a tracery of bright blue filaments that pulsed as they glowed.

These must be blueshell clams, Cade realized. Thousands of them.

He followed the glowing filaments, swimming beside Phineal over the crowded clam beds. The strands thickened and interlinked, converging on one point in the very centre of the lake, where a huge boulder loomed in the glowing blue light. Ten times the size of Cade's cabin, it was encrusted with lake-whelks and barnacles, and festooned with fronds of lakeweed and ribbons of kelp.

As they drew closer, Cade saw that it wasn't a boulder at all, but a colossal clam, bigger by far than all the others. The two huge halves of the shell were almost closed, the ridged line between them open just enough for the orange frill of the clam's body to spill out and ripple up and down in the chill current.

Cade felt a hand on his shoulder. It was Phineal. He pointed to the gourd on Cade's back, which was slack now, the air inside it almost all used up. Tearing his attention away from the glowing clam beds, Cade reluctantly followed the webfoot as he kicked for the surface.

As they rose, it got lighter, warmer. Then, with a splash, their heads burst through into the bright late-morning air far above.

Cade pulled the mask from his face and, treading water, turned to Phineal. 'That clam,' he said. 'It was magnificent.'

Phineal nodded, his crest a dark brooding red. 'The presence of such a blueshell clam in the Farrow Lake is a great gift, Cade Quarter,' he said. 'But also a great danger.'

· CHAPTER SIX ·

How did it go again? Cade went over the chant in his head – the chant that every young Great Glader who had gone through the junior academies of the Cloud Quarter had to recite before dawn class.

Caterbird, Sanctaphrax rock, Great Blueshell Clam,
From Sky and Earth and Water come;
First seeds of life; three Ancient Ones,
Brought from Open Sky by the Mother Storm.

Even now, Cade could hear the chirpy little voices of his classmates as they had chanted the words together. They knew that it was something to do with how life had started in the Edge, but at that time, none of them had really understood what they were saying.

Cade had never encountered a caterbird. The fabled creature began life as a glowing worm that fed on the leaves of lullabee trees, before spinning a cocoon and hatching out as a magnificent crested black and white bird – a bird which, it was said, shared the thoughts of all other caterbirds, both past and present.

The Sanctaphrax rock – that great floating stone, with the ancient city built upon it, and the mighty anchor chain fixing it to the ground – was a different matter. Though Cade hadn't seen it either, he knew all about it, for the rise and fall of the great city of Sanctaphrax was a major part of the history of the Edge, and he had learned all about it in class.

Back in the First Age of Flight, the city had been the centre of science and learning. But when the Mother Storm had returned, threatening to destroy the rock, the chain that held it in place had been cut – and Sanctaphrax had sailed away. Lost. But not for ever.

For it had returned.

Rumours of the fabled floating rock's reappearance had reached Great Glade decades earlier, together with stories of Sanctaphrax being resettled by the poor and the dispossessed from all over the Edgelands. And by descenders.

Descenders were intrepid explorers who climbed down the Edge cliff itself into the inky blackness that lay beneath. This scandalized the academics of Great Glade and was condemned as heresy by the High Professor of Flight, Quove Lentis, who forbade all contact with the city and its new inhabitants. Yet, despite this, the city continued to attract those eager to descend.

Unfortunately for Cade's father, Thadeus, the first and most famous of these descenders was his half-brother, Nate Quarter. He had disappeared into the darkness on his last epic descent before Cade was even born. Then, fourteen years later, news of his return had reached Great Glade, triggering a purge of the academy by Quove Lentis.

Thadeus Quarter's name had been the first name on the high professor's list. Cade's had been the second. His father had never shared Nate's views on descending.

Not that that had saved him . . .

Skytaverns didn't go to Sanctaphrax, and the journey there by other means was treacherous. But even so, Cade dreamed of visiting the floating city one day and meeting the great Nate Quarter for himself.

The caterbird. The Sanctaphrax rock. And then there was the third Ancient One – the Great Blueshell Clam . . .

When Phineal had told him of the destruction of the blueshell clams in the four lakes, Cade was deeply saddened but not surprised. Clams had been gathered for the pearls they contained by Great Glade merchants for centuries, from the steam-pools of the Mire to the wind-canyons of the Northern Reaches, and with little thought to the effect that might have. Only now was Cade beginning to understand just how devastating this mire-pearl trade was to the communities of the Edgelands. His head buzzed with questions.

'Phineal,' he said, his brow furrowed and voice

questioning. 'About this clam. How . . .'

But Phineal raised a hand and his crest turned a shade of indigo that Cade was beginning to recognize was the webfoot's response to potential danger. He was looking over Cade's shoulder, his hooded eyes narrowed as he stared off along the shoreline.

Cade turned to see a distant figure approaching along the lakeside. It was his friend Celestia riding her prowl-grin, Calix. Cade smiled. Celestia lived with her explorer father, the former skyship-builder, Blatch Helmstoft, out in the Western Woods in what the pair of them called the 'tree-cabin' – a description totally inadequate for the magnificent three-storey mansion that was suspended from the branch of a mighty ironwood pine.

'Who is that?' Phineal asked, watching warily as Celestia and Calix came closer.

'That's Celestia Helmstoft,' Cade said. 'We were meant to be going on a ride this morning, but . . .' He frowned. 'She hasn't brought a second prowlgrin with her for me to ride.'

'Please, Cade Quarter.' Phineal's crest flashed ominously. 'Promise me you won't say anything about the clam.'

'But . . . but Celestia's my friend,' Cade protested. 'And she loves the Farrow Lake as much as I do—'

'I'm sure,' Phineal broke in. 'I trusted you because you showed me hospitality, Cade Quarter. Now you must trust me. Nobody must know about the presence of the Great Blueshell Clam – not even your friends – until I'm

able to organize its protection. Promise me you won't say anything.'

The webfoot was clearly agitated. He was blinking furiously, and his crest trembled as it flashed. And when he dropped to his knees and began shoving his belongings into the forage-sack, Cade realized that it was pointless trying to persuade the webfoot that Celestia was trustworthy.

'I promise,' he said.

The approaching prowlgrin was galloping, his paws pounding over the compacted gravel of the lakeshore. Celestia's long black hair streamed back behind her as, gripping the reins with one hand, she raised the other and waved.

'Thank you, Cade Quarter,' came Phineal's low, hissing voice, followed by the sound of splashing, and Cade turned to see the webfoot disappear beneath the surface of the lake.

'Hey, Cade!' Celestia shouted to him as Calix came hurtling straight at Cade, showing no sign of slowing down.

At the last moment, Celestia twitched the reins and, in a flurry of sand, brought the prowlgrin to an abrupt halt, a hair's breadth from where Cade stood. Calix's long wet tongue slurped Cade's face.

'And good morning to you, Calix, boy,' said Cade, half laughing, half spluttering. He looked up to see Celestia grinning down at him.

'What's a webfoot goblin from Four Lakes city doing

out here in the Farrow Ridges?' she said, glancing at the water, where the last of the circular ripples that marked Phineal's dive were fading away.

'His name's Phineal Glyfphith,' said Cade. 'He's just visiting.'

Celestia slid her leg over the saddle and jumped down lightly to the ground. She nodded at the snailskin tent. 'I can see that,' she said. Her green eyes narrowed, and Cade noticed how the sun had deepened her complexion to a honeyed gold. 'The question is,' she said, 'why?'

Cade shrugged. Inside, his head was spinning and, as Celestia continued to stare at him, he had the curious feeling she suspected *exactly* why the webfoot was here. He felt himself turning red.

'He ... he didn't say,' he told her truthfully enough. 'But he took me for a swim,' he added. 'Deep down in the lake. It was amazing. Swimming underwater – and breathing! Phineal had these dried mushrooms, which he put into this sort of leather gourd thing, and when he added water to them, they made air that I breathed in through a tube . . .'

'Fenniths,' said Celestia, nodding.

'That's right,' said Cade.

Of course Celestia had heard of them, he realized. After all, as a herbalist she was familiar with all sorts of plant life found in the Deepwoods.

'Anyway,' he went on, 'with the gourd of air on my back and these raffia flippers on my feet, we went right down to the very bottom of the lake. I saw sleeping snag-tooths. And henchpike. This close!' he added, holding the palm of his hand up to the tip of his nose.

'And did you see anything else?' asked Celestia, an eyebrow arched. She was clearly fascinated.

'Oh, just plants and rocks and stuff . . . I thought we were going for a ride today,' Cade said, changing the subject.

'We are,' said Celestia.

Cade frowned. 'But where's Burrlix?' he asked.

Burrlix was Celestia's second prowlgrin. Older and more powerfully built than Calix, his fur was glossy black, with white threads in his beard.

Celestia smiled and untied a sackcloth bundle from behind the saddle of her prowlgrin. She handed it to Cade.

'For you,' she said.

Cade stared at the bundle. 'What is it?' he asked.

'Unwrap it and see,' said Celestia.

Cade untied the knotted rope and pulled off the sack-cloth to reveal a tilderleather saddle and bridle. It was like the one on Calix's back, but brand-new, with burnished ironwood rivets, buckles, stirrups and a bit that gleamed in the sunlight.

'My father made it,' Celestia said. 'For Rumblix.'

Cade inspected the saddle in his hands. It was lighter than it looked and the smell of the newly worked leather was earthy and strong. He looked up.

'You mean . . . ?'

'Yes,' said Celestia, tossing back her hair. 'It's time you rode Rumblix.'

Cade shook his head. It seemed like only yesterday that he'd seen Rumblix hatch. When the tiny creature had leaped out of the jelly-like egg, he'd been no bigger than Cade's hand. Now, a year and a half later, he was almost as tall as Cade and weighed more than twice as much.

Celestia was looking around. 'Where is he, anyway?'

Cade laughed. 'At noon on a hot day,' he said, 'in the shade under the veranda would be my guess. With Tug.' He looked up at his cabin, put his fingers in his mouth and whistled loudly. Rumblix's head appeared at the side of the stairs. 'Here, boy!' Cade called.

Rumblix came bounding down to the lakeside, his sleek grey fur gleaming in the bright sunshine. He whinnied prowlgrin greetings to Calix, then nuzzled into Cade, sniffing at the saddle and bridle in his arms.

'He can smell the charlock varnish,' said Celestia.

'Prowlgrins love it. And I've coated the bit with some hammelhorn grease so he'll like the taste.'

Cade reached forward and held out the iron-wood bit. Rumblix eyed it warily, his nostrils trembling.

'Gently does it . . .' Celestia whispered, as Cade pressed the bit against Rumblix's mouth until the prowlgrin opened up, then clamped down again.

The prowlgrin's eyes grew wider, and Cade patted his flanks, reas-suring him that, even though it might feel a little strange at first, there was nothing to be feared. And Rumblix, who had started shuffling about uneasily, immediately settled down.

'Now bring the bridle

up over his head,' said Celestia. 'Reins so . . . Stirrups like so, one each side. Saddle behind his nostrils. That's it. Right, now buckle the straps under his belly.'

Suddenly, from the direction of the veranda, there came an agonized cry. Celestia and Cade turned to see Tug standing a little way off, shaking uncontrollably. The great creature moaned softly, tears streaming down his misshapen face as he swayed gently from side to side. Beside him, Cade felt Rumblix shudder with unease and start to pull at the bridle with his forepaws.

Cade turned to Celestia. 'Tug doesn't understand,' he told her. 'In the Nightwoods, the red dwarves used harnesses and whips to control the nameless ones. He thinks the harness is hurting Rumblix.'

Celestia nodded. 'Here's a little trick I learned,' she said.

Leaning over the jittery prowlgrin, Celestia stared into his eyes. And as Rumblix returned her gaze, she blew gently into his nostrils.

Rumblix stopped trembling, and relaxed, the corners of his wide mouth curling upwards and his eyelids lowering. From deep in his throat came low, contented purrs.

Watching intently, Tug wiped his eyes, and when Cade motioned to him, he slowly approached, a look of astonishment on his great misshapen face. When he reached Rumblix, he bent down next to Celestia – and not for the first time, Cade noted the old scars that crisscrossed Tug's broad shoulders. Then, as Rumblix's purrs grew louder,

Tug broke into a lopsided smile.

He turned to Cade. 'Rumblix likes,' he said, tracing the saddle with a fingertip.

'Rumblix likes,' Cade agreed. 'Now, Tug,' he explained gently, taking up the reins, 'Rumblix and Cade are going riding,' and he was about to jump up into the saddle, when Celestia stayed him with a hand on his arm.

'Not so fast,' she said, laughing. 'Rumblix might be ready. But you're not.'

Cade looked down and, for the first time, realized that he was only wearing his breeches. Ideal for swimming, but not for riding a prowlgrin.

'Get dressed, city boy,' said Celestia, her green eyes sparkling, 'and I'll show you something far more spectacular than rocks and lakefish.'

· CHAPTER SEVEN ·

'Go, boy,' Cade said, twitching the reins and
pressing his heels into Rumblix's flanks. With
a whinny of excitement, the prowlgrin leaped forward,
throwing Cade back in the saddle.

Trust your prowlgrin. That was the first rule of prowlgrin riding. The second rule was more obvious: *Hold
on tight* – which is exactly what Cade did as he and his
prowlgrin bounded after Celestia and Calix.

Leaving Tug waving farewell, the pair of them hurtled
up the sloping meadowlands, past Cade's cabin and on
towards the forest. By the time they reached the treeline
they'd overtaken Celestia and Calix, and, as if he'd been
doing it all his life, Rumblix selected a stout-looking lufwood tree and sprang.

His forepaws gripped the rough bark of the nearest
branch, his rear legs came round till his back paws
touched down on the branch, then, with a low grunt, he

launched himself off to the next branch. Then the next, and the next, rising higher as he did so, his sensitive toes telling him exactly how long each branch would bear his weight before snapping. Then, legs outstretched, he jumped to the next tree. And the tree after that . . .

And as they forged their way deeper and deeper into the forest, all Cade had to do was hold on tight – and keep trusting. He heard Celestia laughing behind him, and glanced round.

'Well?' she called to him.

'He's a natural!' Cade shouted. 'Powerful! Fast! Sure-footed!'

They broke through the forest canopy, and Cade saw Gart's sky-platform up ahead, rising high above the tops of the trees – and Gart Ironside himself, hovering in his phraxlighter, some way beyond that. Twitching the reins, Cade steered Rumblix towards the little vessel.

As he approached, Cade saw that the phraxlighter had been roped to a huge ironwood pine with needles like sabres and cones the size of a skytavern's viewing bas-kets. Gart was leaning out from the back of his little craft, a net at the end of a pole in one hand and a long spike in the other. He had positioned the net under a large ball of pinewood resin that was set into the bark like a jewel in a hammerhead matron's brooch, and was attempting to lever it free with the point of the spike. Rumblix, then Calix, landed on a broad branch just above the tethered vessel.

'Morning, Gart,' Cade shouted down to his friend.

The fourthling looked up, surprised, suspicious – then his face relaxed into a smile. 'Morning, Cade,' he shouted back. 'Celestia.' He returned his attention to the resin. 'If you'll just give me a moment . . .'

The clear orange resin glowed with a fiery intensity. Suddenly, with a wet grinding sound, like a tooth being pulled, it came free and dropped into the net. Gart hoicked the resin on board and held it up, triumphant.

'An absolute beauty,' he said, and chuckled. 'If this doesn't earn me a cask of vintage winesap next time the *Xanth Filatine* pays us a visit, then nothing will . . .' He stopped, his eyes resting on Cade's mount. 'Well, well, well,' he said. 'Rumblix, if I'm not very much mistaken.'

Cade laughed. 'We're on our very first ride together.'

'Congratulations!' said Gart. 'Finest pedigree grey prowlgrin I've ever seen, Cade, lad. What do you say, Celestia?'

'He's certainly impressive,' Celestia agreed. 'Which is more than I can say for his rider!' She laughed. 'Follow me,' she called to Cade as she urged Calix to leap from the ironwood pine.

Cade flicked the reins and Rumblix gave chase.

'Enjoy your ride!' Gart called after them.

They continued up over Midridge, Cade happy to let Celestia keep the lead. Ahead of them, glittering in the mid-afternoon sun, loomed a magnificent series of rock pinnacles. Formed of black crystal shot through with veins of red bloodstone, the jagged spikes were a beautiful yet barren curiosity.

The Needles.

Cade could see them from his cabin, and had often sat on his veranda, watching as the sun danced on the angled facets of rock. The place looked enticing, but he had never been there before.

Now, as he and Celestia rose closer, Cade noticed how the sounds of the Deepwoods wildlife faded away. There was no weezit chitter or lemkin howl here. There was no birdsong. Apart from patches of snowlichen, nothing grew, for the crystalline rock was so hard that plant roots were unable to get a hold. And with no vegetation, no creatures had attempted to make the place their home.

The silence was intense and echoing, like, Cade thought, holding an empty shell to his ear. And it was hot, with the black rock soaking up the sun and reflecting it back into the air, making it shimmer like liquid.

'Race you to the top,' Celestia called across to Cade as the pair of them reached the base of the tallest spike.

Gripping the reins tightly, Cade pressed his heels into Rumblix's sides. The prowlgrin leaped forward, and Cade was impressed by how nimbly Rumblix gripped the smooth rock. They jockeyed for position, first Calix ahead, then Rumblix – then Calix again . . .

Then Calix faltered. Lost his grip. Skidded – and Rumblix stormed ahead in a series of short leaps.

'We win!' Cade yelled as the pair of them reached the summit.

He leaned forward and tousled Rumblix's sleek grey fur. He'd raced against Celestia before, and always lost.

But that was on Burrlix's back. Rumblix was a different matter entirely.

'Well done, boy,' he whispered. 'Well done.'

Celestia had been right. The view from the top of the Needles was breathtaking. All around him, the landscape of the Farrow Ridges was spread out like a jewel-encrusted patchwork quilt – the sapphire-blue of the Farrow Lake, the silver threads of the Five Falls, the ruby-ochre of the Levels, and all of it framed by the emerald and jade of the surrounding forest.

Celestia and Calix landed beside him, Celestia's hair blowing in the wind. She was smiling.

'Told you I'd show you something spectacular, Cade. And as for you,

Rumblix,' she said, reaching across and patting the prowlgrin's head. '*You're* spectacular too, aren't you, boy?' And with that, she was off again, careering down the steep rockside. 'Race you to the top of the falls!'

Rumblix ran headlong down the glassy slope, with Cade gripping onto the reins for dear life. Small shards of rock, cracked by sun and frost, clattered down the cliff-face beside them. Close to the bottom of the sheer incline, Calix abruptly took a flying leap across to a great pillow-like boulder. Rumblix did the same, and Cade found himself on the High Farrow.

Side by side, the two prowlgrins hurtled across the broad pavement of nubbed limestone. Pounding over rock slabs and leaping across the deep, shrub-filled fissures between them, the prowlgrins barked and grunted with exertion.

'We win again!' Cade cried out as he and Rumblix skidded to a halt above the first of the Five Falls.

'The *top* of the falls!' Celestia shouted across to him as she and Calix went bounding past. 'That means the highest. The *third* waterfall!'

Cade twitched the reins and Rumblix leaped forward. They scrambled along the narrow rock-strewn pathway, overtaking Calix and Celestia somewhere above the second fall. To his right, Cade heard the thunderous roar of the water plunging down the side of the cliff-face and into the lake far below. As he reached the top of the third waterfall, he turned back to wave to Celestia in triumph – but Celestia had no intention of stopping.

'First one to the Levels!' her voice floated back as she raced by him again.

Down past the fourth waterfall they went, then the fifth, then around a jutting spur of rock and back into the forest. Willoak and rock-ash for the most part, the trees were stunted and sparse. Their branches were spindly, brittle – but Rumblix knew instinctively which would and which would not support his weight, and never hesitated for a moment. And it was he and Cade who arrived down on the soft marshland of the Levels first.

Moments later they were joined by Celestia and Calix. 'You've got a very special prowlgrin there,' said Celestia admiringly. 'The fastest, highest jumping, most sure-footed I've ever seen.'

Cade smiled, his heart swelling with pride as he patted Rumblix. 'Hear that, Rumblix, lad?' he said. 'You're special!'

'We'll head round the lake to Thorne's hive-hut,' said Celestia. 'Keeping to the forest. He's expecting us,' she added.

'He is?' said Cade.

'Of course,' said Celestia. 'He didn't want to miss out on your and Rumblix's first ride.'

Cade smiled. Thorne Lammergyre the fisher goblin was one of the best friends anyone could ever have. He had taken Cade under his wing when he'd first arrived at the Farrow Ridges, wet behind the ears, and looked out for him. Cade knew the fisher goblin would be delighted to see how confident and accomplished Rumblix had become.

Celestia and Calix bounded across to the forest and leaped up into the trees. Cade and Rumblix followed. They climbed high and sped across the treetops, light as thistledown, neither prowlgrin seeming to tire. Then Calix suddenly disappeared back down beneath the canopy of leaves – and Rumblix did the same.

It was gloomy inside the forest, especially after the dazzle of the sun. Dark shadows crisscrossed the tree trunks. The whoop, squawk and chatter of the Deepwoods creatures filled the air.

Calix leaped into a vast lullabee tree, while Rumblix chose an ancient copperwood, its leaves like burnished metal. It seemed to be a good decision. At first.

The branch they dropped down onto was broad and sturdy and barely trembled as they landed. Out of the corner of his eye, Cade saw Calix hesitate, the knobbly bark of the lullabee confusing his aim for a moment. Rumblix jumped again. And again. And was just about to land on a branch on the far side of the copperwood, when there was a sudden flurry of movement.

Cade gasped.

There was a creature on the branch. Hunched. Slurping at rainwater in a hollow. As Rumblix's shadow fell upon it, the creature turned. It hissed, its eyes glowing brightly and long snout dripping.

A rotsucker. A foul carrion-eater, the stench of death clinging to its outstretched leathery wings.

Rumblix caught a whiff and faltered in mid-air. He missed the branch and bounced off the trunk of the tree with a despairing whinny. And Cade realized they were falling. Rolling over in the air. Crashing through branches . . .

Trust your prowlgrin.

Cade's stomach was in his mouth.

Trust your prowlgrin.

The reins slipped from his hands. He clutched the saddle, held on with all his might. He braced his legs . . .

Just then, with a high-pitched yelp, Rumblix seized hold of a low branch. His foreclaws dug deep into the copper-coloured bark and the toes of his hind-paws found purchase. The next moment, he kicked off again, twisted round in the air and came down to land, lightly – and the right way up – on the forest floor.

Glancing round, Cade was grateful to see the top of Thorne Lammergyre's hive-hut poking up through the trees just ahead. Celestia and Calix landed beside them.

Celestia was laughing. 'I know he's a thoroughbred pedigree grey, but if I'd known Rumblix was going to be *this* good,' she said, 'I'd have asked my father to decorate his saddle with mire pearls.'

· CHAPTER EIGHT ·

They completed the final stretch of their journey at a slow trot, steam rising in twists from the damp fur of their prowlgrins' backs and shoulders. Rumblix never once stopped purring.

They entered the clearing set back from the lake. At its centre was Thorne Lammergyre's dwelling, a towering hive-hut of woven willoak with high windows, an arched door and pointed roof. Around it was a tidy arrangement of outhouses and drying racks, and a coop where half a dozen egg-laying lakefowl were penned.

The place seemed deserted. The low sun was casting long shadows.

Cade dismounted. Celestia jumped down next to him, then Calix and Rumblix began lapping water from a long wooden trough. Cade walked across to the hive-hut and knocked on the door. It was unlocked and swung open. Cade smiled as he caught sight of the interior, with its

rich glowing woods and artful carpentry.

Thorne Lammergyre was a highly skilled carpenter and joiner. A master craftsman.

The walls were constructed from thick stakes, fifteen strides long, driven deep into the earth, and clad inside with tongue-and-groove planks. The staircase, which led up to the second storey, was circular, each wooden joint cut with unfailing precision, while the ceiling had been made from alternating blond and dark woods, creating an effect like the rays of the sun, radiating out from an ironwood lantern that hung at its centre.

Cade stepped across the threshold. A faint whirring sound seemed to be coming from somewhere upstairs.

'Hello?' he called.

'Hello?' came the reply.

Cade smiled and turned to Celestia. 'He's in,' he said. 'Hello!' he called again.

'Hello!'

Cade frowned. 'It's me, Cade!' he called.

'It's me, Cade!' came the response, and Cade laughed as he suddenly realized that this was not the grey goblin he was talking to. 'Tak-Tak, is that you?'

'Tak-Tak, is that you?' the words repeated, and Thorne's pet lemkin suddenly appeared at the top of the stairs, his black and yellow striped fur standing on end. His ears quivered. His pointed nose twitched as he sniffed at the air. Then, his darting gaze focusing on Cade in the doorway, the lemkin let out a staccato cry – *tak-tak-tak-tak-tak-tak-tak* – and came scampering down the stairs towards him.

Cade stooped forward and the little creature leaped up into his arms.

'*Tak-tak-tak*,' Cade said, trying his best to copy a striped lemkin's natural call.

And Tak-Tak responded with a repertoire of phrases he had picked up. '*It's easy if you know how!*' '*Come on, city boy!*' '*Where are my spectacles?*' Thorne. Celestia. Blatch Helmstoft. Each of the impersonations was uncannily accurate. With his eyes closed, Cade could not have told Tak-Tak's mimicry from the real thing.

Cade tickled him under his chin. 'Aren't you going

to imitate *me*?' he said.

Tak-Tak cocked his head to one side. 'Aren't you going to imitate *me*?' he repeated, capturing Cade's voice perfectly.

'There's your answer,' Celestia laughed.

'There's your answer,' said Tak-Tak.

'I give up,' Cade laughed, and ruffled the lemkin's fur. 'Where's your master, then?'

Tak-Tak's ears pricked up.

'Master, master,' the lemkin echoed, before suddenly jumping back down onto the floor and bounding out of the door.

Cade and Celestia turned and followed the lemkin. Across the clearing and through the trees they went, down to the lakeside, where they saw the familiar figure of Thorne Lammergyre standing knee-deep in the water.

He had his back to the shore. His breeches were rolled up and he was wearing his old Hive Militia army jacket, the hem a darker grey than the rest where it had touched the water. Using leadwood pegs, he was attaching the last of four plaited fences to the side of a rectangle of stakes that had been hammered down into the mud at the bottom of the lake.

Tak-Tak paused at the water's edge and gave his staccato cry.

Thorne turned and, seeing Cade and Celestia standing on the shore, raised a hand in greeting, his deep-set blue eyes twinkling in his craggy features. 'Cade, Celestia,' he called. 'Just building myself an eel-corral.

Thought I'd try my hand at eel farming.' He patted
the spyglass that swung from the front of his military coat. 'I spotted a new arrival to the Farrow
Lake the other day – a webfoot goblin from Four
Lakes by the looks of him. Practically live on lake
eels, they do, and that's what gave me the idea.'

'Cade's met him,' said Celestia. 'Haven't you, Cade?'
She smiled. 'It's been an eventful couple of days for you,
all told. First you're attacked by that snagtooth. Then you
meet a webfoot . . .'

'A snagtooth?' Thorne climbed out of the water, his eyes wide with concern as he approached Cade and seized him by the shoulders. 'Are you all right, lad? Did you get injured?'

'No, I'm fine,' Cade reassured him. 'Phineal – that's the webfoot's name – he saved me. But, Thorne . . .' Cade's face fell. 'I'm afraid the coracle was wrecked. I'm so sorry. You warned me not to fish at dusk, and I know how much work you put into building it for me . . .'

'Don't you apologize, lad. A snagtooth can be unpredictable when it's riled. You were lucky to escape with your life,' he said, clapping a hand on Cade's back and steering him back up the shore to the hive-hut. 'And I can always make another coracle. Now, come on, you two. You must stay for some fish stew . . .'

'But that's not all,' said Celestia, falling into step with them and taking Thorne's arm. 'Cade and I rode here over the Needles.' They entered the clearing and she pointed over to the water trough. 'Look!'

Thorne's face broke into a delighted smile. 'Rumblix!' he exclaimed and turned to Cade. 'Your first ride together. Tell me, lad, how was he?'

Cade grinned. 'Perfect,' he said simply. He whistled to Rumblix, who came trotting over from the water trough and nuzzled into him. Cade looked at Thorne. 'He's fast, he's sure-footed . . . Even when he got spooked by this rotsucker, he managed to right himself. Didn't you, boy?'

Thorne nodded and patted the prowlgrin on his shoulders. 'No more than I'd expect from a pedigree grey,' he said. 'Finest prowlgrins there are. That friend of yours – the prowlgrin breeder – he certainly knew a thing or two. Rumblix is a natural-born high-jumper if ever I saw one.'

Cade nodded.

High-jumping was the most popular sport in the great city of Hive. It involved racing down a series of jutting wooden ledges, or 'branches', that descended the length of the waterfall that divided the city. Tillman Spoke was the name of the prowlgrin breeder, and he had told Cade all about it back in his cabin. Spoke had owned the batch of prowlgrin eggs that Rumblix hatched from. Cade had been working for him on board the skytavern, the *Xanth Filatine*, tending to the eggs – and would probably still be working for him at the prowlgrin stables he was establishing in Hive.

If it hadn't been for Drax Adereth.

Cade had told Thorne and Celestia the story. How the gang-leader from the depths of the skytavern had framed him. Planted stolen goods on him to make him look like a common thief. Shamed him in front of Tillman Spoke . . .

Cade swallowed. He could still see the look on the prowlgrin breeder's face – a mixture of anger and disappointment when the skymarshal had arrested him. 'I *trusted* you,' Spoke had said to Cade. 'And it seems my trust was ill-judged.'

And there was nothing that Cade could say or do to make him believe otherwise . . .

'He wasn't a friend exactly,' Cade said. 'Like I told you, I worked for him. He was kind to me. I only wish I'd had a chance to explain things to him.' He sighed. 'But if I hadn't jumped from the *Xanth Filatine* when I did, then Drax Adereth would have killed me.' Cade stroked the fur on top of Rumblix's head. 'And you sort of came along with me, didn't you, boy?'

'Well, I'm glad you did jump ship,' said Thorne, 'or we'd never have had the pleasure of meeting you, Cade. Isn't that right, Celestia?'

'He's not too bad. For a city boy,' Celestia added, and laughed. 'Now, where's that fish stew you mentioned?'

'Bubbling away on the stove,' said Thorne, 'and there's more than enough for three. Calix and Rumblix here can have the innards. They've earned them by all accounts.'

'Excellent idea,' said Cade, his rumbling stomach reminding him that he himself hadn't eaten all day.

'It's decided then,' said Thorne, clapping his hands together, and striding up to the door of his home. 'And you can tell me all about your ride over our meal.'

As they followed Thorne inside, Cade was again aware of the strange whirring sound coming from upstairs, and was about to ask, when Celestia brushed past him.

'I'll lay the table,' she announced, and headed for the dresser, with its racks of goblets, plates and bowls, drawers of knives and spoons, and a tall decanter of something dark red which Celestia sniffed and declared to smell 'delicious'.

'And I'll see to the prowlgrins,' said Cade. 'Where are those fish scraps?'

Thorne nodded to a large wooden bowl on the work-bench that had a piece of homespun cloth draped over it. Plump muleflies buzzed lazily around the top, landing briefly on the covered rim of the bowl, then flying off again. Cade gathered it up and stepped outside, to find Calix and Rumblix waiting by the door.

Rumblix's jewel-like yellow eyes were full of expec-tation. Cade set the bowl down on the ground, and the prowlgrins purred loudly as they slurped and gulped at the mess of bones and offal.

'Enjoy,' Cade laughed, watching them for a moment before going back inside.

As he walked through the door, he paused. 'Thorne,' he said, 'what *is* that strange whirring noise?'

Thorne turned from the stove, his face puzzled. Then he smiled and glanced upwards.

'That,' he said, 'is something I've been working on.' He nodded, his face earnest, then added, 'I think you might find it interesting.'

· CHAPTER NINE ·

'What *is* it?' said Cade.

Cade and Celestia had followed Thorne up the stairs to a room on the first floor. Large and windowless, it was packed with shelves and cupboards that contained various tools, bits of equipment and raw materials. Against the far wall was a long trestle workbench. Thorne's old Hive Militia musket lay at one end of the bench, while at the other stood a curious metal object.

This was the source of the whirring noise that Cade had heard.

'Like I said, something I've been working on,' said Thorne, unable to keep the pride from his voice. 'Remember that supper we had, Cade, when I talked about the possibilities contained in your father's barkscrolls? Well, I've made a breakthrough based on his calculations.'

Cade was amazed.

His father, Thadeus, had entrusted him with the four barkscrolls back in the Cloud Quarter of Great Glade on the night Cade had escaped. The scrolls now had pride of place above the mantelpiece in Cade's cabin. The calculations they contained were about phraxchambers, explosion rates and frost conversions, and far too advanced for Cade to understand. But Thorne, with his skill at making things, had been intrigued.

Now, months after he'd first examined them and made notes, he'd managed to make some kind of sense of them.

Cade stooped forward to inspect the object more closely. With its phraxchamber, propulsion duct, funnel and cooling gears, it looked like a miniature version of a phraxengine – the type that was used all over the Edge, from the factory stilthouses of Copperwood and East Glade to the mighty skytaverns that crisscrossed the sky.

Yet this was no ordinary phraxengine. Even Cade could see that.

Instead of the funnel rising up from the top of the chamber and billowing steam, it bent back on itself and was connected to the propulsion duct at the rear of the chamber. Around this central phraxchamber, four smaller spheres circled at different speeds, hovering just above its surface, yet not touching.

It was these spheres that were emitting the whirring noise. Not only that, but they glowed white, then gold, then red, as they did so.

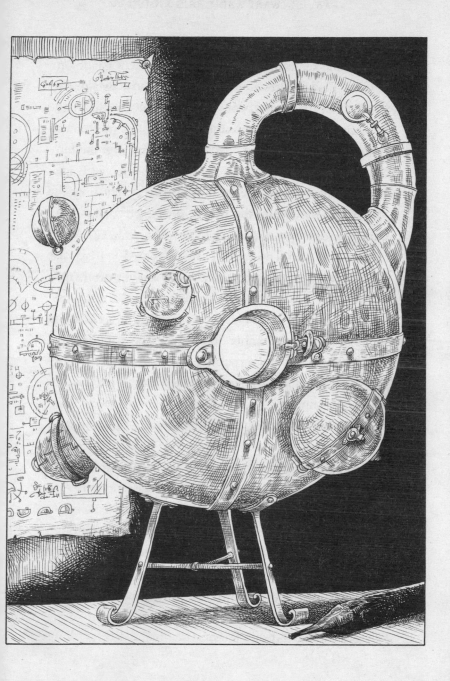

'What does it do?' asked Cade, unable to take his eyes off the object.

'Do?' said Thorne. 'Well, it doesn't exactly *do* anything. Not at the moment.' He leaned forward on the workbench and pointed to the funnel. 'I constructed this model to test the principles contained in your father's calculations.'

'Fascinating,' breathed Celestia. 'By connecting the steam and the flame, the power of the phrax has been changed somehow . . .'

'Exactly,' said Thorne. 'These ironwood spheres are held in place, orbiting the chamber, by that power. Your father, Cade, referred to it as phrax force.'

'It's beautiful,' said Cade, watching the glowing spheres circle the chamber. 'But how is this useful?'

'Don't you see?' interrupted Celestia, unable to contain her excitement. 'If you attached flywheels, pistons and connecting rods to these spheres, each one of them could power machines linked to them. A single phrax-chamber could generate power to run four factories . . .'

'Or four *hundred*,' said Thorne, stroking his chin thoughtfully. 'If the chamber was large enough. And that's just the beginning of what this phrax force could be capable of. I've managed to work my way through the first barkscroll, but there are three more I copied the calculations from that I've yet to master. I've got to hand it to your father, Cade. He truly was a remarkable phraxengineer.'

Cade thought of his father Thadeus: a shy, studious

academic – too gifted not to stand out and earn the envy and hatred of less talented, but more ambitious, rivals in the Cloud Quarter Academy of Flight. He hadn't deserved what had happened to him.

'And yet . . .' Thorne paused, and looked at Cade and Celestia, one after the other. 'We lead a good life here at Farrow Lake, don't we?' he said. 'Fishing the lake. Hunting in the forest. Tilling the land . . .'

'A very good life,' Celestia agreed.

Cade nodded. It was true. Life in the Farrow Ridges was a haven of tranquillity far from the frenetic pace of the great city he'd left behind.

'Beautiful as the phraxchamber is,' Thorne went on, 'I fear it has no place here. I've seen the damage that phrax can inflict . . .'

'Weapons,' said Cade quietly. 'Warfare.'

'Precisely,' said Thorne.

The grey goblin's eyes grew unfocused as he stared off into the middle distance. Cade knew that his friend was reliving the nightmare of the Battle of the Midwood Marshes, where he had watched so many of his comrades cut down on the battlefield – and come close to perishing himself.

'I took the speck of phrax from my old musket and used it in the phraxchamber,' he said grimly. 'And you can see the power it's able to generate. A single speck . . .' His brow furrowed. 'But fascinating as it was to put your father's calculations to use, I can't help wondering if I haven't made a terrible mistake.' He paused again. 'The thing is, science is a one-way journey. Discoveries can't be undiscovered. Knowledge can't be unknown . . .'

Cade watched his friend's troubled face as he wrestled with his conscience.

'Perhaps,' he said at last, 'it would be best if I stowed the chamber away and turned my attentions back to coracle building.'

Celestia was looking at the grey goblin intently. 'But imagine the good such an invention could do,' she said quietly. 'Turning phraxmuskets into steam looms, ploughshares, stilt factories.' She looked at Cade, then back at Thorne. 'With so much power generated from so small a phrax crystal, the phraxmine owners and merchants – not to mention all their cronies in the academies – would no longer control everything.' She jabbed at the air with her finger to make her point. 'This could completely change the Edgelands.'

'That,' said Thorne, 'is my concern.'

Cade shook his head slowly. 'Thorne's right,' he said at last. 'The world isn't ready for my father's discoveries. I don't want everything to change.' He smiled. 'I like Farrow Lake just the way it is.'

'Just the way it is,' echoed Tak-Tak from the top of the stairs. 'Just the way it is.'

· CHAPTER TEN ·

Cade and Tug were outside, hard at work beneath the late afternoon sun. They were gathering in the harvest from the walled vegetable garden that the pair of them had constructed in the meadow behind the cabin.

Boxes filled with sweet red erlberries and crates of tag-nuts already stood in rows at the side of the field, and Cade had turned his attention to the glimmer-onions. They stood in rows, their glossy dark-green leaves just beginning to turn brown at the tips, showing that the bulbs beneath the ground were ready to eat.

The pair of them were making their way slowly along the row, with Cade using a hoe to break up the earth around the individual glimmer-onions. Then, each time he heard Cade's signal, Tug would bend forward, grasp great clumps of leaves in one huge hand and, using his prodigious strength, ease half a dozen or so of the great bulbous glimmer-onions from the ground.

And every time he did so, he grunted, 'Tug.'

Having shaken off the remnants of earth, Tug laid the onions out neatly on a pallet, ready for Cade to choose later which to dry, which to pickle, and which to tie together in bunches that he would hang from ceiling-hooks in his storeroom.

Cade paused, leaned on his hoe and looked around the vegetable garden. He and Tug had been working since sunrise, and it was hot work. What was more, there was a lot more still to harvest. Blue-cabbage. Delberries and sand-apples. Half a dozen types of gladebeet . . . Not for the first time, Cade was struck by how fertile the soil around the Farrow Lake was.

'We'll call it a day when we reach the end of this row,' he said. Pulling his water flask from his back pocket, Cade took a long swig. Then another. Then he handed it to Tug, who drained the flask's contents.

The sun was low in the sky now, and his and Tug's shadows had grown long. Cade's gaze strayed down to the lake where, earlier, Rumblix had been gambolling around Phineal, hoping for scraps from the fish that the webfoot was gutting. Now Rumblix was on his own, perched on a rock at the end of the jetty, fast asleep. The conical snailskin tent by the lakeshore looked deserted.

Pegged to the ground in front of the tent, next to coils of rope, were two enormous globes made of a translucent material that was stretched over a frame of buoyant lufwood. Inside, Cade could make out dark shapes fluttering against the papery sides. He was intrigued – but the webfoot wasn't there to ask about it.

'Where's Phineal?' he asked.

Tug raised an arm and pointed across the meadow-lands. 'The woods,' he grunted.

By the time the remaining glimmer-onions in the row had been loosened, pulled and laid out on the pallet, the sun was down on the horizon, an orange ball seemingly half in the air and half in the water, bisected by the jagged treeline. A wedge of splintered golden ripples crossed the choppy surface of the lake towards him.

'Tug take to store,' said Tug. He hefted the heavy pallet up onto his broad shoulders and set off for Cade's cabin.

Cade picked up two of the boxes of erlberries, one beneath each arm, and was about to follow him when he heard a scream. High-pitched. Terror-filled. Cade's blood ran cold.

It was coming from the woods.

'Phineal!' Cade called out. 'Phineal, is that you?'

The screaming grew louder, more desperate.

Cade dropped the boxes, seized a scythe and dashed towards the treeline. Tug ran with him, his muscular legs crashing through the long grass. The pair of them burst into the forest at the same moment – and stopped in their tracks.

A little way off, in a clearing, was what appeared to be a log covered in gnarled brown bark and clumps of green moss. Except it was hovering two strides above the forest floor. And moving. As Cade watched, it writhed and squirmed, shifting position in the air.

'A logworm,' Cade breathed.

Powerful jets of air were spurting out from two rows of knot-like ducts along its underside, keeping the massive creature airborne as it sucked in air through the gaping mouth that formed one end of its log-like body. The sound was like a phraxchamber letting off steam. Loud. Shrill. Hissing. Pine-needles and fallen leaves caught up in the downdraught rustled and crackled as they swirled.

The logworm's eyes, a ring of bright green orbs that encircled the mouth, glittered as it focused on its prey. Phineal. He was dangling from the branch of a lufwood tree. In his hand was a long-handled moth net, which he was swiping ineffectually at the creature in an attempt to keep it at bay. His crest was flashing orange, purple, orange, purple – the colours of panic and danger – as the logworm arched its great body and prepared to strike.

To distract the logworm, Cade rushed forward, hollering and screaming. And it worked. Following the sound, it swung round to confront him.

'Uh-oh,' Cade muttered as the logworm advanced towards him.

The air filled with the stench of putrid meat, rank and metallic, as the creature exhaled. The next moment, Cade felt a rush of air seize hold of him as the logworm breathed in.

The force was incredible. It was like being trapped inside a whirlwind that was drawing him closer, ever closer, to the dark hole that led deep down into the creature's stomach.

The scythe was torn from his grasp and disappeared into the logworm's gaping maw. For a moment, the ring of eyes bulged as the whirlwind abruptly ceased. Then, with a convulsion and a blast of air, the creature spat the scythe out.

Cade ducked as it shot past him and rebounded off the trunk of a copperwood with a clang.

The logworm inhaled, knocking Cade off his feet and dragging him closer. Scrabbling and kicking out, Cade rolled over onto his front. He grasped at branches, roots, rocks; anything. He dug the toes of his boots into the earth. But nothing slowed him down, and all the while the sound of hissing and sucking grew louder.

'Tug! Tug!' he cried out.

Cade could hear his friend. He was somewhere behind him, grunting with effort. But what was he doing? Why wasn't he helping him?

'*Tug!*' he screamed.

Suddenly, from behind him, a great hand appeared, grasped Cade's shoulder and anchored him to the spot. Then a huge boulder flew over his head and slammed into the logworm's open mouth with a fleshy thud. It wedged itself in its throat, choking it and cutting off the hissing jets that kept the logworm up in the air.

The creature hit the ground hard, writhing and thrashing as it tried to dislodge the great rock. But in vain. With a final wheezing splutter, it fell still.

Cade felt himself being lifted up, then placed gently down on the ground. He turned. Tug was towering over him, his head cocked to one side and brow furrowed. He was staring at Cade quizzically through those dark deep-set eyes of his.

'Cade good?' he asked.

Cade nodded. 'Cade good,' he said.

Tug's face relaxed. The corners of his mouth twitched into what passed for a smile. Then, as if unable to stop himself, he opened his arms wide and wrapped them round Cade in a great hug, lifting him off the ground as he did so. And for a moment they remained like that, the two friends locked together in a warm embrace, both of them overjoyed that the other one was alive and unharmed.

'Not . . . *too* . . . tight . . .' Cade gasped at last.

Tug hurriedly let him go. 'Sorry,' he said, his deep voice filled with sorrow.

'It's all right,' said Cade, and laughed. 'No bones broken.' His face grew serious. 'And thank you, Tug.' He turned and kicked at the side of the dead logworm. 'You saved my life.'

'And mine,' came a small voice from the far side of the lufwood tree.

'Phineal!' Cade exclaimed. 'Are you all right?'

The webfoot was lying on the ground at the foot of the lufwood tree. His face was pale – as was his crest, which flickered a dull muddy green.

'I'm not sure,' Phineal said. 'Something hit me.'

Cade looked down. His scythe was embedded in the webfoot's leg. It looked like a nasty wound, and Cade didn't want to risk making it worse by pulling it out.

'I'll get Celestia,' he announced, jumping to his feet. 'She'll know what to do. In the meantime, Tug'll look after you – won't you, Tug?'

'Tug look after.' Tug nodded vigorously.

Cade turned to go.

'Wait!' Phineal cried out. 'There's something I need you to do for me before the sun goes down.'

Cade paused and turned back. 'Do?' he said.

· CHAPTER ELEVEN ·

Cade worked quickly. Reaching Phineal's camp, he unpegged the two papery globes and let the buoyant wood take them. They floated up high into the air on the end of their long tether ropes – just as the web-foot had instructed. Sky only knew what they were, and Cade didn't waste time finding out.

'We're going for a ride, you and me,' Cade said as he saddled up Rumblix.

Rumblix tossed his head and whinnied excitedly.

Cade jumped up onto his back, flicked the reins – and they were off, speeding towards the tree-cabin in the Western Woods. The sun had set by the time they arrived, and the forest was draped in shadow. Cade brought Rumblix to a halt beneath the hanging cabin and, without dismounting, shouted up.

'Celestia! *Celestia!*'

A second-storey window opened, and a large bald head

with a ruff of white hair over the ears appeared. Spidery fingers fiddled with wire-framed glasses.

'Who's there?' came a small querulous voice.

'It's me, Blatch, sir,' said Cade. 'I'm looking for Celestia. It's an emergency . . .'

A second window flew open, this one on the first storey. It was Celestia herself.

'Where's the fire, city boy?' she called down.

'It isn't a fire,' said Cade. 'It's Phineal.'

'Phineal?' interrupted Blatch. 'Who's Phineal?'

Celestia turned to him. 'A friend of Cade's,' she said. 'A webfoot.'

'A webfoot?' Blatch Helmstoft sounded astounded. 'At the Farrow Ridges? But why?'

'That's what I wanted to know,' said Celestia, 'but—'

'I'm sorry, but we really don't have time for this,' Cade broke in. 'Phineal's injured his leg. Badly. And he needs help.'

Blatch nodded. 'Go, child,' he called down.

But Celestia had already disappeared from the window. Moments later, she reappeared up on the roof, a small rucksack on her back. Quickly securing the saddle, she jumped onto Calix's back and flicked the reins. The prowlgrin leaped up onto the branch that supported the cabin, ran along its length, then headed off into the trees in the direction of the lake.

And Cade went with her.

Despite the gathering darkness, the prowlgrins were sure-footed, never once faltering as they sped through the trees. Back on the shore of the lake, they galloped over the sand and gravel side by side. As they approached Cade's cabin, Cade's eyes grew wide.

'What are *those*?' said Celestia.

Cade stared at the two globes high above their heads. They were glowing with a golden light now as they bobbed gently on the end of their tether ropes, bright against the darkening sky.

'Phineal made them,' he told her. 'He didn't say why . . .'

Cade caught sight of Tug, his great body silhouetted against the line of trees behind him. He was waving furiously. Steering the prowlgrins away from the circle of light, Cade and Celestia sped towards him, dismounting the moment they arrived at his side.

'Phineal not good,' said Tug, his voice gruff.

He turned and ploughed his way back through the undergrowth. Cade and Celestia followed in his wake.

It was Cade who saw Phineal first. He was lying at the foot of the lufwood tree where he'd left him. But Tug was right. The webfoot looked awful. He'd lost a lot of blood; his sallow face was pale and his brow was beaded with sweat.

'I've brought Celestia,' Cade told him gently. 'She'll take care of you.'

Phineal stared back at him, his eyes glittery and wet, and Cade was unsure whether the webfoot had understood, or even heard, what he'd said. Cade leaned forward and placed the flat of his hand to

Phineal's forehead – and winced.

'He's cold and clammy, Celestia,' he said, then frowned when she made no reply. 'Celestia?'

He turned to see that she was staring at the corpse of the logworm.

'Celestia,' he said again.

She turned towards him. There were tears in her eyes.

'You had a narrow escape,' she breathed. 'A logworm this size.' She shook her head. 'I once saw what one did to an entire hammerhead encampment. Devoured them all. Every last one . . .'

'You should have seen Tug,' said Cade, glancing across at his big friend. 'He was so brave. If it hadn't been for him, we wouldn't have stood a chance.'

'Good old Tug,' smiled Celestia, dashing away her tears and leaning over Phineal to examine the scythe embedded in his leg. 'This'll need stitches,' she pronounced, pulling her backpack from her shoulders. She reached inside and pulled out a needle and thread, together with a small pot, which she uncorked. 'Fenbane's good for numbing the skin,' she said as she scooped out a dollop of the oily orange ointment and smeared it all around the wound. 'Lift his leg,' she told Cade.

Cade took hold of Phineal's foot, carefully raised the leg, then held it in place. Celestia gently eased the blade of the scythe out of Phineal's leg, then began stitching. Cade watched her every movement, impressed – as he was always impressed – by how quickly and efficiently she worked. Celestia's mother had taught her all about the healing arts, and clearly had taught her well.

'And this,' she said, finishing the stitches and reaching into the backpack for a second time, 'should prevent infection.' She held up a frosted glass vial, then removed the stopper. 'Stick your tongue out,' she told Phineal.

Phineal shook his head.

Celestia smiled. 'It tastes nice,' she coaxed. 'Come on, now.'

Reluctantly, Phineal stuck out his tongue. Celestia tipped up the vial and let two . . . three . . . four drops splash down onto it.

'That'll do you,' she said.

The effect was instant. Phineal's eyes brightened. His face gained colour and he sat up.

'Thank you,' he said.

Celestia smiled. 'We Farrow Lakers look after each other,' she said. 'Now, try to keep your weight off that leg while it heals.'

Tug lifted the webfoot and carried him back to his tent, followed by Cade and Celestia. As they emerged from the trees, Cade saw that the moon had risen. Full and a silver-yellow colour, it hung low in the sky, a huge shining disc that cast shards of light across the choppy water of the lake and bathed the meadows in a cold, metallic light. Above the conical tent, the two globes glowed equally brightly.

'The moth lanterns,' said Phineal approvingly. 'You did well, Cade.'

'But what are they for?' Cade asked as they reached

the webfoot's camp and Tug put him down.

'They're beacons,' said Phineal. 'I was gathering the last of the moonmoths in the lufwood tree when I disturbed that logworm . . .'

'Beacons?' said Celestia.

Phineal's crest glowed a luminous orange. 'To guide the others,' he whispered. 'Look.'

Cade looked up, open-mouthed.

Coming towards them, filling the sky, were skycraft's of all different shapes and sizes. Huge, diaphanous sails billowed out from tall slender masts, themselves attached to elegant wooden frames, from which trailing ropes and glittering flight weights were suspended.

There was no thrum of phraxchambers, no hiss of steam trailing these skycraft's graceful progress. Only the faint creak of ropes and gentle clink of flight weights broke the silence as their pilots moved nimbly around their decks.

These beautiful vessels, with their delicate construction and intricately carved prows, didn't belong to this, the Third Age of Flight, Cade realized. As he and his classmates at the Academy School had learned, after stone-sickness had caused the flight rocks of the ancient skygalleons to crumble, bringing an end to the First Age of Flight; and before phraxchambers had ushered in the Third Age of Flight, there had been the *Second* Age of Flight – the age of skycraft carved from buoyant sumpwood, then varnished to make them even lighter and stronger. So far as Cade knew, none had taken to the skies for hundreds of years. Yet here, like some ethereal vision from the past, was a fleet of just such skycraft.

At the head of the small fleet was a particularly intricately designed vessel. The sumpwood prow was carved into the head of a rotsucker, with two side sails resembling outstretched wings, and a long curved rudder sweeping out behind it like a tail. The rider, wearing a snailskin flightsuit and dark goggles, was skilfully bringing the skycraft down out of the sky, clearly drawn to the meadowlands at the edge of the lake by the glowing light of the moth lanterns.

Behind the lead vessel, to its left and right, were two more skycraft. One had a prow carved into the shape of a stormhornet; the other, a woodwasp. Their pilots were crouched low on their small decks, perfectly balanced as they lowered their flight weights. And behind them, further apart in the V-formation, were two more vessels. A pilot sat astride one, his skycraft carved from a single lufwood log into the shape of a pearlbug, with wooden feelers jutting out from its angular head. The other pilot's skycraft was just as ornate. With its diamond-shaped scales and curved abdomen spikes, it looked to Cade like some kind of scorpionfly.

The incoming craft were close now, twelve of them, fanning out as they flew low over the lake. The moonlight danced on the tops of the masts and shimmering spidersilk sails, which fluttered like sheets of spun silver and gold, while the carved hulls were uplit by the

golden light of the glowing moth lanterns.

Cade stood spellbound. He didn't think he'd ever seen anything more beautiful.

'Who are they?' he whispered.

Phineal smiled. 'My brother clam-tenders,' he said.

· CHAPTER TWELVE ·

Cade gazed at the skycraft. All of them were beautiful, but for him, it was a sleek, mid-sized vessel that was the most beautiful of all.

It had been carved into the shape of a snowbird. The prow was the head, with a long pointed beak and almond-shaped eyes, which had been painted with gleaming black lacquer. The body was slender, and a scalloped tracery of feathers had been etched into the surface of the wood – a pattern repeated in the stitching of the white sails that billowed from its mast.

Its rider sat tall in the saddle, his hands adjusting the sail ropes and flight weights with such fluid expertise that it looked as though he was not merely flying the skycraft, but was a part of it. Like Phineal, he was a webfoot, but instead of Phineal's slight stature and greenish colouring, this goblin was powerfully built and had scales of a pale, blueish-white.

As Cade continued to watch, the webfoot lowered one sail and raised the flight weights on the port side, bringing the skycraft down through the air in a descending spiral towards the edge of the lake. Two or three strides above the surface of the water, he lowered the second sail and released his anchor stone – a smooth round boulder with a tether rope threaded through the hole at its centre. The rock splashed into the water, sank to the muddy bottom of the lake and held the skycraft fast.

The snowbird was the last of the twelve vessels to descend, and it now hovered above the surface of the lake along with the rest. The white webfoot swung his leg over the saddle and dropped down into the water beside it, then waded ashore.

Phineal turned to Cade and Celestia. 'These are friends of mine from the four lakes,' he said. 'I have much I must tell them . . .'

Cade nodded. He understood that this meant the web-foot wanted to talk to his fellow clam-tenders in private.

'They must be hungry,' said Celestia.

'I expect they are,' said Phineal. 'I caught some fish and lake-prawns earlier . . .'

Cade smiled. 'Then we'll go and fetch some provisions from my store to go with them. Come on, Celestia. And you, Tug.'

Tug turned. He had been as fascinated as Cade by the beautiful skycraft descending out of the night sky, and could hardly tear his gaze away from their web-foot riders. For their part, the webfoots hung back in

the shallows, their crests glowing a nervous green at the sight of Cade's monstrous companion. Cade and Celestia each took an arm and guided Tug along the shore towards the cabin.

At the veranda, Tug grunted a 'good night' and ducked underneath it, then lay down on the mattress of meadow grass beside the sleeping Rumblix. Cade and Celestia climbed the cabin stairs. At the top, Cade turned and looked back.

He saw Phineal limping over to the gathering of webfoots, his crest bright crimson in greeting. Celestia followed Cade's gaze.

'Clam-tenders,' she mused. 'I know about clam-tenders. My father told me all about the webfoot goblins of Four Lakes – and the Great Blueshell Clam they once nurtured. Now there are clam-tenders here.' Her eyes narrowed. 'Tell me, Cade, is there a Great Blueshell Clam in the Farrow Lake?'

Cade swallowed. He felt his face redden. Phineal had asked him not to mention the presence of the clam, but he wasn't about to lie to so direct a question from his friend. Besides, it was Phineal himself who had roused Celestia's suspicions.

'Yes,' he said simply.

There was a pause.

'Have you seen it?' Celestia asked him.

'Yes,' said Cade again. 'Phineal showed me, but he asked me not to tell anyone.'

There was another pause.

'We'd better see about those provisions,' said Celestia, and with that she spun round on her heel and marched towards the door of the cabin. Cade watched her back miserably. He'd let her down, he knew he had. He'd as good as told her he didn't trust her. But then, with her hand resting on the latch, she hesitated. She turned back to Cade. 'I'd have done exactly the same as you,' she told him simply.

Cade lit the storeroom lantern and looked around. It was better stocked than ever, he noted proudly as Celestia inspected the bulging sacks, full crates, and hooks and shelves laden with the produce he'd laid down. The Deepwoods was a wild, dangerous place but, if tended with care and hard work, it could be incredibly bountiful.

'Some of these,' Celestia announced, taking down a string of glimmer-onions. She was carrying a wicker basket she'd unhooked from the back of the door. 'And some of these. And some of this. And this. And this . . .' Sourbeets, nibblick, water-fennel and a large blue cabbage joined the glimmer-onions in the basket.

Cade picked up a small sack of wild barley that he'd harvested, winnowed and stored earlier that year. And a box of oakapples.

'And what about some of this?' Celestia asked, her hand resting on an earthenware flagon of winesap.

Cade frowned. 'Phineal only drinks water,' he said.

Celestia shrugged. '*I* don't,' she said, and rested the flagon on the top of Cade's box of oakapples. 'Besides,' she added, 'this is a special occasion.'

Cade didn't argue.

They left the storeroom and headed through the cabin. Back on the veranda, Cade stopped. Ahead of him, Celestia was striding across the decking, switching her heavy basket from one hand to the other, and was about to descend the stairs, when Cade called out to her.

'Wait, Celestia,' he said, his voice soft but urgent.

'What's the matter?' said Celestia. 'I don't—'

Cade pointed over at Phineal's camp.

The webfoots had been busy. Already, two more of the conical snakeskin tents had been erected, and a couple of webfoots were working together to put up a third. A firepit had been dug, a grill placed over it, and flames were lapping at the bottom of a large pot of water set

above it. Beside it, a white goblin was down on his knees
gutting fish and hulling prawns.

'Phineal's still talking to them,' said Cade.

Celestia frowned, but then nodded.

Phineal, along with a second crested webfoot goblin,
was moving among the group, pausing to talk to each
one in turn. At first, their crests would glow crimson,
but as the conversation continued, the colours began to
ripple with blues and greens, oranges and purples.

'What do you think he's saying to them?' whispered
Celestia.

'He must be telling them about the clam. Their crest
colours show excitement.' Cade frowned. 'But also caution
– perhaps even fear.' Then he added, 'Have you noticed
that some of them look different to Phineal?'

'Of course they do, city boy,' said Celestia. She sounded
amused. 'There are four different webfoot clans. One
from each of the four lakes. Those there putting up the
tent are red-rings,' she said. 'From the lake they call the
Silent One.'

Cade looked at the two squat webfoots. Bathed in the
light from the moth lanterns, the red rings that encircled
the skin of their arms, legs and neck looked black.

'Those on the right are tusked webfoots from the lake
called the Shimmerer,' she said, pointing to three hefty-
looking webfoots with stout yellow tusks that jutted
upwards from their lower jaws. 'And those are white
webfoots. From the Lake of Cloud. They're the muscle,'
she added and laughed.

Cade looked at them. As the tallest and most powerfully built webfoots in the group they certainly looked
the part. There were six of them, each with knives at their
belts and arrow-sacks on their backs. Their lances and
tridents had been thrust down into the ground next to
where they were working.

'And last but not least, the cresteds,' said Celestia.
'Their lake is called the Mirror of the Sky and is by all
accounts the biggest and most beautiful of them all. It
was home to the Great Blueshell Clam.' She frowned.
'I'm surprised there are only two crested webfoots here.'

'Yet they seem to be in charge,' said Cade, as he
watched Phineal and the other crested webfoot con-
tinuing to move from one goblin to the next.

'According to my father, back in the olden days, it was
always the crested webfoots who were the main clam-
tenders,' said Celestia.

Finally, the two crested webfoots seemed to have completed their tour. They withdrew from the others, moved
off on their own and stood at the edge of the encampment, their heads lowered, deep in conversation. Cade
watched them, feeling uneasy as their crests darkened by
degrees to an ominous indigo.

'Do you think something's wrong?' he wondered out
loud.

But then the crests resumed their crimson colour.

'Let's go and find out,' said Celestia, setting off down
the steps from the veranda, and this time Cade didn't try
to stop her.

As they approached, Phineal looked up. He smiled, then nudged his companion with his elbow. The second crested webfoot looked Cade and Celestia up and down.

'This is Firth Thewliph, my second in command,' said Phineal. 'Firth, this is Cade Quarter. And Celestia Hul . . . Hal . . .'

'Helmstoft,' said Celestia, putting the basket down next to Cade's box and sack.

'Cade has shown me great hospitality. And Celestia . . .' Phineal's crest glowed a deeper crimson. 'She is an accomplished healer. The two of them are friends of the lake and forest,' he said. 'We can trust them both.'

Celestia blushed and looked down at her feet, but Cade could tell she was delighted.

Firth nodded and stuck out a hand, which the pair of them shook warmly.

'You are very generous,' said Phineal, looking down at the food and drink.

'Use whatever you like,' said Cade, and Firth took the provisions over to the webfoots on cooking duty at the firepit.

'Is everything all right?' Celestia asked Phineal tentatively.

He nodded. 'Everything's fine,' he said, though the pulsing indigo that returned to his crest betrayed his words. He saw that Cade had noticed it too. 'My friends had a spot of bother on the way here,' he said quietly. 'At a small lake to the west of the grey gorges. Ran into some

Deepwoods traders who wanted to know where they were from and where they were heading. The whites had to discourage them.'

'And did they?' asked Cade.

Phineal nodded his head. 'Yes,' he said, and glanced at Firth. 'So far as we know.'

The peppery smell of the lake moss that the gutted fish had been drenched in wafted over from the firepit as they were laid out on the grill. Cade turned to see that the pot was now bubbling and steaming. Despite the lateness of the hour, his stomach rumbled hungrily.

The moon was high in the sky by the time the meal was declared ready. Eleven of the newly arrived webfoots gathered in a circle around the firepit, pulled wooden bowls and eating boards from their backpacks and sat cross-legged on their snailskin cloaks which were spread out on the ground. The twelfth – a stocky tusked webfoot by the name of Grylth – moved round the circle, serving the fish onto the eating boards and ladling thick barley porridge into the bowls.

Cade was about to tuck in, when Phineal walked over to the two bobbing moth lanterns – trying his best not to limp – and reeled them both in. Flipping a catch and raising the side of first one, then the other lantern, he raised them into the air and shook them gently. The glowing moonmoths scrambled to the opening and took to the wing, flying up from the lanterns and fanning out into the air like droplets of molten metal.

Phineal returned to the circle and sat down between

Cade and Celestia. Then he looked around the ring of faces.

'Welcome, brother clam-tenders,' he said. 'May our time at the Farrow Lake be peaceful.' He turned to Cade, and then to Celestia, then back to the others. 'And may the Great Blueshell Clam be safe in our care.'

'Safe in our care!' the chorus of voices went around, and the webfoots raised their water flasks.

'If this is a toast, then we should use this,' said Celestia, holding up the flagon. 'The finest Farrow Lake winesap, brewed by Cade here himself.'

The webfoots looked at the flagon, then at Phineal. His face was impassive. But then he nodded.

'Just this once,' he said. 'To celebrate our wondrous find.'

The flagon was passed around the circle and, one after the other, the webfoots – red-ringed, tusked, white and crested alike – raised it to their lips and took a swig, to the cheered accompaniment of the others. Then they started eating, all of them making balls of the barley and fish with their fingers and flicking them into their mouths, just as Cade had watched Phineal doing. And since they had no knives or spoons with them, he and Celestia did the same.

'Those skycraft,' said Cade, turning to Phineal and swallowing his mouthful. He nodded down towards the dozen small vessels hovering above the edge of the lake like beautiful, mysterious insects. 'They look as if they come straight out of a history scroll.'

Phineal smiled. 'I thought I told you, Cade,' he said, 'we webfoots want nothing to do with the Third Age of Flight with its phraxengineers and their accursed technology.'

Cade felt the tips of his ears burn as he pictured his father's invention whirring away in the upper room of Thorne's hive-hut.

'Our skycraft do indeed belong to a different age. A time when life was simpler. Purer. The Second Age of Flight.'

Cade nodded.

'Why, the very first skycraft were constructed in your home city, Cade, at the Lake Landing Academy in the old Free Glades. That was more than five centuries ago, back when the settlement had only just been founded and the city of Great Glade was no more than a dream.'

'These days, the Lake Landing Academy's a museum,' said Cade, feeling an unexpected lump in his throat as he remembered his old life.

Phineal sighed. 'Just as at the four lakes, all things change,' he muttered, then smiled. 'At the end of the First Age, when the flight rocks that had kept the ancient sky galleons airborne crumbled with stone-sickness, the creation of wooden skycraft was revolutionary. Back then, they could carry only a single rider, but they ensured that the tradition of sky travel would continue.'

All around the circle, the webfoots nodded and murmured assent, their crests rippling with orange and purple. Phineal wasn't just making his thoughts known

to Cade, but to the entire gathering, as was the webfoot way.

'Those first riders were not merchants, or pirates or
leaguesmen as in the First Age. No, they were questers
after knowledge—'

'The librarian knights,' one of the younger tusked
webfoots interrupted.

'Exactly so,' said Phineal. 'Librarian knights of the Lake Landing Academy charged with protecting and defending the Great Library—'

'Just as we protect and defend the Great Blueshell Clam,' a red-ringed webfoot chipped in.

'Exactly so,' said Phineal again, and Cade had the feeling that this was a story that had been told many times before, around many other campfires.

'Each apprentice librarian knight selected his own lufwood log, from which he carved a flying creature – a creature they were commanded to create, not by their masters, but by their hearts. A ratbird. A stormhornet—'

'A snowbird,' the white webfoot Cade had watched landing butted in, glancing back fondly over his shoulder at his own skycraft.

'Exactly so,' said Phineal, 'for the vessels they created mirrored the spirit of their creators. Just as now.' He paused. 'But the carving of the skycraft and the learning of sail-setting and ropecraft was only half the story. For no skycraft, however buoyant its wood or wide its sails, can become truly flightworthy without the *real* miracle of the Second Age . . .'

'Varnish!' half a dozen voices called out in unison.

'Varnish made from mole-glue and pine-oil, from wormdust and oak pepper. A varnish invented by the wisest and greatest of those old Deepwoods academics . . .'

'Tweezel!' everyone shouted out at once.

Phineal smiled. 'Indeed. Tweezel the mighty spindle-bug. At more than two hundred and fifty years old, and nearing the end of his long life, yet still able to transform his world. Without Tweezel there would be no skycraft.' He turned to Cade. 'And no alternative to this Third Age of skytaverns, phraxengineers and . . .'

Cade looked around. All the crests of the webfoots were glowing a dark and ominous purple.

'Mire-pearlers.'

· CHAPTER THIRTEEN ·

A fter the flagon of winesap had been passed around the circle of webfoots several times, and finally drained, the red-rings and the tusked webfoots fetched musical instruments from their tents. Two reed pipes and a squeezebox. A pot-bellied drum. And a heart-shaped stringed instrument that was strung with fishgut and played with a bow. The night air filled with the sound of music.

First there were reels and jigs that had the goblins tapping their great webbed feet and clapping their hands. At the urging of Phineal, Cade and Celestia joined in. Cade felt self-conscious at first. The complicated rhythms were difficult to follow, and he felt awkward and stiff. Celestia had no such inhibitions.

She was entranced, clapping and swaying to the music, her movements lithe and vigorous. Her teeth gleamed in the moonlight as she laughed out loud, her eyes flashed with happiness and her black hair came undone and fell around her shoulders as she tossed her head.

It was a whole new side to her that Cade was seeing, and he was captivated. Not only was she kind, clever and considerate, but she could also let herself go. He felt so proud to call her his friend.

Phineal and Firth rose slowly to their feet, and the driving music softened into something gentler and full of longing. The two crested webfoots sang, their lilting voices harmonizing both with one another and with the slow, mournful music.

Cade listened closely to the words.

Phineal sang of the Great Blueshell Clam, the Ancient One whose dreams the webfoots had once shared, while Firth sang of the beauty of the Mirror of the Sky and the old world the webfoots had lost. The other webfoots listened attentively, their eyes glistening with tears and their crests glowing with muted colours.

Then Cade noticed the music change again, and with it, the song. It became hopeful, lyrical, and even more beautiful, with Phineal, and then Firth, singing about the Farrow Lake and the Blueshell Clam in its waters. He realized that they were making up a new song as they went along, the words fitting in seamlessly with the music. He heard his name, and then Celestia's, and his heart swelled with pride. And when he looked across at Celestia, she too was smiling. The two of them were friends of the lake and forests, the webfoots sang; they had entered for ever into this song of the clans.

The beautiful music turned to a soft lullaby. Phineal and Firth sat down with the others around the firepit and gazed dreamily into the glowing embers.

Lost in the soothing melody, Cade's eyelids grew heavy. And when he looked round at Celestia again, he saw that his friend was fast asleep, curled up on a snailskin cloak. He lay back, his arm crooked behind his head, and watched the stars that seemed to glitter in the sky like marsh-gems and mire-pearls stitched onto a gown of black silk . . .

It was only when he woke up that Cade realized he'd been asleep. He sat up. It was early morning. Someone had laid a second snailskin over him, and it was wet with dew. He looked around.

Celestia was gone, and so was Calix. Most of the webfoots were up and about. Embers smouldered in the firepit. Phineal was staring down at him.

'Good morning, Cade Quarter,' he said. 'Celestia said to tell you she had to get back to her father. She also said that she's fed your prowlgrin.'

Cade smiled. Rumblix was always hungry, and constantly after as much food as he could get.

Memories of the previous night came flooding back: the eating and drinking, the music and the singing. Cade watched the webfoots as they busied themselves with their daily chores – setting their fishing nets, sharpening their tools, mending their clothes, tending to their skycraft – and Cade recalled the beautiful song of the clans. He felt honoured to have been a part of it.

'There's some honeybroth left if you're hungry,' said Phineal. 'I can—'

'No, thank you,' said Cade, shaking his head as he climbed to his feet. 'I'm not at all hungry.' He frowned. 'Phineal, there's something I've been meaning to ask you,' he said. He nodded towards the twelve skycraft bobbing about above the surface of the lake. 'Where is *your* skycraft?'

Phineal smiled. 'I wondered when you'd ask,' he said. 'Would you like to see it?'

Cade nodded.

'Good,' said Phineal, his crest darkening. 'It'll give me the opportunity to see whether or not my brother clam-tenders were followed. We can only hope those so-called Deepwoods traders were not mire-pearlers after all . . .'

The pair of them made their way back up the meadow. As they passed by Cade's cabin, Rumblix came bounding out from beneath the veranda, barking excitedly, his tongue out and slurping, as though he hadn't had any-thing to eat in a week.

'Nice try,' Cade laughed. 'Now, stay!' he commanded. Rumblix obediently hopped up onto his perch on the veranda railing. 'Good boy,' he said. 'I'll feed you at noon.'

Cade turned and followed Phineal across the meadow towards the treeline. Inside the woods, the webfoot paused for a moment and, eyes narrowed, inspected the ground. Then he took a narrow track that wound its way through the dense undergrowth. When the track forked, he paused again, and this time Cade noticed the marker that the webfoot must have left before to indicate which way to go.

'Knotted grass,' he said, and Phineal laughed.

'Simple but effective,' he said. 'Well spotted.'

Some five hundred strides – and half a dozen more knotted tufts of grass – later, they came to the foot of a tall ironwood pine. The small pebble positioned in the middle of a flat rock at its base confirmed to Phineal that this was indeed the right tree.

The webfoot started to climb.

For a goblin adapted to being underwater, Phineal proved an agile tree climber. He gripped the rough bark with his hands, while his feet seemed to find the best purchase almost instinctively. Cade followed him up the mighty ironwood, trying his best to take exactly the same route.

Gradually, as they climbed higher, it became lighter, until they emerged above the upper canopy of the surrounding lufwoods and lullabees. And still they climbed, past giant pine-cones and clusters of dark green rapier-like needles.

Then Cade saw it . . .

Phineal's skycraft. It was bobbing in the air at the top of the tree, tethered by a plaited rope to one of the ironwood pine's knotty spurs.

The main part of the vessel was made up of two intersected sumpwood beams; silvery grey, covered in decking, and with feather-like patterns carved along their sides. The motif was continued at the stern, with the jutting rudder resembling splayed tail feathers. The prow was fashioned like the head of a mighty bird, with a massive horned bill and a curved ridge that swept back from its bony head. Two eyes, gleaming with purple varnish, seemed almost to stare back at him.

'A caterbird,' Cade breathed.

Phineal nodded. He looked almost embarrassed, Cade thought, and his crest had started to glow a shade of pinky-yellow he had not seen before.

'I had no choice in the matter,' Phineal told Cade. 'When I started carving the block of sumpwood for my prow, I had no idea what I was about to create. Yet it soon became clear.' He smiled modestly. 'It was in my heart.'

Cade nodded. Phineal Glyfphith's calling was to tend to the Ancient One of Water, the Great Blueshell Clam. So when he had created a skycraft to set out in search of it, of course he had carved another of the Ancient Ones – the Ancient One of Air. The caterbird. Water and air. It seemed to Cade a good balance.

'Climb aboard,' Phineal told him.

Cade did so, stepping onto the sumpwood crossbeams and sitting down on one of the two seats fixed below the twin masts. He examined the workmanship of the vessel. There were no obvious joints. No screws or rivets. And it occurred to him just how the skycraft had been built.

Unlike a modern sky vessel, assembled from a thousand different parts, this skycraft had been made from a single sumpwood log. The decking, the crossbeams, the prow and the masts all seemed to flow together, with the grain of the buoyant wood running unbroken from one part to the next in beautiful patterns beneath the silver glow of the varnish.

Close up, it seemed to Cade that the skycraft wasn't a construction at all. It was a carving.

There was a gentle lurch as Phineal untethered the rope, slung it aboard and jumped onto the skycraft, which began to rise slowly through the air. A tingling thrill of excitement passed through Cade's body.

He was riding a skycraft from the Second Age, just like those brave librarian knights centuries before.

When the little vessel had cleared the uppermost branches of the ironwood pine, Phineal, who was standing near the prow, reached up and tugged the slip-knots of first one furling rope, then the other. The sails tumbled down and billowed. Phineal seized the ropes that dangled from their corners as the wind filled the sails, and the *Caterbird* leaped forward at such a speed that Cade was thrown back in his seat.

Phineal sat down on the other seat, his hands playing with the bunch of ropes he was holding. He altered the heights of the dangling flight weights. He aligned the sails. The skycraft reacted to each minor adjustment and soared ahead, faster than ever.

'This one affects lift,' said Phineal, flicking one of the ten flight ropes in his grasp. 'These control direction. These help stability in high winds . . .'

'It all looks very complicated,' Cade observed.

Phineal smiled. 'Twin masts, eight sails, fore and aft flight weights – but after a while, you get a feel for it.' He shot a glance over at Cade. 'Unlike the phraxengineers doing battle with the sky with their fire and steam, we skycrafters ride the winds.'

They continued over the forest, and Cade kept his eyes on Phineal's hands as he adjusted the sails and flight weights. Little by little, it started to make sense to him. Each of the ropes had a purpose: one operated the rudder, one the hull-weights, while four operated the mast sails and four the undersails below the craft. Banking. Soaring. Dipping. Turning. Everything was possible with a tiny tweak of a rope, or a combination of two or more.

With all eight sails set, they wheeled to starboard and headed south. Far below him, Cade made out a tall platform towering above the forest canopy.

'That's where my friend Gart Ironside lives,' he told Phineal. 'He loads supplies onto the passing sky-taverns . . .'

'A phraxpilot,' said Phineal, glancing down, unable to keep the dismissive tone from his voice.

Cade nodded.

Gart's phraxlighter was tethered to the mooring ring of the platform. Compared to Phineal's swift, agile skycraft, so sensitive to every delicate adjustment, it suddenly looked, Cade thought, cumbersome and slow.

They continued on past the Needles and the High Farrow and above the high forest beyond. Looking over the side, Cade saw stands of ironwood pines, groves of

lullabees. Scree-slopes and streams. Jewel-like mountain pools . . .

'Untouched,' Cade heard Phineal whisper. 'So, so beautiful. And let us hope by Earth and Sky that it'll stay that way.' The webfoot brought the skycraft round in a broad arc and headed back in a northerly direction.

'There are caverns behind the falls there,' said Cade shortly after, pointing down at the cave entrances from which the five glistening cascades emerged. 'They're where the white trogs live. They keep themselves to themselves.'

'The best way,' said Phineal.

He brought the skycraft down lower in the sky, taking in the undersails, then skimmed over the surface of the Farrow Lake. To his right, Cade glimpsed Thorne on the shore and waved, but the fisher goblin was too engrossed in his nets to see him. Moments later, they sped past the webfoots – who did wave back. Then, as Phineal adjusted the mast sails, they were up in the air again and speeding high over the Western Woods.

'That's Celestia's house,' said Cade, pointing down at the hanging tree-cabin. 'She lives there with her father. He built it himself.'

'Fine workmanship,' Phineal observed as they passed high over the mighty ironwood pine.

A little further on, Cade pointed again. 'Look,' he said, his voice hushed but urgent. 'Over there, Phineal, in that clearing . . .'

'A hammerhead hive-tower,' Phineal breathed. 'I didn't

realize there were any of the ancient tribes remaining.' He shook his head, then took the skycraft higher still. 'This is truly a remarkable place, Cade Quarter.'

The tiny figures moving around the tall wicker tower at the centre of the clearing didn't appear to notice them. For unlike the phrax-driven vessels, with their billowing steam, roaring jet of fire and mechanical hum, the skycraft was as silent as it was stealthy and swift. And with its pale varnish and iridescent spidersilk sails, it was also almost invisible against the bright backdrop of the sky.

For a second time, Phineal brought the small craft round and they headed south-west. Below them, cast by the high midday sun, their own shadow swept across the green canopy of leaves.

'Would you like to take over?' Phineal asked.

Cade's stomach lurched. Even though he'd been watching Phineal so closely, the thought of actually taking control of the skycraft was daunting – not that he was about to let on that he was nervous.

'I'll give it a go,' he said.

Phineal passed him the cluster of ropes. 'Hold her steady,' he said. 'That's the way.'

The sumpwood *Caterbird* continued her flight over the Western Woods.

'Watch the sails. See how they take the wind. Keep them billowing,' Phineal directed. 'Now use the rudder . . .'

Cade pulled on the rudder rope and to his delight the skycraft came round in the sky – only to be caught by a crosswind, and sent into a downward spiral.

'Ease down the aft flight weight,' Phineal commanded, his voice calm but firm. 'Fill the port sails.'

Cade adjusted the ropes and saw the sails billow out once more. To his relief the skycraft levelled out. Feeling in control at last, a smile spread across his face. All eight sails strained at their ropes and the skycraft sped across the sky. It was so exhilarating it made his stomach churn and his head spin.

The edge of the Western Woods was coming close. Cade knew that when they left the forest, the up currents would change again, and he would have to deal with the new conditions. He gripped the ropes grimly and hoped for the best.

Moments later, it happened.

Suddenly, the forest was behind them. Cade breathed in the warm, tangy odour of the swampy flatlands below them as they flew out over the Levels. At the same moment, the currents of air did change. The wind switched direction. And for a second time the skycraft pitched and went into a spiral.

This time, however, Cade knew what to do, and managed not only to steady the vessel, but also to increase its speed once more. Delighted with himself, he looked across at Phineal, to see that the webfoot was peering down over the side of the skycraft, his brow furrowed and crest flashing an excited crimson and orange.

'What is it?' Cade asked.

Phineal pointed down at the thin strip of land that lay

between the Farrow Lake and the swampy levels behind it. 'It looks ideal,' he said.

'Ideal?' said Cade. 'Ideal for what?'

Phineal's crest flashed deep red. 'Fifth Lake Village,' he said.

· CHAPTER FOURTEEN ·

Cade stepped outside onto his veranda. The morning was cool and overcast, with the ground blurred by a low covering of mist. Raising his spyglass to his eye, he looked out across the lake. It was a ritual he'd been performing every day since the webfoots had started to build their new settlement on the western shore.

That was nearly three months ago.

Now, during the hours of daylight – and occasionally into the night – the sounds of building work echoed across the lake: chopping, sawing, hammering, and the heavy *thump-thump* of great wooden piles being driven deep into the ground.

Two stilthouses had already been completed. Both were tall rectangular buildings with scalloped walls, broad roofs, thatched with lake-reeds, and wooden jetties that stuck out over the lake. A third stilthouse – squatter and smaller than the others – was waiting to be thatched, while the foundations of a fourth were being worked on now, with planks of wood being nailed into position to form a platform.

Cade was still watching the webfoots when there was a loud thud and the veranda shook. He lowered his spyglass and peered over the balustrade, to see Tug rubbing his forehead ruefully.

'Tug hit head again – but Tug all right,' he muttered bravely as he rubbed gingerly at the egg-sized bump that was already forming on his forehead. Cade frowned. His friend had grown at least half a stride taller in the last few months – and was still growing.

'You're just too big to sleep under the veranda any more,' Cade told him. 'So I'm going to build you your own room. On the side of the cabin. And you'll help me,' he added.

Cade glanced back at the industrious webfoots hard at work on Fifth Lake Village. All that building had whetted his appetite for a project of his own.

'I'll get Rumblix harnessed up. You fetch the tools, Tug,' Cade instructed, 'and we'll head up into the lufwood stands for the timber.'

Beyond the treeline, the forest was bathed in shadow and pleasantly cool. A rich smell of pine and damp earth laced the air. But Cade was on his guard. As Tug and he, with Rumblix at his side, plunged deeper into the trees, Cade kept an eye out for any potential danger. Lurking halitoads or spitting quarms in the shadows; or innocent-looking fallen logs that could suddenly hiss into life. Every snapped twig, every rustle of leaves, every creaking branch made him stop in his tracks and peer around uneasily.

Tug had no such concerns. With the sack of tools on his back, he trudged fearlessly along behind Cade, Rumblix bounding close on his heels.

A sudden stirring to Cade's right set his senses jangling. He froze, and hissed at Tug to do the same.

Something was there in the trees. He slipped his phraxmusket from his shoulder and raised it. A low branch trembled. There was a flash of movement.

Cade crept forward, placing his boots down as lightly as he could, attempting to remain silent. He pulled a branch aside – and there in the middle of a clearing stood a small tilder fawn with gangly legs, dappled fur and large brown eyes that stared back at Cade with a mixture of curiosity and alarm. Its nose twitched. Its body quivered. Then, suddenly, kicking up the fallen leaves with its hoofs, it twisted round and bolted back into the shadows.

Cade smiled. 'I'll be scared of my own shadow next,' he said, shouldering his phraxmusket.

Rumblix chased playfully after the fleeing fawn. Overhead, a troupe of lemkins screeched with surprise, and swung off through the branches.

'Rumblix!' Cade called.

The prowlgrin stopped and returned to Cade's side, purring loudly. They continued through the woods behind the cabin, past towering ironwood pines, lush groves of sallowdrop trees and clumps of tanglebriar and thorn shrub. Then, on the far side of a dappled glade, they came to the lufwood stands.

Cade stopped in front of one of the lufwood trees. It was neither too big nor too small; it had a straight trunk and a minimum of branches he would have to strip, and timber that would be light to work, but durable.

'This is the one,' he told Tug.

Tug nodded, dropped the sack of tools to the ground and removed an axe. Soon, chips of wood and the sound of chopping filled the air. Cade unpacked and assembled a makeshift sled he'd taken with him in his backpack and attached it to Rumblix's harness at the back.

'Watch out!' Tug bellowed a moment later, and jumped back.

With a low creak and a dull thud, the lufwood crashed to the ground.

Cade took the axe and began removing the branches and trimming them, then stripped the thick bark from the trunk. Next, with Tug opposite him, he used his double-handled saw to cut the trunk into manageable logs, and the pair of them began shifting the lengths of timber onto the sled.

They worked steadily, the whole process taking most of the morning. By noon, the trunk had been split into sections and the sled loaded. Tug stood beside it with two heavy bundles of logs balanced on his broad shoulders. Around them, the woods were quiet, the noonday sun breaking through the forest canopy in bright shards of light.

Several times throughout the morning, glancing into the darker shadows beneath the trees, Cade had had the nagging feeling that he was being watched. Tug seemed to sense his unease. So did Rumblix.

Now, as they prepared to set off back to the cabin, Cade caught sight of a sudden movement out of the corner of his eye. Rumblix growled, Tug turned stiffly under his heavy load and Cade's hand reached out for his phrax-musket, which he'd left propped up against the stump of the felled lufwood tree.

'Easy there, young feller,' said a voice. It was deep and gruff, and coming from the shadows. 'I ain't carrying no phraxweapon . . .'

A moment later, a tall figure stepped out into a shaft of light a little way off. The stranger stood watching Cade, who stared back nervously at him.

He had a thick beard and long matted hair; his skin was weathered and leathery, the deep lines at his cheeks and his brow black with the woodsmoke from numerous campfires. He was wearing a crushed funnel hat of sleek, oiled quarm fur, from which the skulls of various small animals dangled; and a voluminous cloak that was buttoned up round his thick neck and hung down to his heavy iron-capped boots. The cloak was moss-green, the rough woven fabric covered in patches of tree lichen and sprouting glade grass, camouflaging its wearer perfectly in the shadowy depths of the forest.

'Greetings,' Cade said, stepping back from hisphrax-musket. 'I'm Cade. Cade Quarter.'

For a moment, the figure did not respond. Cade frowned. But then the stranger's thin, cracked lips parted to reveal a mouthful of broken brown teeth, and he spoke.

'Name's Merton Hoist.'

He approached slowly. The odour of his unwashed body mingled with the loamy smell of his cloak to create a pungent, animal-like musk. Cade reached out a hand to greet the newcomer, but there was no response. Merton Hoist's arms remained concealed beneath the cloak.

'Passing by,' he said. He nodded towards the logs and branches heaped up on Rumblix's sled. 'Heard the chopping.'

Cade nodded. Merton Hoist's voice was low and gravelly, and though he seemed to be speaking to Cade, it was Tug he was looking at, his hooded eyes assessing his friend's height and bulk.

'I . . . I live down by the lake,' said Cade, as much to fill the awkward silence as anything else.

Hoist nodded. 'You made your home here,' he said, his gaze never moving away from Tug. 'This place got a name?'

'The Farrow Ridges,' Cade told him.

'Hmmph,' Hoist grunted. His eyes flicked to Cade's for a moment, and Cade flinched under the stranger's cold-eyed stare. Then his gaze returned to Tug. 'Is this your servant?'

'No,' said Cade. 'Tug's my friend. We look out for one another, don't we, Tug?'

Tug nodded. From the look in his eyes, he was feeling

just as uncomfortable as Cade.

But then Hoist smiled. His eyes twinkled and a hand appeared from beneath the cloak and patted Cade on the shoulder. It was large and gnarled, the knuckles and fingers covered in swirling blue tattoos. Something glinted in the depths of the cloak as the hand withdrew.

'You have work to do,' Hoist said. 'And so do I.' He fixed Cade with a dark-eyed stare. 'I should be on my way.' Then, with one last long lingering look at Tug, he turned away. 'Earth and Sky be with you till our paths cross again,' his gravelly voice sounded before he slipped noiselessly back into the sun-dappled woods.

Cade swallowed. He certainly hoped their paths would not cross again.

When he turned away, Cade realized that he was trembling. Tug looked at him, then, shifting the logs he was carrying onto one shoulder, shuffled over to him.

'Cade all right?' he asked tentatively.

'I'm fine,' said Cade with a shaky smile.

He grasped Rumblix's harness. The prowlgrin lurched forward, whinnying with effort. Cade reached out and took hold of one of the sled ropes to help him pull the heavy load. On the other side, Tug did the same. And like that, the three of them pulled the sledload of timber back through the forest and out onto the meadowlands.

As they emerged into the sunshine, Cade felt a great wave of relief wash over him. It was the forest that had made him so nervous, he told himself. Merton Hoist was an old Deepwooder, a solitary wanderer by the look of him, just passing through.

But those dark, calculating eyes staring into his . . .

Cade blanched.

And then it struck him. The glint beneath the heavy moss-green cloak. Had he imagined it or had it been the handle of a phraxpistol? A handle of . . .

Cade came to a sudden stumbling halt.

'Mire pearl,' he whispered.

· CHAPTER FIFTEEN ·

'Tug? Where are you, Tug?' Cade's voice echoed off across the meadow. '*Tug?*'

He looked around.

It was three days later, and work on the extension to the cabin was going well. The ground had been cleared, levelled, and holes had been sunk for the wooden stilts. Having worked late the day before, Cade had slept in, but now he was eager to get back to the job. He arrived to find a stack of newly sawn planks. Another plank lay across two trestles, half cut and with a dusting of sawdust on the ground below it.

Tug had clearly been hard at it. But now he was nowhere to be seen.

'Tug! Tug!'

Where *was* his friend?

Occasionally Tug would go up into the woods to look for the spatchweed that grew among the roots of

140

sallowdrop trees, which he was partial to; sometimes he'd take himself off along the lake.

'TUG!'

Most often, Tug liked to sit at the end of the jetty. He would dangle his feet in the clear water and watch the little fish darting in and out of the lakeweed.

But he wasn't there now. And disappearing like that – it just wasn't like him . . .

Cade turned back to his cabin. Rumblix was perched in his usual place, on the balustrade of the veranda. He seemed to be asleep, though as Cade climbed the steps and approached he opened one eye and watched him, a low purr starting up at the back of his throat.

'Where's old Tug wandered off to, boy?' said Cade, ruffling the prowlgrin's fur beneath his chin.

Rumblix purred all the louder.

Still stroking the creature absent-mindedly, Cade looked back at the trestles and planks and long-toothed saw . . .

He sighed. He was probably being foolish, but Tug's absence was worrying him. It was so out of character. Of course, there was probably nothing wrong, he told himself. Tug was big enough and strong enough to look after himself. But there was nothing he could do about his growing sense of unease.

'Tug!' he bellowed. 'Tug, where *are* you?'

It was no good, he would just have to go and look for his great lumbering friend.

He saddled Rumblix, and the two of them trotted

along the eastern shore, Cade scanning the treeline for any sign of Tug. A wind was getting up, making the lake choppy and sending sand scudding along the shoreline like writhing serpents. As they neared Thorne's hive-hut, the breeze grew stronger, a warm southerly that felt parched and electric. The branches of the trees and shrubs he passed tossed and flapped, and there was a loud rushing sound of the wind blowing through the leaves.

He found the fisher goblin down at the lake. Phineal was with him. The two of them were standing in the lake shallows, their hands resting on the wicker fence of the eel-corral that Thorne had made.

'Have either of you seen Tug?' Cade called.

'Have either of you seen Tug?'

At the sound of Cade's – and Tak-Tak's – voices, both Phineal and Thorne looked round.

'Cade,' said Thorne, straightening up. He shook his head. 'No, he hasn't passed this way.' Then added, 'Phineal brought me a batch of baby eels,' as though he needed to explain why he was standing up to his waist in water.

'Elvers,' said Phineal.

'Elvers,' Tak-Tak mimicked.

'Hush!' Thorne told him.

'Hush! Hush! Hush!' Tak-Tak repeated over and over as he scampered off into the trees.

Thorne turned to Cade. 'To increase my stock,' he said. 'And he's just been showing me how to set the nursery cages at the bottom. Little hideaways,' he explained, 'so they don't get eaten by the larger eels . . .' He turned to Phineal. 'And for which I'm very grateful.'

Phineal's crest flashed a pale green. 'I did see your friend earlier,' he said. 'On my way here. I was swimming across the lake and I saw him on the south shore near the Five Falls.'

Cade brought Rumblix to a halt beside the lake. Tug found the great cascades of water gushing from the caverns and crashing down into the Farrow Lake fascinating. Many was the time he had stood and watched the morning light glistening on them, open-mouthed.

'But that was hours ago,' Phineal added.

'Thanks,' said Cade. He turned Rumblix round and was about to set off for the falls when Thorne raised his hand.

'Stop!' he called. 'Tie Rumblix up. We'll take my coracle. It'll be quicker.'

The fisher goblin seemed to have picked up on Cade's growing unease. Phineal's crest grew darker too as Thorne went up to his hive-hut and returned, carrying his coracle on his back.

Cade and Thorne climbed into the little vessel and began paddling, with steady rhythmic movements, while Phineal swam speedily out in front.

'Tug's never been away this long,' Cade said, breathing heavily.

The lake was choppy and the going was tough, but they were making good progress out across the water towards the thundering falls.

'I slept late ... Lost track of time. Everything just looked abandoned ...'

'Don't worry, Cade, lad,' Thorne reassured him. 'Tug's big and strong. He can take care of himself. Remember the logworm?'

Cade smiled, but as they paddled on, his nagging anxiety only grew.

Phineal led them to the south-west shore, beside the fifth of the mighty falls. They beached the coracle and made their way across the soft mud of the shoreline through a thin mist of spray.

'Wait! Look here ...' Thorne dropped to one knee and pointed.

Cade and Phineal hurried over to him.

'Footprints.' Thorne frowned as he examined the indentations in the blue-grey mud. 'Boots. Heavy ones by the look of them. Nail-studded and toe-capped.'

Cade felt a sudden lurch and flutter in the pit of his stomach.

'Over there.' Thorne pointed along the line of foot-prints.

They followed them. Beneath a copperwood tree, the ground was churned up. Scratch marks, clods of earth, and the signs of something heavy being dragged into the trees.

'Tug was here,' said Thorne darkly, pointing to a set of deep footprints, bare-footed and clawed. 'And there was a struggle with whoever was wearing the boots.'

Cade swallowed hard. 'I've been so stupid,' he groaned. 'I just put it out of my mind, what with the building work on the cabin . . .'

'Put what out of your mind?' Phineal asked, turning to Cade, his crest glowing dark purple.

'A stranger,' said Cade, his face reddening. 'Tug and I ran into him in the lufwood stands behind my cabin three days ago.'

'A stranger?' said Thorne.

'That's right,' said Cade. 'Merton Hoist, he called himself.' He realized his heart was beating fast in his chest at the memory of the character in the forest. How uneasy he'd made him feel. How he'd kept looking Tug up and down. 'You don't think . . . ?' he breathed.

'I don't know,' said Thorne. He wiped the silt from his hands on his breeches. 'Tell me everything you remember about him.'

Cade scratched his head. 'He was tall,' he began. 'Heavily built. Wore a moss-green cloak and . . .'

'And what, Cade?' said Thorne. 'Think!'

'A phraxpistol,' said Cade. 'I thought I glimpsed it beneath the cloak, even though he said he was unarmed. And there was something else . . .'

'Go on,' said Phineal.

'It had a mire-pearl handle,' said Cade.

Thorne shook his head. 'Fancy pistol like that, sounds to me like you came face to face with a mire-pearler,' he said. 'Isn't that right, Phineal?'

'I'm afraid so,' said Phineal, looking down at his feet.

'Could be one of the gang my brothers encountered at the Grey Gorges.'

'And ... and you think he's taken Tug?' Cade said. 'But why?'

Thorne and Phineal exchanged a glance.

'Mire-pearlers don't just deal in pearls,' said Thorne. 'They steal, they trap, they take slaves. Anything they can lay their hands on.'

'Mire-pearlers destroy everything they touch,' said Phineal bitterly. 'We webfoots should know. They ensnare whole tribes and communities at a time. Life is cheap to them, and the natural wonders of the Deepwoods are just riches to be grabbed any way they can. They won't think twice about enslaving a big, strong nameless one like your friend and working him to death.'

Seeing the distress in Cade's face, Thorne reached out and gripped his shoulder.

'Cade! Thorne!' a voice rang out across the lake.

The three of them turned to see a phraxlighter approaching from the east, clouds of steam billowing from the funnel.

Thorne cupped his hands to his mouth. 'Greetings, Gart,' he bellowed into the gusting wind.

Gripping the tiller with both hands, Gart Ironside raised a finger in acknowledgement. He steered the phraxlighter over to the shore, and brought it to a steady hover. Then he raised his goggles.

'What brings you three to the south shore?' he asked.

'It's Tug,' Cade blurted out. 'He's been kidnapped by a mire-pearler!'

'I saw a phraxsloop from my sky-platform not half an hour ago,' Gart said, his voice breathless. 'Spotted its steam trail in the distance. I didn't think anything of it at the time . . .'

'Thanks for telling us, Gart,' Thorne said. 'There hasn't been another phraxvessel in the skies over the ridges for weeks now. It must be him.'

'At least now we know how he's travelling,' said Phineal miserably.

Gart looked at him, an eyebrow raised.

'Phineal here has been fretting about whether or not anyone tracked his webfoot brothers here to the Farrow Lake. And now Tug has disappeared.' Thorne shook his head. 'Seems like this stranger might be guilty on both counts.'

'We've got to go after him,' Cade blurted out. 'We've got to rescue Tug.'

'I'd love to help,' said Gart, 'but that was a two-funnel sloop I spotted, and with his head start . . .' He shrugged. 'We'd never catch up with him.'

Phineal stepped over to Cade and put an arm round him. 'A vessel from the Third Age can't catch him,' he said quietly. 'But one from the Second Age just might.'

· CHAPTER SIXTEEN ·

With his crest flashing orange and yellow, Phineal splashed through the water, seized hold of the side of his skycraft and leaped aboard. Then he turned to Cade, who was still standing on the lakeshore beside Fifth Lake Village.

'Come on,' he called. 'What are you waiting for?'

Cade was about to run into the water after him when Thorne grabbed him by the arm.

'You sure you want to do this, lad,' he asked.

Cade hesitated. 'Tug's my friend,' he said simply.

'I understand,' said Thorne, nodding. He gripped Cade's hand with both of his own, looked him in the eye. 'This is a brave thing you're doing, lad,' he said. 'Sky be with you.'

'Cade!' It was Phineal. 'If that mire-pearler *is* one of the Grey Gorge gang, we can't afford to let him get away. Once Tug's been enslaved, even he won't last long.'

'I'm coming, I'm coming,' Cade shouted back.

He pulled away from Thorne, then trudged quickly through the shallows to the anchored skycraft. Phineal leaned forward and reached out. Cade grabbed his hand and was pulled aboard. He sat down heavily.

'Strap yourself in,' said Phineal. 'We're going to set full sail.'

Cade fumbled for the harness, slipped it over his shoulders and clipped it securely to a ring at the back of the seat. Beside him, Phineal lowered the flight weights, fore and aft, then raised the mast sails, gauging the pull as the gossamer-light material billowed. With all ten ropes gripped in his right hand, he called across to Cade.

'All set?'

'All set,' Cade called back, and hoped that the webfoot hadn't heard the quaver in his voice.

Phineal leaned over the side and hefted the anchor stone up from the lake bed, grunting with effort as he did so. The muscles in his arms, shoulders and neck tensed like cable. The stone thumped down into the bottom of the boat and, unleashed, the skycraft leaped forward.

Cade gripped the shoulder straps of his harness, white-knuckled, as the acceleration shoved him backwards. Every muscle in his body was braced. And, though it seemed impossible, when Phineal released the undersails and the wind filled them too, the skycraft flew even faster, shooting up into the clear blue sky as fast and straight as an arrow.

Jaws clenched, Cade stared straight ahead. The

sailcloth was taut, the masts were bowed. The forest raced past below, a blur of green.

'Look for a steam trail!'

Phineal's voice cut through the hissing rush of air, startling Cade back to where he was: perched precariously on a small, fragile wooden craft that was hurtling across the sky.

When the *Caterbird* finally levelled out, Cade looked down over the side. They were up higher than he'd imagined possible. If there had been clouds, he was sure they would be flying above them. But there were no clouds. Below lay the Deepwoods: tree-fringed ridges, deep valleys, winding streams gleaming like silver threads . . .

Because of their height, it seemed that they were barely making any progress. But Cade knew the opposite was true. Up here, riding the lofty airstreams, the skycraft was travelling faster than any phrax-powered vessel down near the treetops.

'Phineal! Phineal!' Cade shouted out. 'I think I've seen it. There.' He pointed. 'West-north-west.'

There, glistening in the blue sky, were two long streaks of white – the steam trails from a twin-funnelled phraxsloop.

'Well done, Cade,' Phineal said simply, then added, 'Hold on tight. We're going down.'

Cade didn't need telling twice. He braced his legs and gripped the straps of the harness while Phineal realigned the flight weights and pulled in the undersails.

Then, as he pulled on the tiller rope, the skycraft tipped forward – and went into a steep dive.

Speeding upwards had been bad. Hurtling down towards the forest was a thousand times worse, and Cade clung on for dear life as the skycraft plummeted to earth.

The steam trails came closer. Cade pulled out his spyglass and focused it. The outline of a phraxsloop was clear against the dark-green treetops. It was a snub-nosed vessel, with a medium-sized phraxchamber mounted in the middle. Steam billowed from the two funnels that sprouted from the sides. And as they got closer, Cade could make out its pilot. Long hair and matted beard. A greeny-brown cloak. There was no doubt that it was the individual he'd encountered in the forest behind his cabin.

Merton Hoist.

And there, Cade saw, lying in the stern of the sloop, was a large tarpaulin bundle lashed down with rope.

'Tug,' he breathed.

They sailed on, closing steadily in on the phraxsloop. High above it, and sailing soundlessly, the *Caterbird* approached undetected.

Almost above the phraxsloop now, Phineal's hands played with the ropes, pulling on some, releasing others, and bringing the skycraft out of its dive and level in the sky. The webfoot reached down, and Cade's heart missed a beat as he saw the long blade in his hand.

Phineal turned. 'You'll have to steer,' he said. 'He won't hear us coming above the hum of the phraxchamber.'

Cade swallowed, but took hold of the ropes that the webfoot was holding out.

'Keep us above the sloop as we come in,' Phineal told him. 'Steady, and to the stern. I'll board her and free Tug. Be ready to climb as soon as I give the signal.'

Cade levelled the flight weights and, as they got closer, lowered the mast sails a tad to slow the skycraft down. Phineal climbed to his feet and moved to the prow. He tied a rope around his waist and attached the other end to the carved caterbird prow, then, gripping the head with his arms, he swung down and dropped onto the back of the phraxsloop below.

Cade's hands were trembling as he watched

Merton Hoist's back hunched over the controls at the phraxchamber, one tattooed hand on the tiller. He didn't look round.

Phineal worked quickly, the sharp blade cutting through the ropes, and Cade saw Tug's bemused face appear from beneath the flapping folds of tarpaulin. As Phineal tied the rope around Tug's waist, Cade struggled to keep the skycraft steady. He was realigning the under-sails when Tug looked up – and at the sight of his friend, his mouth opened and he let out a heart-rending cry.

'Cade!'

Merton Hoist turned. The look of puzzlement on his face changed to disbelief as he saw Tug and Phineal at the stern, and then the *Caterbird* hovering above.

Suddenly, Hoist sprang into action. Cade watched in stunned horror, everything suddenly moving in slow motion, as the mire-pearler spun round. A wide-barrelled, large-bore phraxpistol was gripped in one hand. And before Phineal could duck, or Cade had a chance to take evasive action, Merton Hoist fired. Once. Twice.

The first shot whistled past Cade's ear. The second struck the port-side mast, splintering it, then ricocheted off and passed through one of the upper sails. The small hole was instantly ripped wide open by the powerful wind, leaving the sail in tatters.

The *Caterbird* went into a spinning dive.

At the back of the phraxlighter, Phineal threw his knife. It struck Merton Hoist in the right shoulder hard, the blade emerging at the back. Hoist fell away from the phraxchamber and clutched at the wound, his face contorted with pain. He fell back against the flight controls, causing the phraxsloop to drop from the sky like a stone, rolling in the air as it did so.

Phineal and Tug jumped.

Side by side, the skycraft and phraxsloop plunged down through the air. And far below, the trees of the forest tossed in the wind as they waited to take the two stricken vessels in their deadly embrace.

· CHAPTER SEVENTEEN ·

The *Caterbird* dropped down out of the sky, Cade gripping hold of the bundle of ropes, wondering what to do.

'Earth and Sky protect me . . .' he breathed as, acting instinctively, he let go of all of the ropes but one. The rudder rope. This he gripped ferociously in both hands. Then, leaning back, he pulled on it with all his might.

Beside him, the phraxsloop plummeted past unchecked. Merton Hoist was hanging onto the port balustrade with one arm, his moss-green cloak flapping like the broken wing of an injured ratbird.

Heart thumping in his chest, Cade felt the *Caterbird* respond to the upraised rudder. He held on grimly to the rudder rope as the sails flapped noisily above him. Slowly, slowly, the skycraft was easing up out of its dive.

All at once, from below him, there came a loud *crash* as Hoist's phraxsloop struck the uppermost branches of the trees. Cade heard the sounds of cracking and splintering, and muffled cries – and looked down to see the sloop and its pilot disappear from sight beneath the leafy canopy of a vast spreading lullabee.

'Cade! Cade!' It was Phineal.

He was below the skycraft, clinging to Tug's shoulders. Tug himself was suspended from the *Caterbird*'s carved prow by the rope, and swaying to and fro like a pendulum.

The forest canopy was no more than twenty strides below him. But Cade was in control now. Keeping a firm grip on the rudder rope, he grasped the sail ropes and lowered the flapping sails in one smooth movement. The *Caterbird*'s descent slowed right down as it approached the top of a towering ironwood pine.

'Just a tad further,' Phineal's voice called. 'Ease off on the rudder.'

Letting go of Tug, the webfoot jumped down lightly onto a jutting branch at the top of the ironwood. Tug was dangling from the rope, head down and eyes shut, his great bare feet grazing the top of the forest canopy. He wasn't moving.

Cade swallowed anxiously, then followed Phineal's instruction. The skycraft dropped down two strides or so and came to a steady hover.

'That's it,' said Phineal. 'Now chuck me the tolley rope.'

Cade threw the coil of rope down to Phineal, who tethered the *Caterbird* to a stout branch. Next, leaving the

skycraft bobbing in the air, its prow lower than the stern under Tug's heavy weight, Cade climbed down gingerly onto one of the uppermost branches of the ironwood pine. It swayed gently beneath his feet, the heavy pine cones hanging below in clusters giving off a rich, nutty perfume.

'Tug . . .' Cade reached out and cupped his hand round his friend's chin. 'Tug, what is it?'

Tug opened his eyes and looked at him from behind hooded lids.

'Tug, speak to me,' said Cade.

Phineal climbed over and joined Cade on the branch. He shook his head.

'It's a classic slaver's trick,' he told him. 'A cloth saturated in a tincture of sleepbane and camphor-root most likely, clamped over his face.'

'Is he going to be all right?' said Cade, alarmed.

'Once the effects wear off,' Phineal assured him. 'Though he's going to be a bit groggy for a couple of hours.'

The webfoot reached forward and grasped hold of Tug beneath the arms, then braced himself.

'I'll steady him,' he said. 'You untie the rope.' Phineal turned to Tug. 'I'm going to swing you round, then I want you to stand on the branch below and hold onto the tree trunk as tightly as you can. Understand?'

Tug nodded groggily.

Phineal manoeuvred him round until his legs touched the branch below, then he lowered him down onto it.

Tug looked down and seemed surprised to find himself standing upright. His legs went wobbly, and he grabbed hold of the tree trunk beside him, with Phineal supporting him. Cade leaned forward and untied the knotted rope around Tug's middle.

'You two wait here,' Phineal instructed. 'I'll bring the *Caterbird* down to you.' His crest glowed a warm orange as he patted Cade on the shoulder. 'Nice flying by the way, Cade Quarter.'

The webfoot returned to the hovering skycraft and climbed aboard, then brought it down to hover beside the ironwood branch. Cade – basking in Phineal's praise – gently guided the disorientated Tug onto the prow deck. The *Caterbird* pitched wildly under his weight. Cade grimaced, but the varnished sumpwood was more than buoyant enough to support Tug's weight.

Tug himself noticed nothing amiss. He sat down heavily, his head slumped onto his chest and he began to snore loudly.

Cade joined Phineal in the flight seats below the masts. The webfoot had his hand raised against the glare of the sun as he scanned the surrounding forest.

'Over there,' he said, pointing.

A little way off, billowing out of the low branches of a lullabee tree, were clouds of steam. And there, halfway down the trunk, was Merton Hoist's phraxsloop, wedged tightly in the fork of two great branches. The prow was dented and the phraxchamber was skewered by a splintered length of branch. One of the two funnels had been badly mangled, hissing steam still billowing out of it; the other funnel had been shorn off completely.

Cade saw Phineal pull a gutting-knife from his belt, and he reached down and untied his phraxmusket from beneath his seat. Then, raising two of the mast sails, Phineal guided the *Caterbird* down towards the wrecked sloop. The hissing grew louder.

'Where is he?' Cade heard him mutter as they drew closer. 'Where *is* he?'

Cade scanned the deck of the phraxsloop. But there was no trace of Hoist. He remembered seeing him dangling from the balustrade, and hearing the grinding crash as the vessel had struck the trees. Could anyone have survived such a collision?

Then Cade saw it.

'Look,' he said, and pointed at the blood; splashes of red, bright against the silvery turquoise of the lullabee leaves.

Phineal nodded, his crest flashing a grim indigo and purple.

'And there's more over there,' said Cade, pointing to the smearing of blood on the branch below them.

Whether it was from the wounded shoulder, or some other injury he'd picked up when he crash-landed, the mire-pearler was bleeding badly. One thing was clear, though.

He wasn't dead.

Phineal brought the *Caterbird* down to land and stepped off the skycraft onto the ground. Cade jumped down after him.

'He can't have got far,' said Phineal, lashing the *Caterbird* securely to the base of the lullabee tree and pointing to the trail of blood that led off across the forest floor. 'We'll track him on foot.'

· CHAPTER EIGHTEEN ·

Leaving Tug slumped over on the foredeck and snoring softly, Cade and Phineal crept forward, following the trail of blood on the forest floor. Beyond a stand of lufwood trees, the trail led into the long grass of a vast clearing.

Phineal stopped, blade in hand, and looked out across the swaying grass. There, pausing and stooping to graze as they went, was a great migrating herd of triple-horn tilder moving steadily across the pasture. Thousands of them. Bucks and does, old and young, with curling horns and glossy butternut-coloured fur; new-born fawns, with spindly legs and three bumps on the tops of their heads, their backs still dappled with blue.

Cade shouldered his phraxmusket, then pulled his spyglass from his top pocket and surveyed the clearing, while Phineal knelt down and dabbed at a pool of blood at his feet. Beside it lay several lengths of cloth from a torn shirt.

'He's been bleeding pretty bad,' said Phineal.

Cade nodded. He looked around, his head swimming at the sight of all the blood, spattering the grass and the leaves of the low shrubs, staining the ground – and then he saw it. A knife, the bloodstained blade glinting in the shards of sunlight. The mire-pearler must have pulled it from the wound.

'Phineal,' he said quietly.

Phineal straightened up, then, catching sight of the knife, stooped down and picked it up. He wiped the blade on his breeches, then turned to Cade.

'Maybe he didn't make it after all,' he said.

'You . . . you think he might be dead?' said Cade.

'That much blood,' said Phineal, his crest glowing a dark purple. 'If he isn't dead now, he soon will be.'

Sky willing, Cade found himself thinking.

The pair of them looked ahead as the trail of blood crossed the clearing and disappeared into the forest.

'Come on,' said the webfoot, stepping out into the sea of rippling grass. 'He must be somewhere nearby. And when we find the body, maybe we'll find some clue as to what those mire-pearlers are aiming to do.'

Cade lowered his spyglass and was about to follow him, when all at once, from somewhere out in the clearing, there came a colossal *crash*. He didn't need his spyglass to see that something had alarmed the great herd of grazing tilder.

And then he saw it. A logworm.

It had appeared suddenly, rearing up out of the long

grass on the far side of the pastures on powerful jets of air, before crashing down directly in front of the herd, blocking its path. The tilder instantly panicked. Those in front scattered, while those following behind turned and stampeded back across the clearing, only to find their way blocked again by a second log-worm, which reared up out of the grass as sud-denly as the first and came crashing down in front of them.

As Cade and Phineal watched, the two log-worms hissed and writhed as they rose back into the air. The terrified herd turned away again and began thundering towards the edge of the clearing where Phineal and Cade were standing. Thousands of triple-horn

tilder, heads down, hoofs pounding down the lush grass-land, desperately seeking the safety of the forest as the two logworms hovered on either side of the herd.

Cade fumbled with the strap of the phraxmusket, only for Phineal to stay his hand.

'Watch,' he said simply.

Suddenly, about fifty strides in front of them, Cade heard a great whoosh of air, and a third logworm rose up out of the long grass – directly in the path of the stampeding herd. As it too crashed down and rose up again in a writhing, undulating movement, the herd turned again and thundered off, back in the direction they'd come.

Penned in on three sides by the logworms now, the tilder raced towards the distant treeline.

Cade raised his spyglass once more and then swallowed hard. There, waiting patiently in the dappled shadows on the very edge of the treeline, were stacks of logs, one on top of another, intertwined and beginning to writhe and pulsate horribly.

More logworms! Hundreds of them . . .

The tilder herd stampeded towards them, their eyes rolling and teeth bared in blind panic. At the very last moment, the writhing wall of logworms rose up in a mighty whooshing hiss, like a squadron of phraxships taking to the air. Unable to stop, the stampeding herd crashed headlong into them.

As Cade watched in horrified fascination, triple-horn tilder were thrown up into the air in waves, only to come crashing down into the logworms' cavernous maws.

'Earth and Sky,' he murmured weakly.

The remaining herd scattered in all directions, but were hunted down by the writhing, rolling logworms, which came tumbling out across the grassland like a moving wall. Lunging after one, then another, and another, the hideous creatures sucked tilder after panic-stricken tilder into their gaping mouths and down to their innards. There, still struggling, they were gripped by rippling bands of powerful muscle which contracted in slow spasms, snapping their bones and crushing the life out of them.

The rapidly thinning herd howled and screeched as the logworms' feeding frenzy grew more intense, rising to a hideous cacophony – before coming to an abrupt stop when the last tilder was swallowed up.

And then there was silence.

Across the clearing, bloated logworms hovered just above the ground in clusters. For a moment, the gorged creatures paused. Then, still hovering, they began to disperse. Slowly, no longer writhing or rippling, but heavy and sagging drunkenly, the logworms heaved themselves in ones and twos across the clearing and into the shadows of the forest.

A couple came lumbering towards Cade and Phineal, causing Cade to reach for his phraxmusket once more, only for Phineal to raise a finger to his lips.

'They won't bother with us now,' he whispered. 'They'll lie up and sleep for weeks, slowly digesting the food in their bellies. Ferns will take root on their backs.

Moss will grow thick and green. They'll look like any other fallen logs – and be just as harmless,' he added. 'Until the sound of migrating tilder triggers another cascade . . .'

'Cascade,' Cade repeated numbly.

'That's what we've just witnessed,' Phineal said. 'A logworm cascade. One of the great and terrible spectacles of these mighty Deepwoods of ours. Never seen one before . . .'

'And I hope I never see one again,' said Cade with a shudder.

The two logworms wheezed by no more than two strides away, the ring of eyes around their mouths heavy and lidded as they went past. Cade and Phineal watched them disappear into the undergrowth.

All at once, from just behind him, Cade heard a noise – a muffled footfall, followed by a sudden movement, and a blow to the side of his head that was so hard Cade saw a rush of shooting stars.

Then everything went black.

· CHAPTER NINETEEN ·

Cade awoke to find himself swaying from side to side. He felt giddy and sick, and his head throbbed painfully at a point just above his right ear. He went to rub it with his fingertips – which is when he discovered that he couldn't move his arms.

He opened his eyes, looked around blearily. Then tried to cry out, but couldn't do that either.

He was gagged and hanging upside down, suspended from a length of bark-stripped branch to which he'd been bound by the ankles and wrists. Two hefty hammerhead goblins were carrying him, one behind and one in front, the ends of the branch resting on their shoulders. Ahead of him, two more hammerheads were carrying Phineal, who had been trussed up just the same. And when Cade craned his neck and looked back, there too was Tug, strapped down to the deck of the *Caterbird*, which was being towed by four more hammerheads.

Cade's head slumped back. There was nothing he could do. Nothing any of them could do.

As the goblins continued through the forest, Cade stared upwards. The sun had set and the patches of sky behind the interlocking fretwork of branches had turned to deepest indigo. Halter bats, with their pointed ears and stalk-eyes, glided from tree to tree on broad leathery wings. And some while later, he spotted a woodcat crouched on an overhead branch.

The creature looked up from the lemkin it had just killed and hissed at the line of goblins passing beneath it – a mistake, as the next moment it fell, its neck pierced by a barbed hammerhead arrow. The woodcat toppled down to the forest floor, the lemkin still clutched in its claws. Just in front of Cade, a hammerhead bent down and proceeded to stuff both creatures into his bulging forage-sack.

Cade sighed. He had no idea how long he'd been tied up like this – although if the numbness of his feet and hands was anything to go by, it had been a considerable time.

It was growing darker by the minute, yet the hammerheads lit no lanterns or lamps. Instead, without easing their pace, they marched on, their keen eyesight and keener sense of smell guiding them through the forest.

They had distinctive brow tattoos, Cade noticed. Dark, jagged blocks of black that resembled tree-lined ridges, and tunics festooned with animal bones and teeth, each stitched firmly into place to form a kind of eerie ivory-coloured body armour. And they were heavily armed too, with serrated broadswords, double-headed axes and blackwood bows, together with quivers full of white-feathered arrows.

The smell of acrid woodsmoke was the first sign that they were nearing their destination. Then there were sounds. Chopping. Hammering. The murmur of voices. And then, as they left the dense forest and entered a clearing, the yellow glow of lamps hanging at the entrance to a tall hive-tower.

As they approached, the tilder hide at the doorway swung back, and dozens of goblin young'uns came running out to greet the returning warriors. Laughing and grimacing, they egged one another onto poke the three prisoners with sticks – until they were chased away by the goblin matrons who had emerged from the hive-tower to see what the hunting party had brought back to eat. Those with bulging forage-sacks handed them over to the females, who scuttled back inside to turn the animals they'd killed into diced meat for the stew pot and skinned pelts for coats, blankets and rugs.

The hammerheads carrying Phineal entered the tower first, and, glancing back, Cade saw the four hammerheads towing the *Caterbird* tie the skycraft to one of the ironwood staves that secured the base of the hive-tower. Strapped to the foredeck, Tug was sound asleep, and the hammerheads didn't disturb him. Then the hammerheads carrying Cade pushed aside the tilder hides and stepped into the hive-tower.

Cade looked around him as he was carried inside. With its wicker framework, raffia-mat walls and central fire, the place was familiar. So was the smell – a mixture of woodsmoke and hammelhorn grease.

He had been a guest in a hive-tower very similar to this one once before. That tower had belonged to the Shadow Clan of the High Valley Nation. He and Celestia had rescued one of the clan's young'uns from a bloodoak and been rewarded by the elders with hammerhead hospitality and bronze rings that marked them out as honorary clan members.

'Put them down over there,' barked a tall, ancient-looking goblin with leathery skin that was almost completely covered in blurred tattoos. He wore a feathered cloak with a collar of snowbird beaks that radiated out from his neck in a spiked ruff. In his hand he carried the carved copperwood staff of a clan chief.

Cade was lowered to the ground beside the central fire, his head throbbing worse than ever. Phineal was set down next to him. The two of them lay on their sides, arms and legs still pulled up above their heads. No one came to unbind them, and some kind of argument was in progress on the far side of the fire. The clan chief stood at the centre of the ring of warriors as each spoke in turn.

'They don't look like the skyfarers . . .' one ventured.

'Looks can deceive. The Stone Clan of the Low Valley Nation warned us to be wary of wanderers . . .'

'I say we make a fire of them – tie them to flametrees and watch them fly . . .'

'The Nightwoods creature too . . .'

'*And* their skycraft.'

Voices were raised in agreement, only for the clan chief to silence them by pounding the foot of his staff on the ground.

'Enough!' he said. 'We cannot take any chances – not after what the skyfarers did to the Stone Clan.' The clan chief turned and looked across the tower to where Phineal and Cade lay, bound and gagged, helpless. 'But we are not savages like the skyfarers,' he snarled. 'We will tie them to flametrees, but we will kill them first.'

The clan chief pointed his staff at two of his warriors, who pulled out daggers from their belts.

'Make it quick and painless,' he instructed. 'Baahl, chief of the Bone Clan of the High Valley Nation, has spoken.'

The two warriors approached Cade and Phineal from the other side of the fire. Cade could see the firelight glinting on their bone armour, and on the blades of the daggers in their hands. He wanted to scream, to lash out with his fists and feet, but he could hardly move.

The first hammerhead knelt down and roughly rolled Cade over onto his back. Then, raising the dagger in one hand, the hammerhead reached down and tore Cade's tunic open, his forefinger locating Cade's rapidly beating heart.

Cade screwed his eyes shut and tense as he waited for the blow to fall.

And waited . . .

Nothing. Just the crackle of the central fire in the hushed hive-tower. He felt a tug at his throat and opened his eyes. The warrior had lowered his dagger and was examining the brass ring on the tilderleather cord that Cade wore around his neck.

'A clan ring,' he said, looking back over his shoulder at his chief. 'This is no skyfarer . : . Unless he stole it.'

Cade desperately shook his head from side to side, and beside him, Phineal's crest glowed red then purple, then red again.

'Let them speak,' said the clan chief, approaching.

The hammerhead warrior raised his blade and cut through first Cade's gag, then Phineal's.

'I didn't steal the ring!' Cade blurted out. 'I was given it! I am a friend of the Shadow Clan of the High Valley Nation,' he went on, hardly pausing for breath. 'I rescued the clan chief's son from the tarry vine . . . I mean the strangle vine,' he corrected himself, remembering the hammerhead name for the deadly creeper. 'The strangle vine and the tree of blood.'

'We are from the Farrow Lake,' Phineal added. 'The skyfarers of which you speak are no friends of ours. My webfoot brothers were ambushed by them in the Grey Gorges beyond the ridges to the south-west . . .'

'That is the territory of the Stone Clan of the Low Valley Nation,' said the clan chief. 'They have suffered much at the hands of the skyfarers since they invaded their lands.' He nodded to the hammerhead warrior, who proceeded to cut the tilderleather straps binding Cade and Phineal.

His arms free now, Cade rubbed life back into his numbed hands and legs. Phineal did the same.

The clan chief ushered them to sit down on tilder rugs by the fire. The clan formed a circle around them, while the chief called for food and drink for the 'friend of Shadow Clan and his companion'. He could not apologize enough . . .

'Shadow Clan are eyes and ears of the two nations,' he explained. 'They roam the farthest of all the clans, and they have told us of you Farrow Lakers. I am sorry we did not recognize you as such.'

'We webfoots have only recently arrived,' Phineal said with a shrug as the food and drink arrived – platters of broiled meat, bowls of fried gladebeet, flagons of woodale and water. 'But we intend to stay and, like you, defend our home from the mire-pearlers.'

'Mire-pearlers?' said the chief, exchanging looks with his warriors. 'So it's pearls that these skyfarers are after.'

'They made slaves of the Stone Clan warriors they captured,' said one of the hammerheads, 'and are holding them in their great phraxship. But we knew such a vessel was too large for mere slavers.'

'A phraxship?' said Phineal, his crest glowing with alarm. 'My webfoot brothers reported being attacked by phraxsloops, maybe three or four in number, but nothing larger.'

'Those are their scout ships,' explained the clan chief. 'Hoverworms compared to the mighty logworm that is their phraxship. It has powerful weapons from the great

city of the glades. Shadow Clan reported that it had
turned away from the gorges and was steaming to the
east . . .'

Phineal's crest turned a colour Cade had never seen
before – a shade of dark, storm-cloud grey. The webfoot
shuddered.

'Towards the Farrow Lake,' he said. 'This is worse
than I feared. With a phraxship that size, they'll be carrying
weapons, phraxengineers and more than enough slaves
to rip every last pearl from the clam beds and leave the
lake in ruins. We're not facing a skirmish with a few mire-
pearlers,' said Phineal grimly. 'We're facing an invasion.'

· CHAPTER TWENTY ·

Gart Ironside's phraxlighter hovered in the misty midday air. Its phraxchamber hummed softly, and a thin wisp of steam rose from its funnel and wound its way round the carving of the hoverworm at the prow. Below the vessel, a sliver of glowing red nestling among the jumble of boulders on the High Farrow Ridge was the only sign of the great network of caverns that lay beneath.

A rope ladder unfurled over the side of the phraxlighter and dropped down into the darkness. Locking the flight levers into position, Gart emerged from the small wheelhouse and climbed down onto the rope ladder, then descended carefully, rung after swaying rung. He was followed by Thorne the fisher goblin, then Blatch Helmstoft, and finally, Cade. Each of them had sturdy packs strapped to their backs.

Stepping onto the ladder, Cade glanced beneath him. His stomach lurched.

Easy does it, he told himself. *One rung at a time.*

As Cade climbed down into the narrow fissure in the rock, he passed through a shaft of daylight that penetrated the cavern below. Anchored to the cavern roof above, and descending just to his right, was a long, pale yellow stalactite, its pitted surface glinting and, at its tapered end, a large red jewel set into the encrusted rock. As the shaft of daylight hit it, the jewel refracted the light into a deep red glow, which gave the cave below its name.

The Cavern of Blood.

That was what the white trogs who inhabited the subterranean system of tunnels and caves called it. For them, this was a place of reverence, where they would gather each dawn to witness the miraculous transformation of this, the highest of their many caverns.

It was this cavern that Gart Ironside had stumbled upon a little over a year ago now, and from which he had removed the sacred jewel in the hope of selling it for a fortune in Great Glade. But the phraxpilot had had a change of heart and replaced the jewel – and just in the nick of time, saving Cade, Celestia, Blatch and Thorne from gruesome sacrifice at the hands of the secretive and superstitious white trogs and their all-powerful queen.

Yet from that first inauspicious encounter an unlikely relationship had begun to grow between the Farrow Lakers and the trogs. And the reason for it was Celestia's cave-cake – a sweet slab of granulated woodwasp honey and mint charlock, perfect for staving off hunger on long cavern explorations. She had put some in her father's pack, wrapped up in oiled paper. When he was captured, the white trogs had found and eaten the cave-cake – and were astounded.

Down in the subterranean caverns, they had tasted nothing quite like it before. And they were desperate for more. In return for slabs of cave-cake, the white trogs were prepared to trade crystals of outstanding beauty and an array of aromatic cave mosses and lichen. And so, once a month, Gart would lower the rope ladder and descend into the glowing red light of the Cavern of Blood with a bulging pack on his back, and trade the cave-cake that Celestia had taught him to make.

It was the first connection with the outside world the white trogs had had for centuries. How fortunate it was, Blatch Helmstoft had observed, that the white trog queen had a sweet tooth.

As Cade climbed past the jewel, he felt the rope ladder tense and jolt beneath him, and he looked down to see that Gart had reached the cavern floor and stepped off the bottom rung. And as he continued to descend, there was another jolt, and then another, as Thorne and Blatch did the same.

Translucent air shrimps with bulbous bodies and multi-eyed heads drifted towards Cade, their long thin feelers trailing over his skin as he continued his shaky descent. Slime snails moved sedately over the surface of the surrounding walls, up and down, leaving iridescent trails behind them.

Stepping down to the floor of the cavern at last, Cade looked around. It was dark and gloomy, the air chill and dank. The red light was much dimmer now than the blood-like glow of dawn, but soon his eyes grew accustomed to the shadows. Gart, Thorne and Blatch had taken off their packs and were removing slabs of cave-cake from them. As Cade did the same, he remembered Celestia's parting words to him. She had taken Tug back to the tree-cabin in the Western Woods to recover, while Phineal had returned to Fifth Lake Village to organize a webfoot skycraft patrol.

'With or without the white trogs,' she had said, her green eyes flashing, 'I am staying to fight for the Farrow Lake.'

His backpack empty, Gart turned and crossed to a low arch on the far side of the cavern, where he picked up an opalescent snail shell that lay at its base. He put the opening of the shell to his mouth and blew hard. The air filled with a deep sonorous sound that echoed down the tunnel beyond. It was answered, moments later, by a similar sound from somewhere far below.

Gart placed the shell back on the ground and returned to the others. 'If the hammerhead tribes are to be believed,' he said, 'we don't have much time to organize our defences.' He eyed the stacks of cave-cake at their feet. 'I only hope we can convince the trog queen to support us.'

Thorne nodded. 'If the mire-pearlers are as strong as

I fear, we need all the help we can get.'

Just then, there was a flurry of movement at the entrance to the cavern. The four Farrow Lakers turned to see one, then two, then a dozen more immense white cave-spiders emerge through the archway with white trog riders perched upon the curved saddles on their backs.

Another blast on a shell sounded from somewhere beyond the cavern, and moments later the largest spider of all emerged through the entrance. Seated on the tall latticed saddle that rested on its thorax, plaited silver thongs securing it round the abdomen and to each of the creature's eight legs, was the queen of the white trogs.

She sat tall and upright, her crystal-shard necklace and spiked crown glinting. Around her shoulders was a long snailskin cloak, clusters of shells emitting flute-like sounds, while beneath it, flowing spidersilk robes glowed in the muted red light.

The white trog queen eyed them imperiously, as did the cave-bat which had swooped in and perched on her arm. She flicked the reins and her spider stepped forward. As it did so, the cave-bat let out a high-pitched whistling cry and flapped its papery wings to regain its balance. The queen raised a hand and stroked it gently until it folded its wings and fell still. She turned to her guards and made a clicking sound with her tongue. The guards lowered their crystal spears, and the queen blinked twice, her painted red eyelids flashing as she did so. Then she cleared her throat.

'You bring much sky sweetness from the upper world,'

she observed, eyeing the slabs of cave-cake on the cavern floor. 'Fortunately, we have ample crystal to trade for it.'

'This time we have a different price, your majesty,' said Blatch, stepping forward – only to be stopped by one of the guards, who lowered the jagged shard of crystal in his hands and jabbed the pointed end into the professor's chest. 'I . . . that is, we,' he said, looking back and gesturing with a sweep of his arm to the others, 'have need of your help.'

'There are evil-doers in the upper world who are heading to the Farrow Lake,' Thorne broke in. 'They are called mire-pearlers,' he said grimly. 'And they mean to destroy the Farrow Lake.'

The trog queen's lips pursed, turning her mouth to two thin white lines.

'It was the hammerhead tribes of the Western Woods who alerted us to the danger, your majesty,' said Cade. 'Many hammerheads have been taken and are being held as slaves.'

The queen reached for the cave-bat on her arm and tickled its ears, then stroked under its chin, her eyes fixed on the top of its little skull-like head. Then she lifted her gaze and surveyed them one by one, her expression impassive. All around her, the mounted guards gripped their crystal-shard lances, waiting for a clicked command.

'What happens in the upper world does not concern us,' she pronounced. 'If these mire-pearlers you talk of do not enter our caverns, we shall have no quarrel with them—'

'But, your majesty,' Blatch blurted out, 'with all due

respect, these mire-pearlers could do untold damage to the Farrow Lake if we do not resist.'

The white trog queen clicked her tongue, and the guard on spiderback closest to Blatch jabbed his crystal-shard spear into the professor's chest a second time.

'If they do not enter our caverns, we shall ignore them,' the trog queen said again, slowly and clearly. 'As is the way of the white trogs.' Her eyes narrowed. 'The sky sweetness you bring from the upper world is intoxicating, but I . . . we, can do without it.'

The words hung in the air.

'The cave-cake is a gift, your majesty,' said Gart Ironside graciously. 'I would only ask that you remember this, should you change your mind,' and with that he turned and headed back to the ladder.

Then, without saying another word, the flute-like shells on her cape echoing sonorously, the white trog queen swung round and, with another twitch of the reins, turned her spider and left the cavern. The guards followed behind, their spiders scuttling down the walls and across the floor after hers.

'Now what?' said Blatch bleakly, as the last of them disappeared, and they were alone again.

'Now,' said Thorne, turning and punching his fist into his open palm, 'we shall face the mire-pearlers ourselves.'

Thorne sounded defiant, but Cade knew better. His friend was worried. Not that he was about to show it.

Looking up, the fisher goblin saw Gart climbing

through the shaft of daylight towards the hovering phraxlighter and he climbed up after him. Cade and Blatch followed close behind.

At the top of the ladder, they emerged squinting into the daylight of the late afternoon and climbed aboard the phraxlighter. Gart was already at the controls and preparing to cast off.

The sun was orange and low in the sky, tipping the jagged treeline with gold. Cade looked down at the Farrow Ridges – the magnificent Five Falls, the tree-fringed Ledges and the lush meadowlands, with the mirror-like Farrow Lake nestling like a jewel in their midst.

Celestia was right. This *was* a place worth fighting for.

Just then, in the distant Western Woods, a blazing luf-wood tree shot up above the forest canopy in a jagged ball of magenta flames and soared towards Open Sky. Cade's heart missed a beat. It was a hammerhead flare! The hammerhead nations had spotted the mire-pearlers and were warning Cade and the Farrow Lakers, just as they had promised.

Cade turned to Thorne, Blatch and Gart. They too had seen the blazing lufwood.

'The mire-pearlers are approaching,' Thorne said bleakly. Then, as his military training in the Hive Militia came back to the old fisher goblin, he began issuing orders in a calm, steady voice. 'Blatch, your cabin will be our headquarters. We'll drop you on the western shore. Inform the webfoots of the impending danger, then tell

Celestia to gather all the medicines she can lay her hands on. I'll meet you there after I've collected the weapons from my hive-hut and picked up Cade's prowlgrin.'

He turned and laid a reassuring hand on Cade's shoulder.

'I want you, Cade, lad, to go with Gart to the sky-platform and help him provision the phraxlighter with all the supplies she can hold.'

Cade nodded. Despite Thorne's quiet authority, the desperation in the fisher goblin's eyes was plain for all to see.

'When the mire-pearlers get here,' he said, 'Sky protect us all.'

· CHAPTER TWENTY-ONE ·

'Drop me off down there,' said Thorne, pointing to the moon-dappled eastern shore. His hive-hut rose out of the forest just beyond. 'Don't worry,' he reassured Cade, 'Rumblix and I will meet you at the tree-cabin.'

Cade nodded as Gart brought the phraxlighter down towards the row of eel-corrals at the edge of the lake. Hovering just above the shallows, Gart kept the little vessel steady as Thorne clambered over the side and splashed down into the ankle-deep water. On the far side of the shimmering lake, Cade could see the skycraft of the webfoots, all twelve of them, rising up from Fifth Lake Village and setting off for the Western Woods.

Blatch must have already delivered Thorne's instructions to them, Cade realized. The plan was for everyone to gather at the tree-cabin – but first he and Gart had a job to do.

Cade waved to Thorne, then turned and joined Gart at the controls as the phraxpilot steered the *Hoverworm* towards the south-eastern end of the Farrow Lake. After a few moments, the sky-platform came into view.

The wooden structure, with its scaffold supports, squat cabin and massive water tank, protruded high above the canopy of trees around it. The lantern that hung above the cabin door, and that Gart kept burning night and day, shone like a lone yellow star against the gathering darkness.

'Let's try to be as quick as we can,' said Gart as they drew closer. 'We need weapons. Phraxmuskets, ironwood bullets. And any bill-hooks, axes or ice-picks you can lay your hands on. You'll find them in the racks next to the hammock.'

He turned the flight wheel and pulled hard on the rudder lever. Instead of heading for the mooring cradle at the side of the wooden deck, Gart brought the small phraxlighter round in the sky and approached the sky-platform from below.

'I'll get blankets and bales of homespun from my stores,' said Gart. 'And then you can help me load the crates of woodgrog. Twenty or so there were at the last count.'

Gart smiled at the look on Cade's face.

'Purely medicinal, Cade,' he said. 'Celestia's setting up an infirmary at the cabin.' His expression darkened. 'In case of casualties.'

A couple of strides below the deck of the sky-platform now, Gart brought the *Hoverworm* to a near standstill. It hung in the air, swaying slightly. Behind him, Cade heard the jet of fire at the propulsion duct fall still; the clouds of steam billowing from the funnel shrank to a thin, serpentine coil.

'Easy does it,' Gart muttered, as he edged the phraxlighter slowly forward between the struts of the tower until they were directly beneath the wooden platform.

The *Hoverworm* bumped gently against a narrow ledge that spanned the crossbeams, and Cade noticed the narrow flight of stairs that was fixed to them, leading up to a trap door in the deck.

'Tolley rope, Cade,' said Gart.

Cade left the wheelhouse and, seizing one of the coiled

ropes from the stern, jumped onto the wooden ledge, then tethered the vessel securely to one of the mooring rings bolted to its side. Gart stepped off the *Hoverworm* and climbed the stairs to the trap door.

'This is the back entrance,' he said, reaching up and releasing the catch. 'A little less obtrusive than the mooring cradle.'

The trap door swung down.

Cade followed Gart and stepped through onto the broad wooden deck. In front of them was the dimly lit cabin, with the dark silhouette of the water tower looming above it on tripod legs. Gart strode across the deck to the door of the cabin and pushed it open.

'Racks are over there,' he said, turning to Cade as the two of them went inside and pointing to the far side of the room.

With its high ceiling, supported by sturdy copper-wood pillars, the cabin was a lot more spacious than it looked from the outside. In one corner was a hammock slung between two hooks, surrounded by hanging scroll-holders stuffed with barkscroll dockets and receipts. On the wall beyond were racks containing a row of eight phraxmuskets, and an assortment of axes, saws, hammers and other tools. Below them were several sacks of ironwood bullets, with stencilled labels that read *Great Glade Militia*.

'Hurry now, Cade, lad,' said Gart. 'We probably don't have much time.'

While Cade took armfuls of muskets and any tools

that might serve as weapons back to the phraxlighter, Gart crossed to the other side of the cabin. There he gathered up bundles of blankets and rolls of roughly woven cloth, then followed Cade out of the cabin, across the deck and back down the stairs to the *Hoverworm*.

It took them each several journeys to stow what they needed on board. Then they started on the crates of wood-grog, which were stacked outside against the cabin wall, awaiting delivery to the next visiting skytavern. Just like Celestia's cave-cake, the woodgrog, supplied to Gart by Thorne and sold on to the skytaverns, was a lucrative sideline. Back and forth Cade and Gart went in relay, ten times, twenty times . . .

At last the *Hoverworm* was packed tight from port to starboard, prow to stern. Having slotted the last crate into place, Cade dragged a tarpaulin out from a locker at the back of the wheelhouse. The oiled material was heavy and awkward to manoeuvre, and it took him some while to spread it smoothly over the cargo and to secure the ties to the bow-cleats. Straightening up, Cade looked around for Gart, who had gone back up to lock and bolt the cabin door – and realized that something was wrong.

The trap door had been closed. He paused. From above his head, he could hear heavy footsteps, and voices. Gruff, angry voices . . .

Gart was talking loudly – for his benefit, Cade realized.

'I'm the only one here,' his voice rang out. 'Take what

you like. I don't want any trouble . . . from either of the *two* of you . . .'

His heart hammering in his chest, Cade slung a phrax-musket onto his shoulders. *Two of them, two of us*, he thought, trying to stay calm. He couldn't use the trap door as the intruders were directly overhead. He'd have to find another route up.

Crossing to the far side of the ledge, Cade clambered onto the wooden struts of the tower. His feet slipped on the angled crossbeams, threatening to pitch him into the yawning depths beneath. But he steadied himself. Then, trying hard not to look down, he began to climb. The plat-form was some ten or so strides above his head. Bracing his legs, Cade climbed up as far as he dared, then, just as he was about to peer over the edge of the deck, he felt a sharp pain in his hand.

It was all he could do not to cry out.

Looking down, he saw that a long splinter from the rough wood of the strut he'd grasped had embedded itself in his thumb. Wincing with pain, Cade pulled out the bloodied sliver of wood with his teeth and spat it away. Then he tried again. This time he took it more cautiously, gripping the struts above gently, then slowly easing himself up. As his head poked above the platform, he peered across the deck.

'Earth and Sky,' he breathed.

Above him, a battered phraxsloop had berthed at the cradle where Gart usually moored his phraxlighter. It must have just arrived, steam still rising from its twisted

and corroded funnel. Its crew were standing outside the cabin, their backs to Cade. One of them was a broad-shouldered flat-head in a heavy leather coat, his hairless skull glinting in the lantern light. The other, a fourthling in a crushed funnel hat of quarm fur and a gaudily decorated topcoat, had Gart pressed up against the door of the cabin, a phraxpistol at his head.

'I won't ask you again, tell me where the others are,' he was demanding.

'What others?' said Gart innocently. 'I don't see anybody from one skytavern docking to the next. Whoever told you otherwise is mistaken. I . . . erm . . .'

At that moment, Gart spotted Cade. He was looking past his interrogator's left shoulder, straight at him.

Slowly Cade slipped the phraxmusket from his

shoulder with one hand and raised it, propping the barrel against the deck to steady it. He took aim at the fourthling.

'I wouldn't do that,' Gart said, his eyes fixed on Cade.

'Do what?' the fourthling snarled. 'Blow your head off for lying to us?'

'There's a much cleaner way to do it . . .' Gart's eyes darted upwards, once, twice, to the water tower looming over the cabin.

'Reckon this one's skytouched in the head,' sneered the fourthling, pressing the phraxpistol into Gart's temple.

Cade suddenly realized what Gart was trying to tell him.

'The release valve,' said Gart. 'One shot is all you have.'

Cade raised his musket to the water tower, aiming it at the round plug at the base of the tall circular drum. He squeezed the trigger.

'Release valve?' The flathead's voice rose in anger. 'What in Sky's name is a release val—'

There was a flash and an ear-splitting *crack* as the bullet struck the plug, which shattered. The next moment, a jet of lake water shot down from the base of the tower in a thundering torrent, sweeping the flathead and fourthling off their feet and washing them over the edge of the deck and down to the forest below.

Cade ducked back down below the deck as water flooded out of the emptying water tower and cascaded over the sides of the platform, like one of the Five Falls in full flow. When the last of the water had poured away, he pulled himself up onto the dripping deck and hurried across to the cabin. The water had swept the platform-keeper's legs from under him, but he was clinging to the handle of the cabin door with both hands.

'Good shot,' he spluttered, as Cade helped him to his feet. 'Now let's get out of here before any more mire-pearlers show up.'

'What about that?' said Cade, pointing to the phrax-sloop berthed at the cradle.

Gart cast an eye over it as he stomped soggily over to the trap door and opened it. 'Hull-rot, chamber-rust and ice-damage to the funnel,' he said dismissively. 'The thing's a death trap.'

They boarded the *Hoverworm* and Cade cast off, a wave of relief washing over him. Relief that he'd managed to climb up the struts of the sky-platform; relief that he'd been able to hit the release valve, and that Gart had held on and, unlike the mire-pearlers, had not been washed from the deck to his death. As they flew low over the treetops, keeping to the fringes of the lake at a low steam to avoid being seen, Cade looked back the way they'd come – and instantly wished he hadn't.

For there, looming up above the Needles and steaming towards the Farrow Lake, was a vast skyship. It was black in colour; decks, fore and aft, snub-nosed prow, high balustraded stern and great central phraxchamber and funnel all coated in pine-pitch. The hull portholes

were tightly shuttered, and the hull rigging sagged under the weight of a thousand twinkling lanterns that clinked against the ship's black sides.

Cade pulled his spyglass from his pocket and put it to his eye as Gart brought the *Hoverworm* to a slow glide and ducked down below the treeline. Up close, Cade could see what these 'lanterns' attached to the hull rigging actually were.

Skulls. Hundreds of them, each one strung on rope, and containing a tallow candle that shone out through the eye sockets. Skulls of goblins and fourthlings, trogs and trolls; skulls of those who had come up against this hideous skyship. And lost.

Now it had arrived at the Farrow Lake to bring more death and destruction. Cade's scalp itched as he imagined his own skull strung alongside the others, a tallow candle set inside it.

No, he told himself bravely. *That shall not happen.*

But then, as he trained his spyglass along the shuttered side and up towards the black prow, his courage drained away. The name of the vessel was picked out in angular blood-red letters:

DOOMBRINGER.

· CHAPTER TWENTY-TWO ·

The moon was full and bright and high above their heads as Gart brought the *Hoverworm* down through the forest canopy, deep in the Western Woods. Shrouded in shadow beneath them was Blatch Helmstoft's tree-cabin, suspended from the mighty ironwood pine. The window-shutters were closed and the place was in darkness. It looked deserted.

As they came down lower, Cade caught sight of Celestia's two prowlgrins, fast asleep on the jutting roof-platform. To their left were the webfoot goblins' twelve skycraft, tethered to mooring rings around the roof of the east turret. And far below on the forest floor, he could just make out the conical snailskin tents that Phineal Glyfphith and his webfoot brothers had erected, nestling in the undergrowth in a tight circle.

Dwarfing the tents, but almost invisible to the untrained eye, were four tall hive-towers. They looked like a part of the forest itself. Three of the towers had already been camouflaged, while the fourth was being worked on, with half a dozen hammerhead goblins clinging to its pointed roof, using lengths of forest vine to tie leafy branches and bunches of pine-needles to the woven matting walls.

The four clans of the Western Woods must have gathered, Cade realized, each erecting its own hive-tower. The Bone Clan and the Shadow Clan of the High Valley Nation, Cade had already encountered, but the two clans of the Low Valley Nation were new to him.

Cade looked down at the hive-towers as Gart brought the *Hoverworm* in to land on the under-balcony of the shuttered tree-cabin. Judging by the pearly fish scales, like droplets of rain, which decorated the entrance of the first hive-tower, and the barbed hooks and coiled nets that hung from the tunics and necks of the hammerheads outside it, this must be the River Clan. The hive-tower next to it was surrounded by shards of flint that anchored it into position. This was home to the Stone Clan, whose members were stocky, thick-set hammerhead goblins, with curious tusk-like teeth protruding from their lower jaws.

The hammerheads of the Bone Clan, with their brow tattoos and distinctive body armour of animal bones and teeth stitched onto their tunics, were outside their own hive-tower, silently preparing their weapons. Warriors sharpened their broadswords and double-headed axes on heavy whetstones; goblin matrons sat cross-legged

on tilder hides, binding snowbird feathers to the ends
of sharpened lengths of blackwood, then storing the finished arrows in leather quivers. Beyond them, members
of the Shadow Clan circled the camp, almost invisible
in the forest gloom as they attached tripwires and
bell-clappers to the surrounding trees to alert them to
intruders; and fish-hooks set at eye-level to punish any
who strayed too close.

As Gart docked the *Hoverworm*, Cade noticed the webfoot goblins in a huddle beside their tents, their crests a
uniform pale green as they gestured to the sky and talked
animatedly. Cade waved to them as he stepped off the
phraxlighter, but the webfoots were too deep in conversation to notice him.

'Come on, Cade,' said Gart, clapping him on the
shoulder. 'We need to tell Thorne and the others what
we saw.'

The pair of them crossed the under-balcony and
climbed the stairs to the first floor of the tree-cabin, where
they emerged in a narrow corridor, dimly lit with wall
candles. A low babble of voices was coming from behind
a polished copperwood door. Gart turned the handle and
pushed the door open, and the pair of them went in.

For Cade, entering Blatch Helmstoft's meeting
chamber was like stepping back in time. At first glance, it
resembled rooms he had known back in the city of Great
Glade.

There were sumptuous satin curtains at the windows
and plush rugs on the polished wooden floor, intricate

patterns picked out in deep reds, greens and blues; there was a detailed tapestry on one wall showing Maris Verginix and the lost children founding the Free Glades. The furniture was made of varnished darkwood: a couch upholstered with leaf-patterned brocade and strewn with silk cushions; straight-back chairs, armchairs and footstools. And there were other items dotted about the chamber. A tall, three-legged table. A glass cabinet containing crystal vases and delicate wood-amber carvings. A broad blackwood chest, inlaid with hammelhorn ivory depicting Deepwoods creatures . . .

This could be a grand salon in a prosperous merchant's mansion on the shore of the New Lake district, Cade thought.

On closer inspection, though, the differences were plain. A startling array of goblin weapons on the far wall, Blatch's magnificent collection of white trog crystal shards on a desk top and an extraordinary splayed skeleton of a rotsucker suspended from the roof beams were all indications of the savage, untamed world of the Deepwoods all about them.

Beneath the skeleton, seated at a black ironwood table, sat a council of war.

Blatch Helmstoft was polishing his wire-rimmed spectacles with a square of blue velvet. In front of him was a parchment notebook, a leadwood pencil lying on an opened page full of diagrams and annotations.

Beside Blatch was Thorne. The fisher goblin was wearing his old military overcoat. Cade saw the patch

stitched to the sleeve, the words picked out in embroidered letters, 1st *Low Town Regt*. Laid out in front of him on
the table were five types of phraxmusket bullets. Phineal
was sitting next to him, his crest glowing the same anx-
ious green as his webfoot brothers outside as he fidgeted
with a copperwood spyglass.

At the end of the table, looming over the others, was
the clan chief Cade and Phineal had encount-ered in
the Western Woods. His heavy brow tattoos and snow-
bird-feather cape marked him out as the high chief of
the hammerhead nations of the Western Woods. And
as Cade and Gart entered, he turned and was about to
speak when the door on the opposite side of the room
burst open and Celestia hurried in, Rumblix at her side.
Tug came lumbering in after them.

'Cade! Gart!' Celestia exclaimed, and she strode across
the chamber towards them, her arms open wide   only
to be knocked aside by Rumblix, who bounded past her
and jumped up at Cade.

'Easy, boy.' Cade grinned, ruffling the prowlgrin's
sleek grey fur as he tickled his back and neck. 'I'm pleased
to see you too. And you, Celestia. And Tug!'

'Tug much better now,' said Tug, a broad smile
spreading across his features. He tapped his head with a
spatula finger. 'Tug was sleepy, but now he's wide awake.'

His friend dwarfed everyone else in the meeting
chamber as he stood before Cade, arms outstretched.
Cade stepped forward and was enveloped in a hefty
embrace.

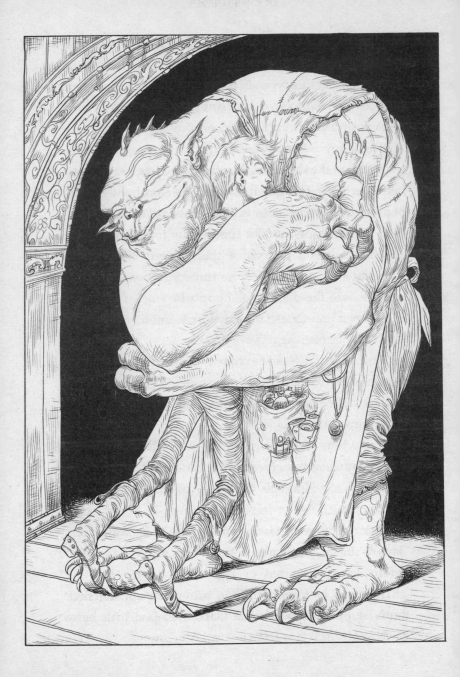

'I'm glad you're feeling better,' Cade said. 'But what's this you're wearing?'

Tug released Cade and looked down at the apron. It was covered in pockets containing vials, wads of bandages and tightly bundled sacks.

'Tug is my assistant,' said Celestia, patting Tug affectionately on the shoulder. 'I've been teaching him how to help me, and he's a quick learner,' she said lightly. Then her face grew more serious. 'Have you brought the supplies, Gart?' she asked. 'The homespun for bandages?'

'It's down in my phraxlighter,' he told her. 'Three bales.'

Celestia frowned. 'You think that'll be enough?'

Gart and Cade exchanged a glance.

'I think we're going to need all the bandages we can lay our hands on,' said Gart quietly.

'And weapons?' said Thorne, looking up from the bullets on the table in front of him.

Gart nodded. 'Some,' he said. 'Eight phraxmuskets and ammunition.'

'Come,' said Celestia, taking Tug by the arm. 'You'll help me unload, won't you, Tug?'

'Tug help,' he said happily as he followed Celestia to the door.

Thorne gestured to two chairs opposite the clan chief. 'This is Baahl,' he said. 'I think you three have met before.'

The clan chief nodded. 'You bring news of the sky-farers?' he asked, peering at Gart, then Cade, his eyes glinting bright beneath his heavy brow tattoos.

Gart sat down, but Cade did not. Instead, he gripped the back of the second chair and took a moment to compose himself.

'The mire-pearlers have discovered the Farrow Ridges,' he said quietly.

For a moment, there was silence. Then Rumblix, sleek and well-groomed, brushed up against him and purred softly.

Cade swallowed. Blatch, Baahl, Phineal and Thorne were looking up at him.

Gart stared down at the table. 'We were surprised at the sky-platform by a couple of their scouts, but Cade here dealt with them,' he said without looking up. 'But then . . .' He paused and glanced at Cade. '*You've* got a way with words – you tell them, Cade. Tell them what we saw.'

'It was a ship,' said Cade. 'Black and shuttered and strung with glowing skulls. As big as a skytavern, but built for war . . . and destruction. We hid below the treeline when we saw it. As we watched, it moored at the sky-platform and then began to open up. Clanking and rattling. Gears grinding. The shutters in the decks slid back and the hatches along the hull rose like a black beetle with a hundred wings. Then the crew came out. Cloddertrogs, flatheads, mobgnomes, fourthlings. All armed with phraxmuskets and pistols, staves and swords . . .'

'I have a thousand warriors,' said Baahl, gathering his feathered cape around him. 'If we strike first . . .'

Cade shook his head. 'Then the final hatch opened,' he said. 'At the centre of the fore-deck. A phraxcannon appeared, on a rotating platform, with four phrax-engineers at the controls. We watched them as they loaded it and trained it on Fifth Lake Village. Then, methodically, they fired it, again and again, and building after building exploded into flaming balls of fire. By the time we crept away, there was nothing left but smoking ruins.' Cade looked across at Phineal, whose crest was now a mournful blue colour. 'I'm so sorry, Phineal,' he said.

The webfoot had his head in his hands.

'Again,' he said, bleakly, raising his head and looking around the table at the others. 'I've seen all this before. At the four lakes. They arrive at a town or city in their skyships and make a show of force. To intimidate the inhabitants, to show that resistance is futile. Then they hole up in their ships, hovering over their intended target, carrying out the occasional raid – but all the while they're plotting. The mire-pearlers eyeing up potential slaves and resources to plunder – and the phrax-engineers working out the best way to harvest them. Then, when they're good and ready, they strike. It may take weeks, months even, but strike they will. And when they do . . .' His voice broke. 'We must prepare ourselves. We must resist . . .'

'But it won't be easy. Not if we're up against a phrax-cannon,' said Thorne, picking up the bullets in front of him in a bunched fist. 'We're going to need weapons of our own – and plenty of them. Enough phraxmuskets and ammunition for a thousand warriors. And even then . . .'

'And where do you propose we acquire such weapons?' asked Blatch, tapping the end of his pencil on the opened notebook.

'Not in Great Glade,' said Gart thoughtfully. 'The place is crawling with mire-pearlers and their like. But maybe Hive?' He turned to Thorne. 'You know Hive, don't you, Thorne?'

The fisher goblin shrugged. 'Old comrades I served with back in the war,' he said thoughtfully. 'They could probably help us find phraxmuskets. But how do we pay for them?'

'Wait.'

It was Celestia. Cade turned. She was standing by the door, Tug beside her, his arms full of bales of homespun. She crossed the room to a carved bureau and opened an ivory inlaid drawer. She reached inside and took out a stunning necklace of mire pearls, interspersed with glittering green marsh-gems. She laid it down on the table.

'What's this worth?' she said, and Cade heard the catch in her voice.

'But, Celestia,' Blatch said softly, 'your mother gave you that.'

Celestia smiled, her eyes as glittery as the gems as she held back tears. 'She would have understood,' she said, then gave a little laugh. 'Besides, it's ironic, don't you think? Using mire pearls to help defeat mire-pearlers?'

Cade noticed Phineal's brow furrow, and he knew that the webfoot felt uneasy about the pearls from any clam being used.

He caught Cade's gaze, and nodded. 'Desperate times demand desperate measures,' he said.

Blatch reached out and patted his daughter's hand, his eyes welling up behind his spectacles. 'She'd be so very proud of you, Celestia, my dear,' he said.

Gart cleared his throat. 'May I?' he asked Celestia, then picked up the necklace and examined it. 'These pearls are exceptional,' he said. 'Should fetch five hundred hivers, I'd say – enough to buy fifty phraxmuskets, with ammunition.'

'Fifty?' said Celestia. 'Is that all?'

Gart shrugged. 'Phraxmuskets don't come cheap,' he said. 'About eight hivers for an old militia model, rebored barrels and reconditioned phrax-mechanisms. Not the finest weapons, of course, but perfectly serviceable.'

They all looked at each other.

'Fifty phraxmuskets,' said Thorne, shaking his head. 'It just isn't enough.'

'I was travelling to Hive when I first came to the Farrow Ridges,' said Cade, pulling back the chair and sitting down. 'The fourthling I was working for told me all about high-jumping . . .'

'Over the central falls, yes,' said Thorne. 'Every two weeks. It's the city's main sport – but what's that got to do with anything?'

'Bets are placed on these races, isn't that right?' Cade went on.

'They certainly are,' said Thorne. 'Fortunes have been made and lost in a day at the Hive high-jumping . . .'

'And how much might one make if, say, one put five hundred hivers on a prowlgrin and rider to win?' Cade asked.

'That would depend on the odds,' Blatch said, scribbling in his notebook. Phineal watched over his shoulder, his crest glowing bright orange. 'An outsider at, say, twenty to one. That would be—'

'Ten thousand hivers, plus your original stake,' Gart broke in.

Cade smiled, his hand trailing over Rumblix's head as the prowlgrin sat purring at his side. 'And that would buy how many phraxmuskets?' he asked.

'A thousand,' Gart announced. 'And more than enough ammunition.'

'That sounds more like it,' Cade said, nodding. 'So all we'd need to do is put our money on the winning prowlgrin. An unknown prowlgrin, so the odds would be high, but a sure-fire winner. A pedigree – possibly a pedigree grey . . .'

Thorne grinned. 'I don't suppose,' he said, looking up as Rumblix nuzzled Cade's hand, 'you might know of such a prowlgrin, Cade?'

· CHAPTER TWENTY-THREE ·

A large bird with a red breast and purple plumage tipped its wings and swooped down for a closer look at the small angular object flying across the sky beneath it. There was the odour of meat in the air. Maybe there was food to be had.

The phraxlighter caught the early-morning sun as it continued north, rose-coloured rays of light gleaming on the windows of its small flight-cabin, on the rudders at the stern, and on the carved hoverworm adorning its prow. From the under-funnel of its gently humming phraxchamber, a ribbon of pink-edged steam trailed back in a sinuous line, bright against the muted greens and browns of the Deepwoods forest below.

It was two weeks since the *Hoverworm* had set off from the Farrow Ridges with four on board, plus provisions – as much as the small vessel could carry.

They'd left the tree-cabin in the Western Woods under

the cover of darkness, flown through that first day and anchored up at dusk for the night, then resumed their journey at daybreak the following morning. It was a routine they quickly got used to, despite the difficult conditions. They'd been plagued by bad weather; high winds and driving rain, freezing fog banks and sudden buffeting twisters. But at last, on this, the third week of their voyage, the conditions had finally begun to improve.

If everything went well, Gart said, they should make it to Hive in another two days. Three at the most.

Unspoken was the fact that time was of the essence. Every delay, every lost day, was more time away from the

Farrow Lake. Sky willing they would make it back – and with weapons – before the mire-pearlers had destroyed their home and enslaved their friends.

Gart Ironside was in the cabin, standing at the wheel. He was wearing his pilot's leather hood and gloves, and there was a scarf wound tightly round his neck. Every time he turned his head to check their latest position, the yellow-tinted glass of his goggles flashed in the sunlight.

Thorne Lammergyre sat next to him, perched on a built-in wooden bench and thumbing through an old notebook that he'd kept years earlier when he lived in Hive. He had a red-lead pencil in his mouth, which he would remove and use to circle anything he came across that he thought might be useful. The address of an old friend. The headquarters of the Hive Militia. A contact on the Sumpwood Bridge . . .

Outside on the aft deck, Cade Quarter was sitting with his back leaning against the stern. His collar was up and he had one of Blatch's fur hats pulled down over his head because, although the sun had risen, the cold of the previous night had not yet released its grip. He'd have been colder still, were it not for the fact that the fourth member of the small group heading for Hive – Rumblix – was crouched down between his legs.

Every so often, Cade would dip his fingers into the jar of grease that sat on the deck by his side, then rub it into Rumblix's joints and feet. Made from a mixture of hammelhorn fat, lakebird oil and woodcamphor, the grease was dark and pungent – but Rumblix loved it, purring so loudly as Cade massaged him that the deck vibrated beneath him.

'Hey, a feathered visitor!' Cade exclaimed as a red-breasted bird swooped down out of the sky and landed on the edge of the cabin roof. 'We should make a wish!' he said, remembering how skytavern passengers believed that birds from the Deepwoods landing on board brought good luck.

The red-breasted bird cocked its head to one side. Then, as Rumblix watched suspiciously, it flapped its wings and landed on the deck – a little too close to the bucket of offal for the prowlgrin's liking. The purring stopped.

Grooming, then food. That was the way it was. First his master would oil his toes, file his claws and brush his fur, and then it was time for breakfast – his favourite part of the morning ritual.

A threatening growl started up in the back of Rumblix's throat as the bird strode jerkily towards the bucket. Cade didn't notice.

The trouble is, he was thinking, *one wish really isn't enough. We need to win a high-jumping race. We need to buy a thousand phraxmuskets – and as quickly as possible. And we need to defeat the mire-pearlers*. Cade was wondering whether a wish for 'success' might cover everything, when Rumblix suddenly wriggled free and, with a yelping bark, pounced at the bird.

There was an anguished squawk and much frantic

flapping. The bucket went over with a crash, spilling the offal, which swirled round the red and purple feathers now littering the deck.

Then everything fell still.

'Rumblix!' Cade barked, leaping to his feet.

The prowlgrin half turned, the body of the bird clamped in his mouth. The next moment, with an audible gulp, Rumblix swallowed it whole – then turned his attention to the spilled offal.

'What's going on?' came a voice.

Cade looked up to see Thorne standing by the door-way to the little cabin. 'Rumblix killed a feathered visitor,' he said glumly. 'Seven seasons' bad luck!'

Thorne shrugged. 'I've never been one for super-stitions,' he said. 'Hungry, were you, boy?' He patted Rumblix on the shoulder. 'You need all the food you can get, don't you?' He turned back to Cade, the notebook raised in his hand. 'There's a tavern in Hive I thought we'd head for first. The Winesap. Run by an old army friend of mine, Rampton Gleep. He'll help us out.'

They sailed on across the green vastness of the Deepwoods during the day, making good time through a cloudless sky. And by the time the sun was once again sinking towards the horizon behind them, and they had started the search for somewhere suitable to anchor up for the night, Gart was confident they were no more than a day and a half away from their destination.

'How about there?' said Cade, pointing to a glade of lullabee trees. With the fading light, the spectral turquoise glow of the leaves was already illuminating the patch of forest. 'We won't have to use the lanterns.'

'Always best not to attract unwanted attention,' Thorne agreed.

Gart seized the rudder levers and steered them down. As the *Hoverworm* broke through the upper canopy, the juicy fragrance of bruised leaves scented the air. Descending further, it came to a hover above a broad branch, its surface a mass of lumps and hollows, the deepest of which were full of rainwater. Thorne and Cade jumped down, and while Gart locked the flight levers, they tethered the phraxlighter, fore and aft.

Rumblix did what he always did when the phraxlighter moored – he leaped from the stern and disappeared into the forest. Cade watched him go. It had worried him the first time Rumblix did this, but as Thorne had explained, the prowlgrin needed to stretch his legs after the long hours spent penned in on the cramped vessel if he was to remain in peak condition. Besides, as Cade knew well, one whistle always had him bounding back to his master's side.

Cade opened the lid of the storage box behind the cabin, pulled out the hammocks, bedrolls and waxed covers he'd stowed there that morning, and went in search of suitable branches to hang them from. Gart remained on the *Hoverworm*, carrying out his nightly maintenance: realigning the rudder ropes, oiling the phraxchamber's cooling-plates and checking the pressure gauges. That afternoon, he'd noticed the thrust faltering on occasions, and he took the opportunity now to clean out the propulsion duct.

As for Thorne, the fisher goblin was on supper duty.

He unpacked the hanging-stove and hooked the chains to an overhead branch. He filled the pot-belly of the stove with chopped wood and screwed-up balls of waxed parchment and lit it. Then, using water from the bark hollows, he filled a copperwood pot and set it over the heat. Soon, the water was steaming, and Thorne added ingredients – gladebarley, woodthyme, and pieces of fish that he'd dried himself.

Everyone knew the tasks that had to be done and, bathed in the turquoise light, the evening routine was carried out quickly, efficiently, and in silence. No one spoke – not until supper was ready.

'Come and get it,' Thorne called.

Cade gave a short, sharp whistle. Moments later, there was a rustling of leaves, and Rumblix burst through the branches and landed beside him. Thorne laughed and patted the prowlgrin on his back.

'Hungry again, eh?'

He poured some of the steaming broth into the empty offal bucket and set it down. Rumblix sniffed at it un-enthusiastically, ate a little, then looked up expectantly.

'Sorry, boy,' said Thorne. 'No feathered visitor this time.'

Rumblix dipped his head back into the bucket.

'That's the way,' said Thorne. 'Eat it all up. We need you big and strong for when we get to Hive.'

With Rumblix slurping noisily, the other three hunkered down on the broad branch. Thorne ladled the fish broth into bowls, passed them round, and they ate. Gart and Thorne talked about the Winesap Inn, and Rampton Gleep, and the last time that Thorne had seen either of them. But Cade found that he was too tired to concentrate. And when he'd emptied his bowl, he said no to the offer of a second helping and turned in for the night.

'Sleep well, lad,' Thorne and Gart called after him.

Cade climbed into his hammock, pulled the covers up to his chin and lay there for a while, his eyelids growing heavy as he tried to count the moonmoths that fluttered above him in the turquoise glow. Three. Four. Five . . .

And then he was asleep.

It was the clatter of pots that woke him. For a moment, Cade thought it was Thorne clearing up after supper. But when he opened his eyes, he saw the new day had already dawned, and that the clatter below was Gart and Thorne packing up the phraxlighter. It was as he was sitting up in his hammock that Cade first noticed the small figure perched on a higher branch behind him.

A scraggy-looking bird creature was staring down at him.

Its eyes were big and yellow. Between them was a hooked beak that looked far too large for the creature's angular head. Feathery tufts grew at the back of its scaly scalp, and there were two long feathers dangling down on either side of its head. They were as bedraggled as the drab plumage that covered the scrawny neck that protruded from a homespun robe. Feathered arms ending in sharp claws were crossed at its chest, while the creature's large feet, with their knotted knuckles and curved talons, gripped the branch firmly.

'Do you plan to stay here long?' it said. Its voice was reedy and nasal.

Cade stared back. 'You're . . . you're a shryke, aren't you?' he gasped.

Cade had never actually seen a shryke before, but in Great Glade, the ferocious bird-creatures were legendary. Once they been a major force in the Deepwoods. But then, centuries earlier, a mighty shryke battle-flock had suffered a devastating defeat in the savage wars that had erupted at the founding of the Free Glades. Then the great shryke city of the Eastern Roost had suffered a catastrophic egg-blight and been abandoned – and along with it, the shryke empire's ambitions to dominate the Edge.

Now, five hundred years later, many believed that shrykes had died out completely. Yet here Cade was, talking to one of these legendary creatures.

The shryke cocked its head to one side. 'I'm not actually a shryke,' it said. 'I'm a shryke *male*.' He flapped a feathered arm behind him. 'My shryke mistress lives just over there.'

'Your shryke mistress,' Cade muttered, remembering that in shryke society, the females were in charge.

He climbed from his hammock and peered into the foliage where the shryke male was pointing. At first he saw nothing, but then caught sight of what looked like a walkway, half concealed by the trees, and beyond it, some kind of construction.

'That's your house?' said Cade.

'The shryke mistress's roost,' the shryke male corrected him. 'Along with the nest-huts of her sisters.'

'You talking to yourself up there, lad?' came Thorne's voice.

'No,' Cade replied. 'To . . .' He turned to the bird creature. 'I don't know your name.'

'Gwilp,' he said. It sounded like a small burp.

'Gwilp,' he called back. 'Gwilp is a shryke.'

'A shryke!' Gart and Thorne cried out. The next moment, they appeared beside him, phraxmuskets in hand, with Rumblix between them. They eyed Gwilp up and down. Gwilp stared back at them with obvious unease.

'A shryke male, actually,' he corrected them.

'A shryke male,' said Thorne, then smiled delightedly. 'Never thought I'd see the day . . . Delighted to make your acquaintance, Gwilp. Do you roost around here?'

'Over there,' Cade answered for him.

Thorne and Gart exchanged glances.

'Shrykes of old had a fearsome reputation,' said Gart. 'There was a time when the mighty battle-flocks seemed certain to conquer the entire Deepwoods . . .'

Thorne was nodding. 'What kind of a welcome would we receive if we were to visit your roost?' he asked, turning to Gwilp. 'We have items we might barter,' he said. 'Pots, knives . . . For food – and a little offal, perhaps,' he added, reaching down to stroke Rumblix's glossy fur.

'You'd be most welcome. The shryke mistress loves to trade,' said Gwilp. 'If you want to meet her, I can take you.' He paused. 'You three,' he said. 'Not the leaper. The shryke mistress might get the wrong idea and eat it.'

Cade blanched. Eat Rumblix! He saw the same look of concern in Thorne's face.

'Gart, you stay here with Rumblix. Keep him tethered,' Thorne said. 'I'll take Cade. And I want us ready to leave the moment we get back.'

Gwilp waited while Thorne threw a few of their belongings into a pack, then the three of them set off for the shryke roost. Climbing from branch to branch, they soon came to the start of the shryke walkway that Cade had glimpsed through the trees.

Constructed from ropes and planks of wood, the suspended bridge snaked its way through the lullabee glade. Cade's gaze darted nervously around as he followed the others. The whole area seemed devoid of life.

No birds. No creatures. Gwilp's comment about what might happen to Rumblix echoed ominously in Cade's head, and he was about to ask Thorne what they should do if the shrykes proved to be as ferocious as it was thought when the walkway abruptly emerged into a concealed clearing at the heart of the glade.

A circle of trees had been felled to create it, with a single tree left standing at its centre that had been stripped of its branches and sawn off at the top of the main trunk. Platforms had been attached to the inner ring of trees and modest nest-huts built upon them, their roofs consisting of large, intricately woven bowls, supported from below by circular walls of sun-baked clay, from which roosting poles protruded. Encircling the clearing and crisscrossing the air at different levels was a series of walkways that connected one shryke nest-hut to the next. The largest nest-hut of all rested on top of the pillar-like tree at the centre of the clearing, with yet more walkways radiating out from it in all directions, like the spokes of a wheel.

It was to this central nest-hut that Gwilp was headed, with Cade and Thorne following warily behind. Gripping the rope balustrade tightly as the walkway swayed, Cade looked up to see two shryke females perched on a roosting pole in front of their nest-like construction.

Compared to the shryke male, these shrykes were huge, three or four times larger than Gwilp. And unlike Gwilp, they were finely clothed. Generous swathes of material, decorated with feathers, teeth and claws, were wrapped around their shoulders; richly

patterned fabric aprons and cloaks matched their gaudily bright feathers, while separate pieces of cloth formed elaborate head-dresses. Their hands ended in sharp, curved talons, as did their feet, which they tapped rhythmically on the wooden boards of the platform as they talked.

Then they noticed Gwilp.

'Ah, visitors!' said the taller of the two shryke matrons, stepping down off the perch and motioning for Cade and Thorne to approach.

'I found them, Mistress Hinnygizzard. In the lullabee grove.'

'He *found* them, Sister Plume,' the matron said to her companion, then turned to Thorne and Cade. 'Did you realize you were lost?' she asked, and cackled with laughter.

Cade sighed with relief. Given everything he'd heard, he had expected the legendary shrykes to be far more intimidating. Yet these two seemed affable enough – despite their savage-looking beaks and claws.

'We are travelling to Hive from our home at Farrow Lake,' said Thorne. 'I am Thorne. This is Cade. We would like to trade, for food—'

'Trade!' Mistress Hinnygizzard squawked delightedly. 'Oh, we shrykes *love* to trade, don't we, Sister Plume? You come from Farrow Lake, you say. Where in Sky's name is that?'

Cade blushed under the two shrykes' yellow-eyed stare. 'It's . . . it's a new settlement, south-west of here. Just a few dwellings, and a skytavern platform.'

Mistress Hinnygizzard flapped her emerald and blue arm feathers in excitement. 'Skytavern platform! How glamorous. We would love to take a journey on a skytavern, wouldn't we, sister? But we're simple forest folk, making a living as best we can. Nothing left over for such luxuries.'

She hopped back onto the roosting pole, her expensive fabric skirts rustling as she did so. Sister Plume settled down next to her.

'How different from the olden days,' Mistress Hinnygizzard sniffed, her yellow eyes growing heavy-lidded and dreamy. 'Once, shrykes ruled the forests, you know,' she mused. 'With our great travelling markets we controlled the trade of half the known Deepwoods, while our magnificent city at the Eastern Roost was the envy of all the Edge . . .'

Cade held his breath, wondering where this was all leading. But then she paused, and her eyes grew bright.

'So you wish to trade,' she said, turning to Thorne. 'What do you have to barter?'

'We need food,' he told her. 'More specifically, offal, if you have it. And we have these.' He pulled his pack from his back, dropped to his knees, and began removing the contents. 'A copperwood bowl, perhaps,' he said, running his thumb around the rim. 'Intricately engraved. Finely turned ironwood spoons. These goblets, inlaid with amber . . .'

As Mistress Hinnygizzard eyed the contents of Thorne's pack keenly, Cade looked around him and saw several more shrykes. Shryke matrons perched on roosting poles in front of a couple of the smaller nest-huts; a shryke male scuttling along one of the walkways from one nest-hut to the next, an earthenware pot balanced on his feather-tufted head.

'We have no need for copperwood bowls, finely engraved or otherwise,' Mistress Hinnygizzard was saying. 'Nor spoons. Nor goblets. As I said, we're simple folk, aren't we, Sister Plume?'

'We are indeed, sister,' her companion nodded.

'But, what's this?' Mistress Hinnygizzard asked, plucking the red-lead pencil from the top pocket of Thorne's jacket and examining it in her claws.

'It's . . .' Thorne began.

But the shryke matron was not listening. Instead, she reached inside the folds of her silken cloak and drew out a hand-mirror, which she held up to observe her face. 'A little, so,' she said, drawing a red line on the side of her beak. 'A line here. And here. And here . . .'

She turned to Sister Plume, her large hooked beak a blaze of red. 'What do you think?' she asked.

Her companion nodded admiringly. 'The great Mother Muleclaw the Third herself could not have looked more magnificent as she led her flocks into battle,' Sister Plume said softly. '*You* look ready for battle, my dear,' she said. 'Or, at the very least, a cruise on a skytavern.'

The two shrykes squawked with amusement.

'Gwilp!' Mistress Hinnygizzard commanded. 'Supply these fine traders with all the offal they desire.'

· CHAPTER TWENTY-FOUR ·

'It hasn't changed at all,' shouted Thorne, twisting round to Gart and Cade as he led the three of them through the dense crowd that packed the Winesap Inn. 'Half of Low Town seems to be in tonight,' he laughed.

The tavern was vast, with richly carved wooden pillars rising up to support equally ornate roof beams high above their heads. By the far wall a staircase led up to a balcony where well-dressed goblins sat at tables and were served by scurrying oakelves in tall conical bonnets. Below, goblins of all types clustered around troughs that lined the walls, dipping long-handled ladles into them and drinking the golden winesap that gave the tavern its name.

Cade wrinkled his nose. The flickering tallow candles gave off a rancid odour and the winesap troughs smelled sour and musky – a smell that intensified each time a group of drinkers called for their own trough to be filled.

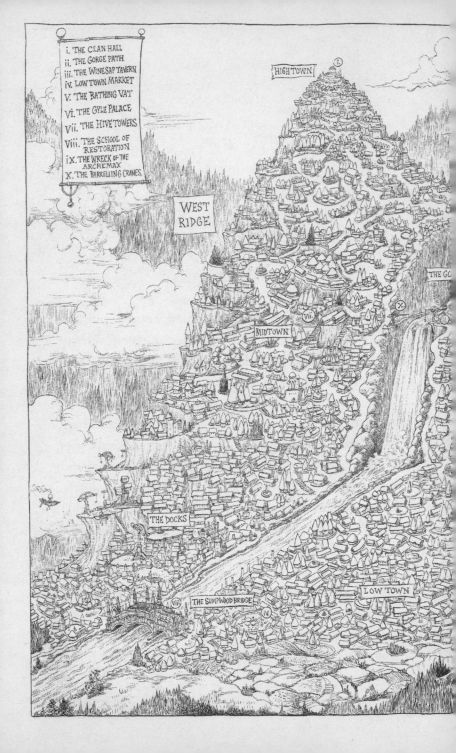

i. THE CLAN HALL
ii. THE GORGE PATH
iii. THE WINESAP TAVERN
iv. LOW TOWN MARKET
V. THE BATHING VAT
VI. THE GYLE PALACE
Vii. THE HIVE TOWERS
Viii. THE SCHOOL OF
RESTORATION
iX. THE WRECK OF THE
ARCHEMAX
X. THE BARRELLING CRANES

WEST RIDGE

HIGH TOWN

THE GO

MIDTOWN

THE DOCKS

THE SUMPWOOD BRIDGE

LOW TOWN

Stacks of barrels lined the walls, and when the shout went up, a goblin in a dirty white apron would hurriedly climb a stepladder and turn a spigot, sending a fountain of glistening liquid down through the air and into the trough below.

All around them in the crowded tavern, the residents of the Low Town district of Hive were taking refreshment after a long day spent hard at work in the pressing mills and sap-sheds that produced the wines Hive was famous for. Cade looked about him at the different faces. A tufted goblin with thick black hair sprouting from the tips of his ears. Pink-eyed goblins, with their wide milky stares. And a couple of low-belly goblins, their enormous stomachs supported by the 'belly slings' slung from their shoulders . . .

Once they would have lived in separate warrior clans in various parts of the Deepwoods, each with their own chosen weapons and battle dress, and constantly at war with one another for territory. Now they were city folk, living and working together, and all dressed in the blue-dyed jackets of winesap workers.

It seemed a world away from Cade's quiet little cabin beside the tranquil waters of Farrow Lake. His stomach churned as he thought of his friends back there, and how they were all depending on him, Gart and Thorne – and Rumblix of course – for their very survival.

They had set off from the shryke roost at noon the previous day and, owing to the good weather, Gart had suggested they fly through the night. After more than two weeks on board the cramped *Hoverworm*, Cade and Thorne were happy to agree, and all three of them had taken turns to pilot the phraxlighter through from dusk to dawn.

Sitting at the wheel, the steady thrum of the phrax-chamber below him and the carved hoverworm prow in front, Cade had gazed out at the Deepwoods and marvelled at the vastness of the mighty forest. Once, the city of Great Glade had seemed huge to him – his entire world. But not now. However magnificent its buildings, it was just a pinprick in this endless expanse.

As dawn broke, Thorne and Gart had joined him in the wheelhouse. Gart had passed Cade his spyglass, which he'd put to his eye. And there, far away on the horizon, Cade had caught his first glimpse of Hive, a seemingly chaotic jumble of buildings crowded one on top of another on the towering slopes of two mountain peaks, a thundering waterfall pouring down the gorge between them.

And as they drew closer, Thorne had taken Cade to the prow and pointed out landmarks. Cade could hear the pride in the fisher goblin's voice.

'That's High Town at the top of West Ridge, where the rich folks live. Large mansions, terraced gardens, spectacular views,' said Thorne, pointing to the top of one of the mountain peaks. 'See that building there? It's the Clan Hall. Where the High Council meets. Used to be dominated by the clan chiefs, but after the war we changed all that . . . And there,' he said, nodding towards the top of the mountain opposite, 'is the Peak.'

Cade found himself looking at an impressive palace, seemingly fashioned from gleaming wax. 'Who lives there?' he asked.

'That's the Gyle Palace. It's where the Sisterhood of Grossmothers and their gyle goblin followers live,' Thorne told him. 'Over there are the Docks,' he continued. 'And that's the Sumpwood Bridge, home to the Hive Academy – a lot like your academic district in Great Glade . . .'

Cade stared at the magnificent bridge, with its grand facades and pointed towers, spanning the river at the bottom of the gorge – and he found himself thinking how different life might have been if his father had been an academic *there*, rather than in the School of Flight run by the treacherous Quove Lentis . . .

'Down there is Low Town, my old district,' Thorne said, pointing to a docking-tower at the foot of East Ridge, where the sprawl of buildings ended and the fields with their neat rows of winesap vines began. 'It's where the finest winesap in all the Edge is produced.'

Gart pulled on the rudder lever and brought the *Hoverworm* down close to the roofs, the smoke from a thousand chimneys making their eyes water, then descended to the docking-tower and manoeuvred the *Hoverworm* into a gap between two barges, each one laden with winesap barrels.

Thorne jumped onto the platform and cleated the little vessel securely. After paying the dock warden, a rotund goblin with a fat belly and large tufted ears, the four of them – with Cade holding Rumblix on a leash – set off down the steps of the mooring tower and followed Thorne through the labyrinth of narrow alleys beyond.

'That's the house I grew up in,' said Thorne, stopping in front of a squat, timber-framed house with shuttered windows. 'Twenty-three of us in two rooms, there were, with little enough to eat, and long hours at the sap-press to look forward to.' He shook his head. 'But times changed after the war . . .'

They walked on and, as Thorne guided them from alley to alley, Cade noticed how the goblins they passed would nod or doff their caps when they saw the old grey militia jacket that Thorne was wearing. At last, they came to a tall building flanked by warehouses, hooks and pul-leys dangling from their fronts, and packed inside with huge winesap casks.

The sign above the door confirmed that they'd come to the right place. *The Winesap Inn.*

As Thorne pushed open the tall doors, which were cov-ered in carved vines laden with grapes, and went inside, Cade felt Rumblix pull on his leash and yelp excitedly.

'Easy there, boy,' he reassured him, patting his head. 'I know it's strange – it's strange for me too.'

He followed Gart and Thorne inside, with Rumblix sticking close at heel, his nostrils flared and tongue lolling as he took in the unfamiliar sights and smells.

Suddenly a whispery, yet oddly penetrating, voice sounded, so close to Cade's ear it was as if it was inside his head.

'Well, well. If it isn't Militia Private Lammergyre,' it said.

Cade looked up and saw a slight whey-faced creature with large black eyes and red-veined ears perched on a high seat that had been carved into one of the upright pillars above their heads.

'Artifuce!' Thorne exclaimed and thrust out his hand in greeting. 'My favourite tavern waif!'

'It's been a long time,' the waif said, his bony hand lost in the fisher goblin's grasp. 'Heard you'd left the city, returned to the Deepwoods.' The waif's black eyes grew large as he peered down from his seat into Thorne's face. 'Seems you have found a measure of peace at . . . Farrow Lake.'

'Indeed I have, old friend,' said Thorne. 'We must catch up, but first . . .'

'You want to see the boss,' said Artifuce, his ears fluttering. 'You'll find Sergeant Gleep up in the barrel-wood balcony. I'll tell him you're here.' The little waif closed his large eyes and tilted his head to one side, but didn't move from his seat.

'As I live and breathe!' came a booming voice moments later. 'Thorne Lammergyre!'

A ruddy-faced mobgnome with red plaited side-whiskers, wearing a leather apron over his jerkin and checked breeches, came striding down the stairs towards them. Cade noticed the soft-peaked cap he was wearing, the ornate *H* of the Hive Militia embroidered on its front.

'Sergeant!' said Thorne, smiling broadly, but standing to attention and giving a salute.

Pushing his way through the crowded tavern, the mobgnome threw his arms around Thorne and patted him hard on the shoulder. 'Thorne, old comrade, it's good to see you looking so well,' he said. He stepped back. 'How long has it been?'

'Nearly fifteen years,' said Thorne. He turned to Cade and Gart. 'This is my old comrade-in-arms, Rampton Gleep. Rampton, these are my neighbours from Farrow Lake, Gart Ironside and Cade Quarter.'

Rampton shook their hands enthusiastically. 'Any friends of Thorne's . . .' He turned back to Thorne and his face assumed a look of utter shock. 'Fifteen years!' he exclaimed. 'It hardly seems possible! But come, follow me, we must drink a toast to old times with my best sapwine!' He took Thorne by the arm and strode back up the stairs to the balcony, the drinkers stepping aside and doffing their caps in respect as the two old soldiers passed.

Gart and Cade, with Rumblix pulling on his leash, followed them. Up on the balcony, Rampton called loudly for sapwine, and several oakelves, their conical bonnets nodding, came hurrying towards them. A cloth was thrown over a round table, stools pulled up and goblets set down. A cork popped close by Cade's ear, making him jump – and Rumblix bark – and looking round, Cade saw an oakelf holding a foaming bottle of red sapwine almost as big as she was. She filled their goblets and Rampton raised his high above his head.

'To old comrades and the Glorious Revolution!' he announced.

'To the Glorious Revolution!' The toast was taken up from table to table on the balcony, then spread down to the drinkers at the troughs below.

'The Glorious Revolution!'

'*The Glorious Revolution!*'

Cade saw Thorne flinch, and realized that old, long-suppressed feelings were being reawakened.

'To the Glorious Revolution,' he said quietly, and drained his goblet.

Cade did the same. The sapwine was delicious, the bubbles exploding on his tongue, leaving intense flavours of sweet, sun-ripened grapes; meadowgrass, mulled spices, a hint of smoked oak. They sat down, and Rampton refilled their goblets from the enormous bottle.

'You were in a bad way when you left,' he said, laying a hand on Thorne's shoulder. 'You never got over the Midwood Marshes fight, I know, but you acquitted yourself bravely. I only hope your new home has given you some peace of mind.'

'It has, Rampton,' said Thorne. 'At least, it had until now . . .' He paused, then nodded to Gart, who reached inside his flight coat and took out a small leather wallet. 'Our home at Farrow Lake has been invaded by mire-pearlers from Great Glade, and we need all the phraxmuskets we can buy to fight back.'

Rampton's face grew serious, and he fiddled with a plaited side-whisker as he listened intently while Thorne described the *Doombringer* and exactly what they were up against.

'I've got contacts at the militia armoury,' he said thoughtfully when Thorne had finished. 'I can certainly get you phraxmuskets. But they don't come cheap.'

'We know,' said Gart, opening the wallet and sliding it across the table to the tavern keeper. 'Which is why we need the best price we can get for this.'

Rampton's eyes lit up as he looked down at Celestia's string of pearls and marsh-gems. '*Very* nice,' he said, then sucked in air through his teeth as he wound the side-whisker round his little finger. 'There *is* someone I know . . .' he said. 'A connoisseur, you might say, who'd pay extra for such fine workmanship – more a work of art than just a necklace.'

Rampton glanced around to make sure no one was observing them as he flipped the wallet closed and pushed it back across the table to Gart.

'Keep those out of sight and close to your chest,' he advised, then leaned over to Thorne. 'The Sumpwood Bridge Academy,' he said. 'Ask for a professor of phrax studies by the name of Landris Bellwether.' He winked. 'And keep that old militia jacket on if you want the best price.'

Thorne smiled. 'I will, and thank you, old friend,' he said.

On the far side of the balcony, an oakelf had opened the shutters and a cool breeze wafted into the tavern. Suddenly, with a high-pitched, excited yelp, Rumblix, his nostrils quivering, launched himself up into the air, yanking the leash from Cade's hand as he did so.

'Rumblix!' Cade shouted as the pedigree grey prowlgrin scattered the oakelf servers and disappeared through the open window. 'Rumblix! No!'

· CHAPTER TWENTY-FIVE ·

Cade dashed down the stairs as fast as he could, barging past the drinkers below. He burst out through the carved doors and into the street. His head was fizzing; his stomach churned.

Then he saw him. Rumblix. Galloping off over the rooftops on the other side of the street. Cade put his fingers to his lips and whistled. The prowlgrin ignored him, and disappeared over the pitched roof of a warehouse on the corner.

'Rumblix!' Cade called despairingly, as their best hope – their *only* hope – for making enough money to buy the weapons they needed vanished into the bustling city.

'I won't give up! I can't give up!' Cade told himself as he gave chase, running as hard as he could up the sloping street.

Rumblix, his beloved prowlgrin, whom he'd nurtured and trained from the moment the little creature had hatched from his egg: Rumblix was gone. The poor thing must be panicking in this great city, overwhelmed by the noise and smell and bustle of the place. He must be so frightened.

Cade reached the end of the alley and caught sight of the pedigree grey prowlgrin jumping over the rooftops further up the steep mountainside. Gasping in lungfuls of air, he dashed up the street after him, the distant roar of the Hive river in his ears as it plummeted down the gorge.

A couple of doughty cloddertrog matrons stepped smartly aside to let him run between them; a hammel-horn cart skidded and swerved, its driver shouting at him to watch where he was going. But Cade didn't even hear him.

'Rumblix! Come back, boy!' he was shouting. *'Rumblix!'*

He reached the end of the street and kept on running. Open-fronted shops with displays of ironware, wooden utensils, bolts of cloth blurred past him; bustling market stalls laden with fruits and vegetables, trinkets, footwear, pots and pans. Their stall-owners, bellowing too-good-to-miss bargains, fell still as he dashed by. Breathing hard, Cade came to a square. There was a well at its centre, where a gathering of trog females with leather aprons and knotted headscarves were chatting to one another as they filled their water pails.

Cade stopped, looked around.

'Rumblix!' he shouted desperately as he saw the

prowlgrin land on top of the roof of Chandler Natwick's
– a candle-making shop on the opposite side of the square
– then gallop along the pointed roof-ridge with a curious
mixture of care and determination. Cade put his fingers
to his mouth and whistled again.

Two hammelhorns in harness skittered anxiously at
the noise, while the trog females at the well stopped what
they were doing and looked round. And up on the chandler's roof, the prowlgrin paused, turned his head and
eyed him intently.

'Rumblix, boy,' Cade called out, his voice as calm and
measured as he could make it. Then, his unblinking gaze
fixed on the jittery prowlgrin, he ran headlong across the
square.

He'd hoped that Rumblix, reassured by the sight of
his master, would leap down from the roof and come
bounding over. But instead, as Cade watched, the prowlgrin sniffed the air, then turned away and jumped from
the candle-maker's roof onto the adjoining roof, then
onto the next one, then the one after that . . .

Panting loudly, Cade continued the chase, darting up
street after street. He kept his head raised and his eyes
peeled for the tell-tale streak of grey, high up on the
rooftops, as Rumblix galloped on over the slate tiles and
smoking chimneys of Low Town.

Close to exhaustion now, Cade rounded a corner at
the end of a long and winding alley – and stopped in his
tracks. There was a rich, earthy scent in the air, a mixture
of fresh dung, damp fur and the tang of wet straw – a

warm Deepwoods smell that was at odds with the acrid ironwood smoke and molten metal from the city's furnaces and workshops. It was a familiar smell, one Cade knew well.

It was the smell of prowlgrins.

Cade followed his nose. Just round the corner was a broad courtyard, at the centre of which stood a prowlgrin stable. Cade stared up at the large open-fronted building with its weathered timber walls and sloping ironwood roof. Inside was a framework of stout horizontal roost-beams, each one with a trough clamped to its front. Narrow walkways, with ladders connecting the different levels, gave access to each of these individual roost-beams – and to the prowlgrins perched upon them.

Forty pairs of large jewel-like yellow eyes stared down at him. The prowlgrins shifted from foot to foot on long sensitive toes that were as glistening and well-oiled as their fur was sleek and shiny . . .

And grey.

Cade gasped. These were pedigree grey prowlgrins, forty of them, all roughly the same age and size as Rumblix. Each one had a collar around its neck, with a name picked out in silver against the black leather. *Matrix, Codix, Matafix, Emblix* . . . names that were repeated on the small painted plaques nailed to each of the wooden troughs. And there, skittering about, nuzzling up to one prowlgrin, then another, then hopping from one roost pole to the next, was Rumblix.

His Rumblix! Cade didn't think he'd ever heard the

young prowlgrin purring so loudly.

'So, you picked up their scent?' Cade called up to him. 'Couldn't resist, eh, boy?'

'Who are you?' came a voice, and Cade looked round to see a young fourthling on a magnificent-looking white prowlgrin approaching him.

She had a snub-nose, and thick fair hair gathered together in a single rope-like braid that hung down her back. Reaching Cade, the rider swung her feet from the stirrups and expertly dismounted to stand facing him, hands on her hips.

'My name's Cade Quarter,' Cade said. 'And that's my prowlgrin, Rumblix, up there.' He pointed at the purring prowlgrin.

'So it is,' came a familiar-sounding voice from the shadows of a walkway, high up in the roost-house, just above where Rumblix was perching. 'I didn't think I'd ever see the two of you again.'

· CHAPTER TWENTY-SIX ·

Cade stared up at the familiar figure of Tillman Spoke standing on the walkway at the top of the open-fronted roost-house – the well-tailored frockcoat; the salt-and-pepper hair, oiled and styled in the Great Glade way, giving its owner an unmistakable military air; the piercing green eyes . . .

The last time Cade had looked into those eyes, they had been full of anger and disappointment. And, at the sight of his former employer now, Cade was suddenly back in the cabin on board the *Xanth Filatine* when the pearl necklace that had been planted in Cade's backpack was discovered by a brutal skymarshal.

'I believed you. I *trusted* you,' Tillman had said coldly when the skymarshal arrested Cade. 'And it seems my trust was ill-judged.'

They were words Cade could never forget. And now, here he was, looking up at his former employer.

'Don't go anywhere, I'll be right down!' Tillman called, striding to the end of the walkway, where a rope and pulley system was attached to the side of one of the wooden uprights.

Tillman slipped one foot into a stirrup-like attachment, grabbed hold of the ropes and, as the ironwood counter-weight rose, sank quickly down through the air. At the same time, Rumblix jumped off the roost-perch he'd been sitting on and started leaping down the wooden framework.

Cade watched them descend. Tillman Spoke, his waisted frockcoat fluttering in the wind, and Rumblix, leaping down from strut to strut. They reached the ground at the same moment. Rumblix landed with a thud. Tillman stepped lightly off the pulley-stirrup.

Cade realized his own legs were shaking. He and the prowlgrin breeder had parted on such bad terms . . .

'Cade!' Tillman said, and grasped Cade's hesitantly outstretched hand with both of his own. 'I can't tell you what it means to see you standing before me here in Hive, safe and well.' The prowlgrin breeder was beaming at him – but there were tears in his eyes. 'Can you ever for-give me, Cade,' he said, dabbing at his face with a striped handkerchief, 'for thinking you were a thief?'

'So you know I didn't steal that necklace?' said Cade, tears of his own filling his eyes.

'I know everything,' said Tillman. 'It was the work of a gang from the lower decks. It all came out after you dis-appeared – the murder of two academics on board was the last straw. The skymarshals arrested the gang leader down in the depths of the skytavern . . .'

'Drax Adereth,' said Cade dully.

'That's the fellow.' Tillman shook his head. 'Unpleasant piece of work. Turns out he was in the pay of the High Professor of Flight, Quove Lentis. I've felt guilty ever since . . .' Unable to contain himself, Tillman Spoke wrapped his arms around Cade and hugged him so tightly it took Cade's breath away. 'It's *so* good to see you, Cade!'

Beside Cade, Rumblix nuzzled at him and purred loudly. Tillman released Cade and stepped back, smiling broadly as he looked at the prowlgrin.

'And you, Rumblix! I can hardly believe it!' he said. 'Look how you've grown. And the two of you still together – it's more than I could ever have hoped for!'

Tillman looked up at the prowlgrins roosting above their heads.

'And now you've found your brother and sisters, all grown up, just like you. Remarkable, eh, Whisp?'

The fourthling girl, who'd been standing stroking the heavy-set white prowlgrin, her eyes fixed on Cade all this time, nodded.

'He's as fine as any of them,' she said, her voice soft, almost shy. 'You've raised him well,' she told Cade.

'That's high praise coming from my head groom,' said Tillman warmly.

Just then, there was the sound of footsteps, and Cade turned to see his two friends come running round the

corner into the courtyard. Gart was bright red, his moustache wet and drooping, and Thorne's scalp was beaded
with sweat. They came to a halt in front of him.

'Is he here?' Thorne panted, gazing up at the rows
of identical pedigree prowlgrins on the roost-perches.
'Cade, is Rumblix here?'

'Right here!' Cade laughed, stepping aside to reveal
the prowlgrin standing behind him.

'Thank Sky for that!' Thorne exclaimed as he bent
double and struggled to catch his breath. 'You gave us a
fright, Rumblix . . . taking off . . . like that.'

'These are my friends from Farrow Lake,' Cade told
Tillman. 'They helped me after I had to jump ship.'

The contrast between Gart in his weather-stained
longcoat and Thorne in his old grey militia jacket, and
the elegantly dressed Tillman Spoke, was marked. Cade
saw Tillman catch sight of the fisher goblin's jacket and
stiffen, before holding out his hand.

'We fought on opposite sides in the war,' he told the
goblin. 'I served in the Free Glade Lancers – but I'm now
proud to call Hive my home.'

'This is Tillman Spoke,' Cade broke in. 'He breeds
prowlgrins. I worked for him on the skytavern. Rumblix
picked up the scent and led me here.'

Thorne and Gart exchanged glances. They both
remembered the story they'd been told of Cade's mixed
fortunes on board the *Xanth Filatine*.

Thorne's face clouded over. 'So, Rumblix is *yours*,' he
said.

Tillman Spoke laughed. 'No, no,' he said. 'Rumblix has only one master – the first person he saw and imprinted on when he hatched. And that's Cade Quarter, here.' He clapped his hand on Cade's shoulder. 'But, Cade,' he said, 'you haven't told me what brings you to Hive.'

Cade was about to explain about the mire-pearlers and the threat to Farrow Lake when a look from Thorne stopped him. By his guarded expression, it was obvious that his friend was suspicious of this elegant fourthling from Great Glade.

'Cade is here to ride Rumblix in the next high-jump,' Thorne answered for him.

'By Earth and Sky, another coincidence!' exclaimed Tillman Spoke. 'Whisp here is entering the next high-jump too!'

· CHAPTER TWENTY-SEVEN ·

Cade crossed the courtyard, his feet sinking deep into the straw that covered the cobblestones, and made his way round the strange contraption in the middle of the small square.

Three large wagon wheels were mounted horizontally on vertical axles above a high-sided metal tank of water. Overhead, a pipe snaked up from the tank, ending in a broad downward-pointing nozzle, like the seedhead of a drooping glade-plant. As Cade passed, droplets of water fell from the nozzle and plinked on the spokes of the wheels, before dripping down onto the surface of the water in the tank below.

Cade reached the zigzag stairs at the back of the roost-house and climbed them to the top walkway, which bounced slightly beneath his feet as he walked along it. And when he went through the doorway at the far end, the smell of prowlgrins – that distinctive mixture of wet fur and meaty breath – enveloped him.

He'd spent the previous night as Tillman Spoke's guest. Thorne had returned to the Winesap Inn, where his old comrade had provided him with rooms, while Gart Ironside had preferred to sleep in his hammock on board the *Hoverworm* docked at the Low Town platform. They'd all agreed to meet up at noon the next day at the eastern end of the Sumpwood Bridge. Whisp, the head groom, had settled Rumblix on a perch in the roost-house and then made herself scarce, leaving Cade to have supper with Tillman in his small house on the far side of the courtyard.

They had dined on Hive Pie – a dish of glimmer-onions and diced riverfish, followed by rich, crumbly tilder cheese with small hard-baked biscuits – and had talked late into the night. Cade told Tillman about his simple life in the small lakeside cabin, about meeting Tug and raising Rumblix, and his prowlgrin rides with Celestia in the Western Woods – but was careful not to mention the mire-pearlers.

'He seems a decent sort, your prowlgrin breeder,' Thorne had said quietly before leaving. 'But I'd rather our business was known to as few folk as possible, Cade.'

For his part, Tillman had told Cade about settling into the stables, just in time for the hatching of his prowl-grins; then running into Whisp, when he was about to despair of ever finding a groom who could match his high standards.

'Her father bred prowlgrins for the Grossmothers

up in the stables of the Gyle Palace in the old days, back before the war,' Tillman had said, cutting himself a sliver of the pungent tilder cheese. 'But after the Glorious Revolution of theirs, he lost his job and ended his days as a sap-trader here in Low Town. But he taught Whisp well,' he said. 'Her real name is Feldia, but my gyle-goblin grooms gave her the nickname, and it stuck.'

'Why Whisp?' Cade had asked, trying to stifle a yawn.

Tillman had smiled. 'I'll leave you to find that out for yourself.'

Cade looked around at the rows of sleepy-looking prowlgrins on their roost-perches. It was early, and they were still waking up, but already three small goblins with enormous noses and heavy-lidded eyes were hard at work.

These must be the gyle-goblin grooms that Tillman had spoken of the night before, he thought.

To his right, one of the grooms was down on his knees, the empty buckets behind him. Next to him was a basket, its assortment of contents – rags, brushes, curry-combs, files, tweezers – spilling out onto the boards. And crouched in front of him was a grey prowlgrin, eyes closed and purring throatily as the goblin massaged one of its feet with what looked to Cade like hammelhorn grease.

As Cade approached, the goblin looked up. He didn't look pleased to see him.

'Emblix,' said Cade, for want of anything better to say. He nodded to the plaque on the prowlgrin's trough.

'Ay, Emblix, sir,' said the goblin, returning his attention to the prowlgrin foot clamped between his knees.

'A pedigree grey,' said Cade.

'Ay, a pedigree grey, sir.'

Cade couldn't tell whether the grey goblin was being surly or was nervous in his presence.

'My name's Cade,' he said.

The goblin paused, then looked up again. He was frowning, and for a moment Cade thought he was going to ask him to go away. But then he nodded.

'I'm Glitch,' he said.

'Good to meet you, Glitch,' said Cade. 'I . . . I'm a friend of Tillman Spoke's. That is . . . well, I used to work for him. Like you.' He laughed. 'The last time I saw Emblix here, he was an egg lying in a tray on a bed of ice. So he wouldn't hatch too soon,' he added.

'She,' said Glitch.

'She,' Cade repeated. He paused, then crouched down next to the goblin. 'Tell me,' he said, 'that grease there. There's a minty smell I can't . . .'

'Burberry oil,' said Glitch.

'I see,' said Cade. Conversation with the goblin was not proving easy, and he was about to cut his losses and leave, when Glitch turned to him.

'It strengthens the skin, but doesn't reduce the sensitivity,' he said. 'Important for a racing prowlgrin, that. Strong toes to grip, but sensitive toe-tips to sense slipperiness – which is what you need on a high-jumping gallop down the falls.'

'The idea is to gallop down the falls as fast as you can, isn't it?' said Cade, encouraged by the fact that the gyle goblin had opened up – if only a little.

'Ay,' said Glitch. 'Down the banks of the gorge, from ledge to ledge, against the minute-glass.'

'I haven't seen the course yet,' said Cade. 'But from what Tillman told me, it's pretty spectacular.' He frowned. 'The prowlgrins go one at a time, is that right?'

'Ay, one at a time,' Glitch said patiently, 'crisscrossing from bank to bank. And then, when everyone has raced, the two fastest go head to head in the grand race-off.' The gyle goblin switched to the prowlgrin's other foot. 'Now that's quite a sight to see, I can tell you, and a real test of rider and prowlgrin's skill.'

'Is it dangerous?' Cade couldn't stop himself from asking.

'Oh, very dangerous,' the goblin nodded without looking up. 'Tumbles, broken heads, drownings . . . But the rewards are high, especially for a prowlgrin breeder like Mister Spoke. At least, that's what we're all hoping.'

Tillman Spoke had been so excited back on board the *Xanth Filatine* when he'd talked about setting up his very own prowlgrin stables in Hive, Cade remembered. 'A new life', he'd called it.

'All hopes are resting on Whisp and the old white,' Glitch was saying. 'They're rank outsiders, but if they win the next high-jump, the Hive Militia have pledged to buy all forty pedigree greys we've been training. As their roost-marshal said . . .' Glitch put down the oil and turned to Cade, his eyes wide with excitement. 'If the Spoke Stables can win the high-jump with an old gyle mount, then the Hive Militia can trust the quality of our training. Mister Spoke's fortune will be made . . .'

The goblin's face fell.

'Of course, if Whisp and the old white fail, then he'll have to shut the stables. He's down to his last hiver – not that you'd know it to look at him.'

Just then, from outside, Cade heard a metallic clinking and hissing. Cade climbed to his feet – only for the goblin groom to seize him by the ankle.

'You won't say nothing, will you, Cade, sir,' he whispered. 'If word spreads that he's broke, Mister Spoke's creditors will be round here taking anything they can grab.'

'I won't say a thing,' Cade assured him.

Cade stepped out of the roost-house onto the walkway and looked down. His gaze fell upon the huge wooden contraption that stood at the centre of the straw-covered courtyard. The white prowlgrin was standing on one of the horizontal wagon wheels, with Whisp sitting in the saddle on his back.

She was wearing tight white breeches and a scarlet satin shirt that shimmered in the early-morning sun. On her head, secured under her chin by a black leather strap, was a helmet of burnished copperwood, with a crest of white feathers.

As Cade watched, she reached up and pulled the cord that dangled from the pipe overhead. A cascade of water poured down from the wide nozzle and the wheel at the prowlgrin's feet began to turn. Whisp took hold of the reins. Cade noticed how she looped them round her thumbs, then leaned forward and, her lips moving, whispered to the white prowlgrin.

The wheel began to move faster, the spokes becoming a blur as the prowlgrin broke into a gallop and leaped over them. With water showering down all round them, prowlgrin and rider jumped across to the second wheel, which moved even more quickly, and then to the third. Almost standing in the stirrups, her legs clamped to the white prowlgrin's flanks, Whisp was leaning forwards, her chin resting on the top of his head, whispering as she did so.

Faster and faster the two of them went as the wheels whirred. And all the while, the torrent of water poured down around them, creating a halo of spray in the morning light as the prowlgrin galloped over the spinning spokes of the wheels.

Cade smiled to himself. He understood the nickname the grooms had given her now.

'*Whisp*,' he murmured. 'Short for whisperer.'

· CHAPTER TWENTY-EIGHT ·

W hat was happening back at Farrow Lake? Cade wondered, and not for the first time. An emptiness churned in the pit of his stomach.

Above the whirr and clatter of the prowlgrin practice-wheels, and the splish-splash of the cascading water, Cade heard his name being shouted. Leaning over the walkway balustrade, he saw Tillman Spoke in the courtyard in front of the stables. He was sitting at the front of a wheelless open carriage constructed of buoyant sumpwood and pulled by a russet-coloured prowlgrin in harness.

'I've got business to attend to in the Bridge district if you'd like a lift,' the prowlgrin breeder called up.

'I'll be right with you,' Cade called back.

He stepped into the stirrup, released the pulley rope and descended to the ground past purring prowl-grins, full from their morning feed and awaiting the attention of the grooms.

Tillman shifted along to make room as Cade climbed up onto the wooden bench of the floating carriage, then twitched the reins. The prowlgrin trotted forward. They left the stables and joined the other traffic – more prowlgrin-drawn carriages made of expensive sumpwood, and heavy ironwood wagons with metal-rimmed wheels, pulled by teams of yoked hammelhorns. The wagons were laden with sacks of vegetables, cords of wood and barrels of ale; the ornate floating carriages were driven by uniformed mobgnomes, elegant fourthling matrons peeking out through the curtained windows behind them.

Tillman expertly steered the little carriage through the narrow streets of Low Town, while overhead, funnelled phraxvessels crisscrossed the sky, leaving a latticework of steam trails.

Behind Cade, two large barrels clinked emptily in the open carriage as it weaved in and out of the traffic. He glanced round, to see the words *Bartlett Rind & Nephew – Purveyors of Finest Prowlgrin Offal* painted on the side of both barrels in a slanting red script. Tillman noticed him looking.

'Only the best for my pedigree greys. Costly,' he added with a frown, then smiled, 'but I wouldn't have it any other way.'

With his expensive clothes and sumpwood carriage, if Tillman Spoke did have money troubles, thought Cade, he showed no sign of it.

'How are the stables doing?' he asked. 'The prowl-grins look magnificent.'

'Fine, fine,' said Tillman, pulling on the reins and taking them down a broad street teeming with traffic. 'Over there's the Low Town Meeting Hall,' he said, neatly changing the subject as he pointed across to a squat bell-roofed building with a Hive flag – a white *H* on a green background – fluttering at its top. 'Since the Glorious Revolution, each Hive district has its own individual council.'

Cade remembered the toast that had reverberated through the Winesap Inn the day before. 'What *was* the Glorious Revolution?' he asked.

Tillman laughed dryly. 'The one good thing to come out of that accursed war,' he said. 'The Great Glade Militia defeated the Hive Militia at the Battle of the Midwood Marshes, which was fought for control of the lucrative sumpwood forests. The returning Hive soldiers led a revolt against the clan chiefs – up there.'

Tillman pointed to the great building at the top of the left-hand mountain peak.

'They threw the lot of them over the gorge in barrels,' he continued. 'These days the ordinary Hivers elect their leaders – one from each district council – and very proud of it they are too. If only Great Glade had followed their example,' he added bitterly, 'perhaps it wouldn't now be in thrall to the academics and their merchant cronies.'

'Oi, watch where you're going!' came an angry voice, and Cade looked back to see a woodale-dray drawn by four hammelhorns bearing down on them, its driver, a red-faced cloddertrog, shaking a clenched fist angrily.

Tillman tugged at the reins. The prowlgrin lurched to one side, and the two vehicles grazed one another as they passed, but there was no damage done.

'The revolution was fifteen years ago,' Tillman commented. 'These days, Hive's on the up and up, and no mistake.'

Ahead of them, the roar of the Edgewater River plunging down over the gorge grew louder as they drew closer. Cade looked down the street for a view of the river itself, but before he could catch sight of it, the air suddenly filled with a rank, metallic odour, and Tillman pulled up in front of two open ironwood gates, the painted sign at the top – *Bartlett Rind & Nephew* – matching the name on the barrels behind them in the carriage.

'You can take a shortcut to the Sumpwood Bridge through Fish-Gut Walk,' he told Cade, pointing across the road to a narrow opening between two grimy warehouses.

Cade thanked him and jumped down, then headed for the alleyway. Glancing back, he saw that a portly, officious-looking goblin in a belly sling had appeared at the gates and was barring Tillman's way.

'I'm very sorry, Mr Spoke, sir,' Cade heard the goblin saying, 'but until you settle your existing bill, my uncle said no more refills.'

'You have explained that the Hive Militia has promised to purchase my entire flock, haven't you, Brinley?' Tillman answered smoothly.

'Uncle says, come back after race day, when promises

become payments . . .'

Cade turned away and entered Fish-Gut Walk.

The alley was aptly named. It was narrow and slippery underfoot, and smelled of fish, rancid and oily. At the far end, it opened up onto the riverbank – a thin strip of dirty sand, lined with warehouses and cut across by scores of rickety-looking jetties, bargeboats tethered to them, and swarming with brawny dockworkers. And, some forty or so strides to his left, rising up from a narrow base on extraordinary buttresses that floated in mid-air, was the Sumpwood Bridge.

Anchored at either end to the river banks, with stairs leading up to a central walkway and buildings on either side, the Sumpwood Bridge resembled a row of mighty skytaverns bolted together, rather than a river crossing. But then this was no mere bridge, Cade realized as he gazed up at it. This was home to the Hive Academy.

The airy towers with their conical light-turrets and gargoyle-fringed rooftops reminded him of buildings back in the Cloud Quarter of Great Glade. And it wasn't only the architecture that was familiar. There was something else about the place that Cade recognized; the robed academics scurrying this way and that, heads down, lost in thought, barkscrolls tucked under their arms, created an atmosphere that was a curious mixture of feverish activity and hushed reverence.

Cade stopped at the foot of the wooden stairs and looked around him. It was almost midday, but there was no sign of either Gart or Thorne.

On the walkway, Hive folk were crossing the bridge in both directions, going about their daily business. Judging by the crowds, Cade guessed that this must be the main thoroughfare connecting the East Ridge part of the city to the West Ridge part. He climbed the sweeping steps that led up onto the bridge and wandered along the walkway, the wooden academy buildings rising up and towering over him on either side.

To Cade's left, the School of Buoyant Materials, its name carved into a broad crossbeam above triple doors, was bedecked with floating statues. Ornate sumpwood carvings of winged creatures and galleons from the First Age of Flight bobbed about at the end of chains that

were attached to every ledge and cornice of the elaborate front facade. A little further along, the broad latticed
doors of the Academy of Water offered him a view of a
small inner courtyard where glittering fountains, spirals
and columns of water – siphoned from the river below –
seemed to defy gravity as they danced in the air. It was
an astonishing sight, and a large group of passers-by had
stopped to take it in.

Approaching the middle of the bridge, Cade came to
two huge archways, one opposite the other, on either side
of the bridge, which served as entrances to narrow pas-
sageways between the magnificent buildings. Set upon
fluted columns, each arch had a large carved eye at its
centre.

Intrigued, Cade went through the arch on the south
side of the bridge, and emerged from the shadows
moments later onto a broad gantry that jutted out over
the river. Leaning on the balustrade, he stared down-
stream, past the bustling and smoky lower reaches of
Low Town and the Docks, where the great city gave way
to lush farmland: meadows, orchards and fields pep-
pered with grazing hammelhorn, truffling woodhogs
and flocks of squabbling fowl.

He turned, crossed back over the bridge and went
through the second great archway. This time, as he
reached the north-facing gantry, the sound of rushing
water became deafening. Looking down, he saw the tur-
bulent river rushing between the bridge supports, while
further upstream, roaring like a wild beast, the mighty

torrent cascaded endlessly through the steep gorge that divided the city.

Cade shielded his eyes from the sun and gazed up at the top of the mountain, where the Edgewater River cascaded over the lip of rock at the top of the falls and came crashing down into the roiling pool at the bottom, spray billowing up in great white clouds. He pulled his spyglass from his pocket, put it to his eye and focused. Panning up the sides of the gorge, he made out the series of wooden beams, as broad as tree trunks, that had been hammered into crevices in the rock face and that zigzagged from side to side, from the top of the gorge to the bottom.

'The "branches",' he murmured, remembering the name Tillman Spoke had given these wooden supports. He swallowed uneasily. Spaced wide apart and with water showering down onto them, they looked as if they would test even the most stout-hearted and sure-footed prowlgrin.

'There you are,' came a voice, and Cade felt a heavy hand clamp his shoulder.

He spun round to see Thorne and Gart standing behind him on the gantry. Thorne nodded towards the falls.

'Checking out the high-jumping course, I see,' he said approvingly. 'It's certainly an impressive sight.'

'Daunting,' Cade replied quietly. 'I'm not sure Rumblix is ready for such a challenge.'

'Remember why you're here and do your best, Cade,' said Gart, smiling. 'It's all you, or any of us, can do.

Talking of which, let's see how much we can raise with Celestia's necklace.'

Thorne smoothed down the front of his old military tunic which, Cade observed, had been freshly laundered and pressed. 'Let me do the talking,' he told the other two.

The three of them returned to the central walkway, and after walking a little further, Thorne stopped and pointed to a building. It was tall and windowless, with numerous jutting turrets and roof-spires giving it a cluttered but imposing appearance. Standing atop fluted plinths on either side of the grand entrance were huge hexagonal ironwood phraxlanterns, bright with dazzling light, even now, at midday.

'This is the one,' he said. 'The Academy of Phrax Studies.'

The glowing phraxlanterns warmed Cade's ears as he passed between them, following Gart and Thorne up to the door. Thorne rapped on the darkwood panel. Before the echoing knock had faded away, the door opened slightly, and a gnokgoblin with small darting eyes peered out through the crack.

'Tradethmen'th entranthe at the rear,' he lisped.

Thorne steeped forward and wedged his foot in the door before the gnokgoblin could close it. 'We're here to see the Professor of Phrax Studies . . .'

'There are many profethorth of phrakth thtudieth,' the gnokgoblin responded irritably, glancing down at Thorne's boot.

'Professor Landris Bellwether,' said Thorne amiably enough, though making no move to unblock the door.

'You have an appointment?' the gnokgoblin said, then sighed, and Cade sensed he knew he was beaten. 'You'll find Profethor Bellwether on the fourth floor,' he said, and stepped back to allow them to enter the hallway.

Inside, Cade's eyes widened in amazement. Although the academy had no windows, the interior of the building was ablaze with light. Phraxlanterns of every shape and size jutted out from the panelled walls on ornate iron-wood sconces, all glowing brightly. And as the three of them headed for a spiral staircase at the back of the hall, Cade recognized the distinctive scent of toasted almonds that always accompanied the use of phrax crystals – as well as the mighty lightning storms that produced them.

He felt a hard lump in his throat. It was a scent he had grown up with: the scent that had pervaded his father's academic robes back in the Cloud Quarter.

The entrance hall to the Academy of Phrax Studies was lined with glass cabinets filled with objects that had come into existence since the harnessing of the power of phrax crystals had ushered in the Third Age of Flight. There were, Cade noticed, models of stilthouse factories and foundries, and skycraft of various designs, from tiny phraxlighters to magnificent skytaverns, every intricate detail reproduced in miniature. Cade paused in front of the last cabinet he came to.

Inside it, the history of the darker side of the Third Age was on display. The weapons of war. There was a range of phraxmusket bullets, some long and pointed, some round, some snub-nosed, some grooved; there were phraxcannonballs; there were cluster-grenades and explosive mines. And, in pride of place, raised above the rest on a crystal stand, rested a single lightly rusting metal sphere.

A PHRAXFIRE GLOBE, the card before it announced. *The first phrax-explosive device to be used in the Edge. Its inventor, 'the Armourer', developed these globes for use by the enemies of the Free Glades. Subsequently, laboratory work carried out on them by Xanth Filatine, High Master of the Knights Academy, ushered in the Third Age of Flight.*

Cade shuddered.

How strange it was, he thought, that everything good that had ever come from phrax power had started off with this single weapon. He found himself thinking of the extraordinary phraxmachine that Thorne had constructed from his father's blueprints, with its four glowing spheres spiralling in orbit around the phraxchamber.

Would his father's invention herald a new age? he wondered. And if so, what wonders and terrors might it bring . . . ?

'Come on, lad,' Thorne called, and turning to see that he and Gart were already heading up the circular stairs, Cade hurried after them.

They climbed the staircase, which spiralled upwards, each flight interrupted by a landing off which long, high-ceilinged corridors ran. Everywhere Cade looked the air was bright – and fragrant – with the glowing phrax-lamps. At the top of the stairs they came to a door. Thorne knocked, and it was opened by a gnokgoblin, identical to the one downstairs apart from a pair of half-moon spectacles, which he peered over questioningly.

'We're here to see Professor Landris Bellwether,' said Thorne briskly. 'He should be expecting us.'

The gnokgoblin frowned, and Cade could see that he too was going to challenge them, but at the same moment there came a voice from inside the study.

'I *am* expecting visitors, Deeg,' it said. 'See them in.'

The gnokgoblin's mouth opened and closed indignantly. Thorne brushed past him, and the three of them entered the professor's study, a brightly lit chamber with sloping ceilings and a varnished wooden floor, where every piece of furniture – desk, chair, couch, chest, bookcase and cabinet – was floating at the end of chains.

A fourthling with slanting eyes, a sharp aquiline nose and a shock of grey hair was reclining on a broad sump-wood couch that hovered in the middle of the room. He was wearing a green velvet jacket and black breeches, but his feet were bare in traditional goblin fashion, while around his neck were several chains, each one with some kind of spectacles or magnifying eyepiece at its end. And lying open on his lap was a large leather-bound book of yellowed barkscrolls.

Smiling vaguely, he looked at each of his visitors in turn before his gaze came to rest on Thorne. 'I take it *you're* Rampton's old militia comrade,' he said, setting the book aside and climbing to his feet.

'First Low Town Regiment,' said Thorne, nodding. 'We served together in the war.'

Suddenly there was a raucous screech from the corner of the study. Cade looked round to see a scraggy-looking bird of prey with a fiery crest and serrated hooked beak launch itself off a floating sumpwood desk and swoop towards them.

'*Thunderbolt!*' Landris Bellwether barked at the creature, and he tugged hard on the leash in his hand. A barely visible silver chain twanged taut, and Cade saw that it led from the leash to a ring secured around the crea- ture's scaly ankle.

Its dive interrupted, the bird flapped in mid-air for a moment, then landed on Landris Bellwether's shoulder, where it eyed the three intruders malevolently.

'Not the most amiable of pets, vulpoons,' Landris commented. 'Or the most obedient, come to that,' and he pulled back the sleeve of his velvet jacket to reveal an angry-looking scar on his forearm. He tickled the creature under its beak. 'But Thunderbolt and I have grown used to each other. Haven't we, boy?' He turned back to Thorne. 'I understand from Rampton you have something that might interest me.'

'A necklace,' said Thorne.

Gart reached into the inside pocket of his jacket for the wallet, which he handed to Landris Bellwether – keeping a wary eye on the vulpoon as he did so.

Without saying a word, Landris shuffled across to his desk, the vulpoon flapping on his shoulder for balance as he did so, then laid the wallet down. He selected a stubby magnifying-lens from the range of eye-wear dangling around his neck and put it to one eye, which he screwed up to keep the lens in place. Then he opened the wallet and removed Celestia's necklace.

Cade, Gart and Thorne watched the professor intently – as intently as the professor himself was scrutinizing the necklace. Landris Bellwether was in no hurry. Slipping the necklace slowly through his fingers, he examined it pearl by pearl, mire-gem by mire-gem: he even spent time examining the gold clasp, lips pursed and brow creased.

Finally he looked up. Cade and the others waited.

'It's certainly a beautiful piece,' he said, stroking the necklace, seemingly reluctant to give it back. He removed his eyepiece and his eyes narrowed. 'First Age, I'd say. From the viaduct workshops of the ancient academies of Old Sanctaphrax. Normally, for such a piece, I would offer . . .' He paused. 'Two hundred hivers. Two twenty at a push . . .'

Cade's heart sank. It was less than half the amount they'd been counting on.

'In normal circumstances, that would be a fair price,' said Landris, nodding earnestly at Gart. 'Even for a historic piece like this.' He frowned. 'And yet for the famous Thorne Lammergyrc, hero of the Glorious Revolution . . .' He turned to Thorne, and the vulpoon on his shoulder squawked as he reached out with his hand. 'Five hundred hivers,' he said, and smiled. 'And that's my final offer.'

· CHAPTER TWENTY-NINE ·

The mattress was soft, the dorm was dark and quiet, Cade had eaten well – but he couldn't get to sleep. Just could not. There was a constant chatter inside his head.

'Balance. Keep your feet in the stirrups. Shorten the rein and pull back into the leap. Avoid the topple . . . Avoid the topple . . . Avoid the topple . . .'

He tried blocking the words out. He tried counting hammelhorns. He tried to hum the lullaby his mother used to sing to him.

But it was no good. Nothing worked.

'Avoid the topple . . .'

Cade's stomach lurched as the image of Rumblix galloping down the falls played out in his head, leaping from ledge to jutting wooden ledge down the sides of the great gorge as Cade clung helplessly to his back. First the stirrups went, then the reins whiplashed from his grasp, and Cade was losing his balance, toppling over as Rumblix and he fell down towards the thundering white torrent below . . .

Cade shuddered, wide awake again. He was clammy with cold sweat. He rolled over, then back again.

It was just no good.

Throwing back the covers, Cade pushed open the double doors and climbed down the ladder from the sleeping closet. It was one of six, set into the copper-wood-panelled walls. Behind three of the other doors, the gyle-goblin grooms – Grint, Grub and Glitch – were snoring rhythmically. Cade padded across the floor to the window, his bare feet feeling the warmth of the stove in the kitchen below coming up through the floorboards.

He looked out of the window at the courtyard below him, where the light of the waning moon was edging the store sheds and cobblestones with silver, and throwing blurred shadows from the prowlgrin practice-wheels. With the very existence of Farrow Lake depending on him, the pressure he felt was almost unbearable.

He had to stay calm, he told himself. Calm and focused.

He stared anxiously at the now familiar wooden contraption, with its water tank and three horizontal wagon wheels. He'd spent hours in the saddle on Rumblix's back over the previous two days, getting both of them used to leaping from spoke to spoke as the wheels spun and the water poured down onto them.

But had it been enough?

Tillman's voice, together with those of the gyle-goblin grooms, echoed once more inside his head.

'*Balance! Balance! Keep those feet in the stirrups. Shorten the rein – no, not too much! . . .*'

They were trying to be helpful, trying to prepare him for what was about to come, but more than once their instructions had served only to confuse him and send him toppling from Rumblix's back into the water tank below. And more than once, as he broke the surface, spluttering and coughing, he'd looked up to see Whisp, the head groom, looking down at him, her head tilted to one side.

What *was* that expression he saw in her clear grey eyes? he wondered. It wasn't amusement, or sympathy. Was it surprise? Or even disappointment? Cade couldn't tell. She had barely said two words to him since he'd arrived.

Pulling on his jacket and boots, Cade abandoned the sleeping chamber and descended the staircase to the large kitchen below. The lufwood blazing in the central stove bathed the saddles, harnesses, reins and halters hanging from the ceiling in a purple glow. Cade crossed the kitchen to the door, opened it quietly, stepped outside and set off across the courtyard.

The air was cold and crisp, and smelled of the rain that had only recently stopped falling. The straw was slippery beneath his feet. As he passed the practice-wheels, he trailed his fingers over the surface of the water in the tank, and shivered. Pausing in front of the open-fronted roost-house, he looked up to see Rumblix hunkered down on his perch on the second storey, eyes shut, and snoring softly.

At least one of us is getting a good night's sleep, Cade thought, and was about to return to the stable quarters when he noticed the lantern glow coming from one of the upper perches. He climbed the zigzag stairs, and found Whisp crouched down beside the old white prowlgrin, carefully oiling his paws.

'Oh, it's you,' she said, looking up. 'You couldn't sleep either?'

Cade shook his head as he knelt down next to her. 'Can't stop thinking about tomorrow,' he said.

'The high-jumping race,' Whisp said softly, turning her attention back to the old white's feet. 'You do realize that nobody's expecting us to win. Either you or me.' She glanced back at Cade and he saw a glint in her grey eyes. 'But we might just surprise a few people tomorrow.'

'You think so?' said Cade. He watched Whisp kneading Dominix's toes with expert fingers.

'Yes, I do,' she said. 'Dominix here is old. My father hatched him out himself in the Gyle Palace stables. Grint, Grub and Glitch were with him too. They took Dominix with them when the revolution came. Settled down here in Low Town.' She stroked the white prowlgrin's flank and smiled. 'We were raised, Dominix and me, side by side in a sapwine hovel in Barrel-Makers Yard. We understand each other, don't we?'

Dominix gave a deep growling purr, and swivelled his blue eyes to look into hers.

'Which is why we're going to surprise them in the race.'

'And what about Rumblix and me?' said Cade ruefully. 'You've seen me on the practice-wheels, toppling from the saddle enough times.'

Whisp looked up at him, and Cade saw that look again. Surprise? Disbelief?

'You really have no idea, do you?' she said, then smiled as she saw Cade's bewilderment. 'No idea how good Rumblix is. He's the finest pedigree grey I've ever seen. He has allowed you to ride him, and now your job is that of any good rider: to accept that gift fully.' Her eyes were bright with passion. 'You were at his hatching, Cade. The two of you have a bond and you must trust that bond when you ride.'

'But the practice-wheels,' Cade protested.

Whisp shrugged. 'They're to build up stamina. Dominix needs them at his age, but Rumblix . . .' She shook her head, her eyes wide with wonder. 'I've never seen a more gifted jumper. And you, Cade Quarter, you understand him. You're just like Dominix and me.'

Whisp flexed her prowlgrin's toes, one by one, and rubbed the minty burberry oil in between them, while Dominix purred all the louder.

'So why *do* I keep toppling?' said Cade miserably.

The high-jumping race was tomorrow. Thorne had entered Rumblix and Cade in the scroll of jumpers and riders that morning; Gart had gone to check the best odds at the betting benches, the five hundred hivers tucked away in a concealed pocket of his topcoat.

Everything was riding on Cade and Rumblix's perfor-
mance. There was no going back.

And yet, however talented Rumblix might be, Cade
still worried that his own inexperience might let them
both down.

Cade stared out across the courtyard, over the rooftops of Low Town and towards the distant sound of the
thundering gorge. Whisp stood up and leaned towards
him, and he felt her breath on his cheek.

'Cade Quarter, you're trying too hard,' she whispered.
'Don't grasp, don't cling, don't fear the fall but . . .' Her
voice softened to a soothing lilt. 'Breathe, feel, and . . .
fly.'

She stepped back and looked at him, a faraway look in
her eye. Cade stared back at her; at this strange fourthling
girl who sounded so much wiser than her years. Tillman
had told him that her real name was Feldia; that Whisp
was just a nickname . . .

'What *do* you whisper to Dominix when you're riding?'
he asked.

Whisp turned her gaze to him, a smile plucking at
the corners of her mouth. 'But, Cade,' she said, 'I've just
told you.'

· CHAPTER THIRTY ·

Cade glanced down and realized that he was gripping Rumblix's reins so tightly his knuckles were white. Beneath him, he felt a shiver of excitement ripple through his prowlgrin's body.

'Easy, boy,' he whispered, patting Rumblix's gleaming grey fur. 'Not long now.'

They were second from the end of a line of shuffling, snorting prowlgrins and their nervous riders, climbing the 'Stairway to Eternity'.

Before the revolution, when the tyrant Kulltuft Warhammer and his clan chief cronies had ruled Hive, these stone steps leading up to the top of the falls had been the final walk for many brave citizens of Hive. The Stairway to Eternity ended at a jutting lip of rock, a place of execution, from which those accused of speaking out against the clan chiefs were 'barrelled'. Tied up, placed in winesap barrels, then dropped into the waterfall, those hapless victims who were not dashed to pieces on the rocks below were used as target practice by Warhammer's elite guards in the Bloody Blades, positioned along the gorge path.

These days, though, the stone steps led to the covered high-jump gantry. And today – one of the two-weekly race days – the sides of the gorge path below were thronging with an expectant and excited crowd decked out in their best finery.

Back near the end of the line, inching slowly forwards, Cade had had plenty of time to absorb the atmosphere. Trogs, trolls, fourthlings and every variety of goblin had turned out to cast their eyes over the jumpers and riders as they made their way patiently along the gorge path and, step by stone step, up the Stairway to Eternity.

Cade's gaze rested for a moment on the goblin matrons in mob-caps waving the wager sticks they'd purchased from the betting benches, and attempting to stroke the prowlgrins they'd just bet on for luck. And on the haughty long-haired goblins in expensive top-coats, who whispered to each other as they assessed the merits of each prowlgrin that passed by them. And once, glancing over his shoulder, he'd seen the huge figure of a Grossmother, her glistening eyes sparkling from beneath folds of fat, being carried through the crowd by fifty tiny, but attentive, gyle goblins.

'Two thousand hivers on Spave and Verginix!' Cade heard her booming voice rising above the hum of the crowd.

The Grossmother wasn't the only one. It seemed all the smart money was being placed on the experienced orange and black prowlgrin ridden by a colonel in the Hive Militia to win. They were at the head of the line and would be the first to jump, followed in decreasing order of fame and experience by the other twenty-one pairs of jumpers and riders.

Back in twenty-first place in the line, the unknown Cade Quarter looked up. He and Rumblix had reached the top of the Stairway to Eternity. Whisp and her prowlgrin, Dominix, were just in front of them. On the slow progress up to the top of the falls, she had glanced back at Cade several times, her face calm and radiant.

'You'll be fine, Cade,' she'd told him, mouthing the words slowly. 'Fine . . .'

But Cade didn't feel fine. His stomach churned, his mouth was dry, and beneath the heavy copperwood helmet his face was bathed with sweat. And all the while, the thundering sound of the mighty Edgewater River grew louder and louder, until it drowned out all other sounds and filled Cade's mind with a numbing dread. Somewhere down there in the crowd jostling around the finishing rock were Thorne and Gart, their eyes trained on the high-jump gantry, waiting to catch sight of him.

He couldn't let them down.

With a twitch of the reins, he urged Rumblix forward. They followed Whisp and Dominix out onto the covered gantry. The air was pungent with prowlgrin breath and toe grease, excited whinnying and low grumbling growls. Over the helmeted heads of the riders in front, Cade could see the bright light at the end of the dark tunnel.

'Colonel Thebius Spave and Verginix!' the jump-marshal announced, and somewhere below, a klaxon boomed.

It was greeted by a tremendous roar from the crowd, followed by cries and shouts, sudden gasps; then all at once by a crescendo of cheers. The line of jumpers and riders took a step forward.

'Rove Duggett and Felvix!'

The roar from below rose again.

Cade and Rumblix shuffled forward, Cade's heart thumping in his chest. He desperately tried to go over the course in his mind, picturing the branches as they zig-zagged down the gorge. On the way up he'd attempted to memorize them all – where the jump was narrow, where it was wide; where it went in front of the falling water and where behind; where it was in direct sunlight, where in shadow; where the gradient increased . . .

They shuffled forward. Another roar. Another step forward. Cade's mind was whirring. He felt an ominous paralysing panic beginning to grow within him. He wasn't up to this high-jumping race. What in Earth and Sky had he been thinking?

He turned in the saddle. Behind him was the last jumper, a broad-faced lop-ear groom in a shabby topcoat and battered helmet. The lop-ear smiled back at him and gave a shrug.

'Don't worry about it, friend. We're the tail-enders,' he said and winked. 'I mean, what's the worst that can happen?'

'Feldia "Whisp" Dace and Dominix!'

The klaxon sounded. At first, there was polite applause and a few shouts – but then gasps and cheers that rose in volume and intensity to a huge roar, which grew and grew . . .

'Names?'

'What?' Cade looked round.

'I said, names?' The jump-marshal, a tall long-haired goblin in a crimson topcoat covered in gold braid, looked at him tetchily.

'Um . . . Cade Quarter and, er . . . Rumblix,' said Cade numbly.

'Take your position,' said the jump-marshal, pointing to the circle of light at the end of the gantry.

Cade swallowed hard and pressed his heels gently into Rumblix's flanks. The prowlgrin moved slowly forward to the very edge of the gantry. Cade looked out through the opening at the great city of Hive – at the tree-fringed terraces and domed mansions of the peaks; the white-fronted clan-houses and clusters of hive-towers of Mid Hive; the jumble of warehouses, foundries and crowded alleys of Low Town.

And, thundering down through the heart of it all, the great swirling torrent of the Edgewater River. Cade felt its spray, cold and refreshing, on his burning face.

What was the worst that could happen? He and

Rumblix could stumble and fall to their deaths . . .

Or . . .

Whisp's voice from the night before came back to him. *You really have no idea how good you and Rumblix are . . .*

'Cade Quarter and Rumblix!'

Cade leaned forward and pressed his mouth to Rumblix's ear.

'Breathe. Feel,' he whispered. The klaxon sounded. '*Fly . . .*'

As if in answer, Rumblix launched himself off the platform to the first branch, a wooden beam that had been driven into the sheer rock on the western side of the gorge. He gripped on with his front paws, then brought his back legs round at an angle, till he was all but facing back the way he'd come. His feet touched down for a moment – then he pushed off a second time, hurling himself back across the void, in front of the waterfall, to the second branch.

'Breathe, feel, fly,' Cade whispered

in his prowlgrin's ear as they flew through the air.

The third branch was wet with spray and slippery, but Rumblix didn't falter. His sensitive back feet gripped the wood effortlessly, then swivelled, and he jumped onto the fourth branch, then the fifth, then the sixth . . .

The twelfth leap meant passing behind the waterfall. For a moment, everything went dark and echoey.

'Don't fear the fall,' Cade whispered, relaxing in the saddle, his heart racing.

They emerged on the other side. Rumblix gripped the branch for an instant, then kicked off again.

The gorge was reaching its widest point, and the leaps between the branches were at their longest. Rumblix increased his speed, zigzagging back and forth across the yawning gap below, while the thunder of the falls drowned out all other sounds.

Then suddenly, in a blur of spray, Cade saw they were approaching the roiling white water at the foot of the falls. One more branch to go . . .

'Fly!' he whispered, rising in the stirrups and feeling Rumblix's powerful leg muscles ripple as the prowlgrin stretched to seize the jutting beam of wood that seemed to rise up to meet them. The branch shot past, Rumblix's toes barely grazing the wood . . .

And they were falling!

Cade shut his eyes and leaned forward, his arms spread as he embraced his prowlgrin. Rumblix's wet fur was soft against his cheek; his breath, hot and pungent, filled his nostrils; and, with his chest pressed hard to the creature's round body, Cade felt his prowlgrin's beating heart against his own. Rumblix shuddered, muscles rippling then relaxing, and gave a whinnying snort of triumph.

Cade opened his eyes.

They were standing on the finishing rock, the white water bubbling around them. They'd made it. And in one piece. Cade didn't know how fast their time had been, but the crowds on the banks of the Edgewater on either side were going wild. Cade pulled off his helmet and looked up at the branch high above their heads, then back down at the rock they had landed on. It was an astonishing leap.

He slumped forward and hugged Rumblix tightly. 'You flew!' he whispered.

· CHAPTER THIRTY-ONE ·

'You did it,' said Whisp, her grey eyes fixed on Cade.

'*We* did it,' he said, and smiled. 'You and me, Dominix and Rumblix.'

The crowd could scarcely believe their eyes. Two pairs of unknown prowlgrins and their riders had taken first and second place. And the timekeeper – an academic from the Sumpwood Bridge – had been the most astonished of all.

He was standing on the west bank of the Edgewater River next to the minute-glass. The tall contraption, with its two long glass vessels set one above the other so that the sand in the upper one would stream down into the one below, gleamed in the sunlight. The flow of sand had been stopped the instant Cade completed the course. Now the timekeeper was examining the minute-glass to make sure he'd read its calibrations correctly.

He had, he confirmed to the jump-marshal.

The twentieth and the twenty-first jumpers had beaten the rest. What was more, their performances had been so astonishing that the twenty-second rider did not bother to jump, but disappeared from the gantry and went in search of the betting benches to lay a wager of his own on the grand jump-off.

This second leg of the competition was a simple race between the two fastest jumpers. It was different from the timed jumps. Instead of completing the course by zig-zagging back and forth between the branches, unable to miss any out, the jumpers were now allowed to select their own individual route down the gorge.

Cade frowned. He and Whisp were back on the covered gantry, sitting astride their respective prowlgrins. Rumblix was skittish and excited, full of energy and eager to jump again. Dominix was breathing more heavily, his tongue lolling and flecks of spittle bubbling at the corners of his mouth. His age, Cade could see, was telling against him, but as he watched, Whisp leaned forward, massaged his great white brow and whispered quietly to him. The old white's eyes brightened, and his powerful legs rippled and braced in response. Despite his age, with a rider like Whisp, Cade knew that Dominix would make a worthy opponent in the coming race.

And that was the problem.

'You and Tillman have been so kind to me,' Cade told her. 'And I know how important this race is to you . . .'

'I have to win,' Whisp said simply, holding Cade's

look. 'The Hive Militia roost-marshal is down there with a bill of sale in his hand. Tillman will lose everything if Dominix and I don't win. I'm sorry, Cade.'

'So am I,' said Cade quietly, thinking of the terrible situation back at Farrow Lake. 'Everything I hold dear is riding on this race. I wish it wasn't.'

Whisp smiled. 'Then you must jump to win, Cade Quarter.' Her grey eyes flashed. 'And I shall do the same!'

'Take your positions!'

The jump-marshal stood by the opening. Cade noticed how the tufts of his hair had been freshly oiled and knotted for the occasion, and the buttons of his topcoat given an extra polish.

Rumblix padded up to the edge of the gantry next to Dominix. And as he looked down, Cade felt a sense of elation, quite different from the terror of the first jump.

The klaxon sounded, and Rumblix and Dominix leaped high into the air. Instead of landing on the branch closest to the gantry, though Cade saw Whisp direct Dominix off to the right, where he hopped lightly down the glistening rocky outcrop, then landed on a branch further below.

'Come on, boy!' Cade urged, twitching Rumblix's reins, and the two of them dropped down to the branch directly beneath them. Then, with a jutting spur of rock making it impossible for him to do the same again, he pulled Rumblix round and the two of them leaped out for the other side of the gorge, the spray from the waterfall splashing into Cade's face as they did so.

From there, he did a second direct drop, then another, then flew back across the gorge – *behind* the waterfall this time.

All at once, there was a flash of white as Whisp and Dominix crossed past them in mid-air. Rumblix landed on the twenty-eighth branch, while Dominix, completing a prodigious jump, landed on the thirtieth.

On either side of them, the crowd on the gorge path was going mad, waving arms, flags, jumping up and down; everyone shouting out the name of their favoured prowlgrin.

'Dominix!'

'Rumblix!'

The mist and spume that billowed up from the water-fall as it crashed down into the pool at its base filled the air. Cade could no longer see Whisp. He could only hope that they wouldn't crash into one another and topple down into the water below. With his legs braced in the stirrups, Cade hunched forward in the saddle, his chin resting on Rumblix's head.

'Breathe. Feel,' he whispered. 'Fly!'

With a burst of exhilaration, he felt Rumblix respond with a sensational leap, down, down, down towards the finishing rock below. He was going to do it! He was going to win! . . .

Suddenly, and seemingly out of nowhere, Dominix soared out of the flying spray across their path. The great white prowlgrin passed so close to Cade that he felt the warmth of the creature's body. Brushing past them,

Dominix landed on the finishing rock, a fraction of a second before Rumblix himself landed – and Cade felt a sickening lurch in his stomach as he slumped back in the saddle.

'I'm sorry, Cade,' Whisp's voice sounded close by his ear. 'I had to do it.'

She twitched the reins and Dominix, his mouth foaming and nostrils flared, leaped across the rocks to the west bank of the river, where the crowd was cheering. Cade stared after her. He could see the race-goers laughing and waving, their mouths open as they bellowed and roared. But he couldn't hear them. All he was aware of was the thundering roar of the falls and its echo – the clamour of failure which pounded inside his head.

He'd failed.

Failed.

Looking up, he saw Thorne and Gart standing on the river bank. Rumblix trotted over the rocks and jumped down to join them. Cade slipped out of the saddle miserably.

Over by the timber platform, the timekeeper was leaning against the large minute-glass, applauding, as goblins in green and gold uniforms gathered around Whisp, Dominix and Tillman Spoke. The prowlgrin breeder was grinning delightedly, but Whisp stared fixedly at the ground.

'I'm so sorry!' Cade began – then stopped when he saw the look on Thorne and Gart's faces.

Gart reached into his topcoat. 'The odds on both

Rumblix and Dominix were forty to one at the beginning of the first round,' said Gart, a frown on his face. 'They thought that Dominix was too old and Rumblix too young. But I knew better. Just one look at them parading along the gorge path and up the Stairway to Eternity and I could see the pair of them were head and shoulders above any of the others in the field. So I split my bet and put two hundred and fifty on each of you.'

'You mean . . . ?' said Cade.

'Yes,' said Gart, handing Cade one of the two wager sticks he was holding, and tossing the other one away.

Cade looked down. *Dominix to win*, it said in black letters.

'Two hundred and fifty at forty to one! Ten thousand hivers!' said Gart delightedly.

'You might have lost the race, Cade,' said Thorne, his eyes gleaming. 'But thanks to Gart here, we won!'

· CHAPTER THIRTY-TWO ·

The *Hoverworm* pitched and rolled. Savage winds swirled around the vessel, howling and roaring like a pack of ravenous whitewolves, while banks of black storm clouds, as tall as mountains, closed in from every direction. Forks of dazzling red lightning split the sky and hurtled zigzag down to the forest below. Thunder followed, split-seconds later and so loud that the trees trembled and the sky pulsated visibly with strange shimmering ripples of energy.

'What are *they*?' Cade gasped, the hairs on the back of his neck standing on end.

He, Thorne and Gart were in the wheelhouse of the tiny vessel, staring out of the windows. One minute they had been sailing westwards into a cloudless sunset. Then this. Hurricane winds, red lightning, thunder – and now these extraordinary rings spreading out across the sky.

'Magnetized air currents,' said Gart, one hand gripping

the flight wheel, the other the rudder lever, as he struggled to keep the overloaded phraxlighter from turning turvey. 'We're in a blood storm, and a bad one at that.'

'Can't we land?' asked Cade desperately.

Gart shook his head. 'In these conditions, and with this load on board, the *Hoverworm* would be smashed to pieces in the treetops,' he said. 'If we could find a clearing maybe—'

The phraxpilot was cut short by a blinding flash of red light that exploded on the starboard side. For a moment it was as though the entire sky was awash with blood. Then waves of magnetized air currents broke over the phraxlighter. Cade felt a strange tingling sensation course through his body. A loud rattling sound erupted at the stern and, looking back, Cade saw that the tarpaulin they had used to secure the cargo was writhing. It looked as if some great beast was trapped beneath and was trying to punch and kick its way out.

A thousand phraxmuskets and twenty-five crates of ammunition were clattering and clanking against one another.

Just three days earlier, the little phraxlighter had steered a path through the crowded skies of the great city of Hive towards the armoury, a vast circular building that nestled in the shadow of the Clan Hall, close to the top of West Ridge. They'd moored at the rear, where they were met by the quartermaster of the Hive Militia, Tove Gripply.

A heavily built fourthling with thick ginger hair and a waxed moustache, he wore a light grey uniform with embroidered chevrons bearing the names of the battles he'd served in. As he greeted Thorne warmly, Cade read the stitched letters – *High Pines*, *The Two Gorges*, *Ambris Bluff* and *Midwood Marshes*. The last one, bigger than the rest, on the right-hand sleeve, said simply: *Revolution*.

'Thank you for this,' Thorne had said as the quarter-master led them inside.

'I hear you're after old militia phraxmuskets, no questions asked,' he'd said.

'You heard right,' Thorne had replied.

The armoury was vast, with phraxweapons of all types hanging from floating sumpwood racks that were anchored to the floor with chains.

'Anything for a hero of the Glorious Revolution, like your good self. And besides,' he'd said and laughed, 'your money's as good as the next goblin's.'

Gart had stepped forward and handed Tove their winnings. After counting through the fat wad of hivers, the quartermaster had stuffed them greedily into his pocket.

'That'll buy you five hundred phraxmuskets and a dozen cases of ammunition,' he'd announced, stopping beside a winch and beginning to turn the wheel.

Above them, a cluster of sumpwood racks had slowly descended from the great domed ceiling. Cade had seen Thorne's eyes narrow and his fists bunch. The fisher goblin had carefully adjusted the collar of his militia tunic, so old and worn compared to the quartermaster's, and then stared pointedly at the embroidered chevrons.

'Make that a thousand muskets and twenty-five cases

of ammunition,' Thorne had said, and Cade had heard scorn mixed with suppressed anger in his friend's voice. 'And I won't rip those unearned battle honours off your sleeve.'

Tove Gripply's face had turned as red as his hair. 'Perhaps I was a little hasty,' he'd blustered, avoiding Thorne's steely gaze. 'A thousand it is,' he'd said, then added, 'Those of us who sat behind desks did our bit too, you know . . .' He frowned. 'And twenty cases, was it?'

'Twenty-*five*,' Thorne had said.

They had loaded the phraxmuskets onto the phraxlighter in bundles of fifty, together with the crates of ammunition, and secured the whole lot with the tarpaulin. Then they'd returned to the prowlgrin stables, to find Tillman Spoke and Whisp waiting for them.

Whisp had given Cade a tub of the minty burberry-oil grease for Rumblix, then knelt down beside his prowlgrin.

'You are the finest jumper I've ever seen,' she'd whispered. 'Fly high and keep your master safe.' Her eyes had filled with tears.

'May Earth and Sky protect you!' Tillman Spoke had called after them, his hand on Whisp's shoulder, as the pair of them waved after the departing phraxlighter.

Now, though, as the force of the magnetic storm gripped the *Hoverworm* and the tops of the Deepwoods trees thrashed back and forth, both Earth and Sky had become suddenly deadly.

A tailwind was driving them westwards across the sky at breakneck speed. The whole of the Edgelands had turned red, with the magnetic currents pulsing through the air and jagged forks of lightning pouring down to earth like streams of blood.

'Watch out!' Thorne bellowed as a mighty ironwood pine rose before them.

For a moment, Cade thought that the *Hoverworm* had been driven down to the forest and was about to crash. But no. They were still airborne, high up above the forest canopy. The tree had come to them.

Gart wrenched the rudder lever to starboard and the *Hoverworm* missed the ironwood pine by inches, only for two more to appear directly in their path. Seized by the powerful magnetized air currents, whole sections of the forest had been wrenched from the earth and yanked up into the sky. As Cade looked around, he saw dozens more of the huge ironwoods hissing across the sky towards them.

Teeth clenched and eyes narrowed as he stared ahead, Gart focused all his energies on steering the *Hoverworm* through this terrifying aerial forest, while Cade knelt beside a trembling Rumblix, enfolding him in his arms. He shut his eyes.

'Earth and Sky protect us.'

Suddenly, from behind them, there came the sound of ripping fabric.

'No!' came Thorne's anguished cry.

Cade opened his eyes. A bundle of phraxmuskets had

come loose, cut through the tarpaulin and, gripped by the magnetized air currents, were tumbling up into the crimson night in all directions. And as he watched, open-mouthed, unable to speak, the muskets were followed by one of the crates of ammunition, bullets scattering to the wind. The *Hoverworm* creaked and rattled as it hurtled on faster than ever.

'We've got to do something!' Cade cried, pushing Rumblix aside and clambering to his feet.

He staggered to the back of the pitching vessel, grabbing a coil of rope from a stanchion-hook as he went. Seeing him, Thorne went with him, taking a rope of his own. They tried to tie down the tarpaulin; to stop the precious cargo breaking free.

But it was hopeless. The *Hoverworm* was still gaining speed.

The sharp-edged phraxmuskets were tearing through the thick, oiled material as if it was mere spidersilk, and hurtling off into the darkness, followed by crate after crate of ammunition.

'I can't stop them!' Cade wailed. 'Thorne, there's nothing I can do . . .'

All at once there was a blinding flash. Then another. And another and another, until the sky behind them was lit up by dazzling splashes of light, white against the crimson, as the muskets' phraxchambers exploded. Then, like erupting seed-heads, the ammunition crates went up, sending constellations of glowing bullets spiralling out across the blood-red sky.

It would have been spectacular if it hadn't been so heart-breaking.

The phraxmuskets they had travelled so far to find and worked so hard to buy were gone. All of them. How were they going to defeat the mire-pearlers now?

In the wheelhouse, Gart stared ahead as the last of the lightning-struck ironwood pines rose up before them. He gripped the wheel with both hands as he steered the now lighter and more agile *Hoverworm* past the blazing trees, the storm-force winds still driving the little vessel on.

Thorne and Cade pulled themselves back along the deck, tore open the wheelhouse door and collapsed inside. The fisher goblin bolted the door shut behind him and slumped forward, his head in his hands. Cade buried his face in Rumblix's fur and fought back his tears.

An hour passed. No one spoke. Outside, the clouds thinned, the winds dropped and the blood storm slowly faded away behind them.

'It's over,' Gart announced at last, his voice bleak. He was hunched over the flight wheel, the lever of the broken rudder dangling uselessly behind him. 'I've never sailed through a storm like it. Not in all my years. It's a miracle our phraxchamber didn't explode like the phraxmuskets ... All those phraxmuskets ...' He stopped, unable to continue.

Thorne flinched. Then, seeming to gather himself, he rose to his feet and straightened his tunic. Cade found himself looking at the faded patch on the sleeve: *1st Low Town Regt.*

'We've had a setback,' Thorne said through clenched teeth. 'A terrible and unfortunate setback. But the fight must continue.'

Cade stroked Rumblix. 'I'm sorry, boy,' he murmured. 'For dragging you all the way to Hive; for making you train, and jump the falls – all for nothing . . .'

'Not for nothing!' said Thorne fiercely. 'Our journey to Hive has taught each of us valuable lessons.' He managed a rueful smile as he reached out and stroked Cade's prowlgrin. 'You and Rumblix here have discovered a courage that will serve you well in the challenges that lie ahead. And you, Gart.' He turned and laid a hand on the phraxpilot's shoulder. 'You have proved more than a match for the worst the sky can throw at us. I'm honoured to have you at my side.'

'And you, Thorne?' said Cade. 'What has all this taught *you*?'

The fisher goblin stared out of the wheelhouse window. He sighed. 'I joined the Hive Militia despite my family begging me not to. I didn't care. I wanted adventure, excitement . . . The war was a bad time for me,' he said quietly, 'but it wasn't the worst. When we came marching home, Hive had changed. Its inhabitants felt betrayed by the clan chiefs and Kulltuft Warhammer, their leader. There were riots in Low Town when news of our defeat reached Hive, and Kulltuft was ruthless in suppressing them. He sent in his guards and massacred whole families . . .'

Thorne paused, his jaw clenching and unclenching.

'My family was among them. I only discovered this when I arrived back, muddy and footsore, from the Midwood Marshes. I hadn't been there to protect them.' Thorne's eyes blazed as he stared out of the window. 'So I gathered my comrades, and others, and I led them all up the mountain to the Clan Hall. We broke down the door and we took our revenge . . .

'The Glorious Revolution, they called it.' Thorne gave a bitter laugh. 'It was brutal, bloody. Kulltuft Warhammer was beheaded . . .' He paused. 'He was dead, but so too were the ones I loved. My family. As long as I remained in Hive I knew I could never move on. So I ran away.'

He turned to Cade.

'Our journey to Hive has taught me to confront my past, Cade. We have lost the phraxmuskets, but we still have each other. You, me, Gart, Celestia, Blatch, Phineal . . . *You're* my family now, and I won't run away – not again. Not ever.'

Gart brought the *Hoverworm* down in a clearing, and the three of them patched her up as best they could. They worked in silence. Despite Thorne's rousing words, Cade was unable to shake off the feeling of failure. Their situation was dire. They had gone to Hive to get the weapons that would have given them at least a fighting chance against the mire-pearlers, but now they had nothing.

Taking to the sky once more, they pressed on, limping towards their destination. The storm had driven them on with tremendous speed, and they were much closer to

Farrow Lake than any of them had thought possible.

'More than two weeks it took us to fly to Hive,' Gart told the others as he pored over his navigation charts. 'Yet we've made up so much time . . .' He frowned. 'We should arrive back tomorrow.'

It was late afternoon when, having flown high over the shimmering green of the forest canopy for hours, the Farrow Ridges came into view far ahead. There on the horizon were the Needles, jagged against the orange sky; there were the High Farrow and the Western Woods, with the Farrow Lake nestling between them like a glittering marsh-gem; and there, the Five Falls, the cascades of water tumbling down from the water caverns like rivers of gold. Cade's heart soared.

He couldn't help it. He was home.

But as they drew closer and Gart brought the *Hoverworm* down low, to conceal their flight in the tree-tops, Cade caught sight of the great black skyship, and his heart sank.

Vast, black and sinister, the *Doombringer* hovered in the sky, moored to the sky-platform at the end of a great chain some hundred strides long. It was shuttered, and clustered around its sides, like suckling woodhogs, were tethered phraxsloops. The sound of raucous laughter and drunken shouts rose from the upper cabins as the skull lanterns outside clinked against the ship's black hull. And there was another sound which mingled with the crew's carousing. A low mournful wailing that came from deep within.

Cade felt the hairs on the back of his neck stand on end. It was the anguished moaning of the slaves imprisoned in the hold. There must be hundreds of them, he realized.

He counted the phraxsloops. There were eight in all, each one capable of carrying – what? Four . . . five at the most. Which meant there were probably no more than forty mire-pearlers on board.

Forty mire-pearlers enslaving hundreds from all parts of the Deepwoods, Cade thought, and every chained prisoner a living testament to lives and communities ravaged and destroyed. The great black phraxcannon stood jutting out from the prow, a black finger pointing towards the open pasture of the levels on the far shore.

What chance did anyone stand against its terrible firepower?

Glancing over at the Five Falls, Cade noticed black barrel-shaped objects stacked on the lip of rock at four of the cavern mouths. At the fifth, the tallest and largest cavern, scaffolding and ropes suggested it was still being worked on.

'Phraxmines!' Gart exclaimed. 'They're after the clam beds. They're going to dam the falls and drain the lake. We've got to stop them.'

'How?' said Cade bitterly. 'If it hadn't been for that blood storm, we might have stood a chance. But now . . .'

'If it hadn't been for that storm,' Thorne broke in, 'we would have arrived too late.'

· CHAPTER THIRTY-THREE ·

C ade took out his spyglass and trained it on the *Doombringer*. As he watched, a hatch on the fore-deck opened, and two hammerhead goblins stumbled out, followed by a tall figure in a crushed quarm-fur hat and a moss-green cape.

'Merton Hoist,' Cade breathed. 'He's alive.'

The mire-pearler chief had a whip in one hand and a phraxpistol in the other. He pointed it at the defiant hammerheads who, Cade now saw, were chained and shackled. Hoist cracked the whip across the backs of the hammerheads once, twice, until they knelt and began cleaning and polishing the great phraxcannon.

Cade was horrified, yet transfixed.

The three of them were silhouetted against the fading gold of the sunset. Then Hoist suddenly turned and seemed to stare directly at Cade. Cade started back.

'Your spyglass!' said Thorne sharply, reaching out

and snatching it from Cade's hands. He nod-ded towards the setting sun. 'The reflection on the glass,' he muttered, closing the spyglass and handing it back to Cade. 'I hope they didn't spot us.'

'So do I,' said Cade, staring down at the spy-glass, shame-faced. He'd been careless. And he hated that. The initials carved in the brass seemed to wink at him in the sunlight. N.Q. Nate Quarter, the uncle he'd never met; the famous descender who now lived in the floating city of Sanctaphrax...

Gart was flying as close to the forest canopy as he dared, weaving a course through the jagged treetops that rose all around them. Beneath him, Cade felt the uppermost branches graze the hull. Roused from his thoughts, he looked up. Immediately in front of him, he saw a patch of forest devoid of trees. It wasn't large enough to be a natural clearing, and as they flew over it, he looked down to see jagged shorn-off tree trunks and, at the centre of them, a deep crater gouged out of the earth. A little further on, to port, was another crater. And on the starboard side a little beyond that, a cluster of three or four more . . .

'That's the work of the *Doombringer* and its accursed phraxcannon,' Thorne commented.

Gart sighed, and raked his hair back from his forehead. 'Somehow, we've got to figure out a way to disable the cannon,' he said. 'Otherwise any attempt to stop the detonation of the caverns will be futile.'

Cade found himself glancing back at the hovering *Doombringer*, his heart hammering like a drum inside his chest as the *Hoverworm* left the Farrow Lake behind and entered the Western Woods.

The three of them stood in the wheelhouse of the phraxlighter. Gart was concentrating hard, his brow creased as he shifted the rudder lever this way, that way, deftly steering the phraxlighter between the angular treetops.

'What we need to do is create a diversion,' Thorne mused. 'Get the mire-pearlers to leave the ship . . . Then a few of us could board the *Doombringer* and put the cannon out of action, while others could scale the falls and stop the detonations . . .'

'This diversion,' said Gart. 'Sounds a lot like the rest of us coming out into the open and asking to get shot at. You saw those shell craters back there.'

Cade shuddered as he thought of Celestia, and Tug, and everyone else back at the hanging-cabin.

'Do you think the others are still safe?' he said, reaching down and ruffling the fur around Rumblix's neck.

'We'll find out soon enough,' said Thorne grimly.

Cade became aware of a change in the pitch of the hum coming from the phraxchamber and, glancing round, saw that Gart's hands were a blur as they danced over the flight levers, slowing the *Hoverworm*, then lowering it beneath the forest canopy.

Looming before them, hidden from view from above, was the magnificent three-storey building that Thorne had helped Blatch Helmstoft build all those years ago, suspended from the horizontal branch of the mighty ironwood pine.

They came down slowly, past the roof and upper storeys, the hammerhead hive-towers and the conical snailskin tents of the webfoots perfectly camouflaged on the ground below. Gart eased the flight lever back, bringing the phraxlighter to a hover next to the under-balcony. Then Thorne left the wheelhouse and hastened to the stern, where he uncoiled a tolley rope.

Before he had a chance to tether the little vessel to a mooring ring though, a webfoot goblin appeared on the boards of the under-balcony. He was one of the burly white webfoots, clutching a loaded crossbow. He stared for a moment at the phraxlighter, his eyes wide and crest flashing an excited orange and red – then turned and ran up the stairs.

'They're back! They're back!' Cade heard him calling.

Moments later, there came the thumping of boots on stairs, and the under-balcony began to fill. There was Blatch, clutching his parchment notebook, the leadwood pencil behind one ear – and Cade noticed the spider's web of cracks that spoked out across one of the lenses of his wire-rimmed spectacles. There were Phineal and Firth, along with the third webfoot, their crests all flickering a luminous hope-filled green. And the hammerhead clan chief, Baahl, gathering his feathered cloak around him against the cold night air as he stepped towards the balustrade and peered into the darkness at the hovering phraxlighter.

Cade stared back, then lowered his gaze, unable to face the look of hope in their eyes.

'The phraxmuskets?' They were the first words out of Blatch's mouth as he stepped forward to meet them. Then he saw the state of the phraxlighter, the tattered tarpaulin and the empty cargo bay, and Cade saw his face fall. 'What happened?'

'We lost them all,' Thorne said bitterly, stepping off the phraxlighter and securing the tolley rope to the mooring ring. 'A thousand of them . . .'

'A thousand!' Phineal blurted out, his crest glowing a sick-looking yellow.

'In a blood storm,' said Gart, his shoulders slumped

as he stepped off the battered *Hoverworm*. 'There was nothing we could do.'

Cade followed him. He'd never seen Gart look so dejected.

'But at least you made it back in one piece,' said Blatch, clapping a bony hand first to Gart's shoulder, then Thorne's, before embracing Cade. 'You must have had quite an adventure, the four of you,' he went on, tickling Rumblix under the chin.

Cade knew that Celestia's father was trying his best to be cheerful, but he could hear the disappointment in his voice.

'And we'd love to hear all about it,' he went on, 'but that will have to wait. As you must have seen, time is running out for our beloved Farrow Lake.'

'The phraxmines,' said Thorne, nodding. 'We have to disable them.'

'That's easier said than done,' Phineal broke in. 'We can't get near the falls. We've tried, and the mire-pearlers' phraxcannon has driven us back each time. And what the cannon doesn't destroy, their phraxsloops finish off. I have lost all but two of my brothers,' he added, his voice breaking. 'And if the mines explode . . .'

Cade stared at the balcony floor, unable to bear the sorrow in the webfoot's face. He knew how important it was for Phineal that the mines did not go off. If they did, the avalanche of rocks would block the falls and dam the river – allowing the phraxengineers to drain the lake and the mire-pearlers to plunder the clam beds. That is when they would discover that the Farrow Lake was home, not only to the clam colonies, but to the Ancient One itself: the Great Blueshell Clam.

'My warriors have suffered grievous losses too, though the hope of phraxweapons coming sustained us.' Baahl's deep voice sounded weary as it broke into Cade's thoughts. 'But now, with no weapons . . .'

Cade bit his lip. Reaching out, he stroked Rumblix's fur. His faithful prowlgrin had done everything that he'd asked of him, and more.

Baahl's voice grew softer, more intense. 'It hasn't been done for generations,' he said, 'but now we shall have to risk the old ways. To call on the deep, dark savagery of the forests . . .'

'Cade!'

Suddenly Cade was plucked from the balcony and enveloped in a powerful embrace. Bottles clinked, and instruments and bundles pressed against his face. Then, just as abruptly, he was released, and looked up to see Tug's great misshapen face smiling down at him. It blurred as Cade's eyes filled with tears.

'Tug!' His voice was thick with emotion. 'Tug! I've missed you, old friend.'

Tug was wearing the apron Celestia had given him, festooned with the glass phials, medicinal bundles and rolls of bandages – and spattered with what could only be dried blood. Cade wiped away his tears.

'Celestia?' he asked.

'Tug take you to her. We been busy. Very busy.'

'Go to her,' said Blatch, smiling at Cade before turning back to the others, his face careworn and grave. 'Come, we must make a plan.'

Cade followed Tug down the rope ladder from the under-balcony to the forest floor. Down on the ground beneath the hanging-cabin, they crossed the clearing, passing three hive-towers, each one heavily clad in the pine branches that camouflaged them, then stopped in front of the fourth.

It was smaller than the others, yet the most ornately decorated. The fish scales, gleaming like oil on water, that were stitched around the frame of the doorway and up the woven fabric of the walls, had been laid out, Cade now saw, in intricate patterns. There were spirals and concentric circles, and parallel wavy lines, depicting the eddies and flow of the Deepwoods river the River Clan had adopted as its totem.

Two hammerheads, fish-hooks on the front of their tunics and nets hanging round their necks like scarves, were hunkered down outside the hive-tower, deep in mournful conversation. At Tug and Cade's approach, they looked up, and Cade expected to be challenged. But instead they rose to their feet and greeted Tug with great respect. Reaching out, one of the hammerheads grasped the corner of the snailskin curtain that hung at the entrance, and pulled it aside.

'Enter, Tug, friend of the river,' he said. 'She needs you. Glave is worse.'

As Cade followed Tug into the hive-tower, the air

inside wrapped itself around him like a heavy blanket. It was hot, an open fire blazing at the centre of the floor, and laden with smells: fish-oil and eel-grease, lamp oil and pungent meadowgrass and glade hay . . . and something darker, muskier and sweet, like toasted almonds. Cade swallowed.

It was the smell of phrax.

Cade kept close to Tug as they crossed the hive-tower. Beyond the bright flicker of the fire, where groups of hammerhead matrons were preparing soups and broths, and on into the shadows they went.

Wounded figures lay groaning on beds of glade hay. The glow of lamplight played on bandaged heads and swaddled bodies; on bloody wounds and eyes that stared unseeing into the distance.

Cade felt a mixture of pity and rage. So much had happened while he was in Hive; so many atrocities that now demanded to be avenged. But how?

'Cade,' said Tug softly, and gestured ahead.

Cade looked, and there, kneeling beside a young hammerhead warrior, was Celestia, her black hair tied back and her topcoat, like Tug's apron, covered in medicine bundles, bandages, and small clinking bottles of tincture.

She glanced up, and Cade saw how worn and tired she looked.

'Cade!' Her green eyes flashed. 'We've been so worried . . .'

The hammerhead beside her groaned and, looking down, Cade saw that his arm was a bandaged stump, and the side of his body was blistered with phrax burns, the skin red-raw and puckered.

'Tug, come help me,' Celestia said.

Tug lumbered over and knelt beside her. Then, with great tenderness, he plumped up the glade hay beneath the hammerhead.

Celestia reached over, unhooked a bottle from Tug's apron and began applying salve to the warrior's burns.

'It's been terrible, Cade,' she said as she worked. 'With the falls being mined, we couldn't wait for you to get back. So we mounted an attack. Then another.' She swallowed. 'The clans were decimated . . .'

Cade saw a tear escape and fall, glistening, into her lap as she continued

to apply the salve. She didn't look up.

'So were the webfoots . . .'

The wounded hammerhead moaned softly. The white bandage wrapped round the stump of his arm was rapidly turning red as blood seeped through the material.

'Scissors, Tug,' said Celestia, 'and bowl.'

Her voice was suddenly firm and business-like. She took the pair of scissors that Tug handed her, then Tug placed a copperwood bowl beneath the arm while she cut through the bandages. The blood flowed freely from the wound.

'Tourniquet,' Celestia said, holding out a hand.

Tug untied a length of tilderleather from his apron pocket, and Celestia tied it at the top of the arm. The blood kept flowing. Without being told, Tug stepped forward and, using a short length of wood, tightened the tourniquet further.

'I don't know what I'd have done without Tug,' said Celestia, without looking up. 'He has a gift.'

Tug grunted.

'A natural healer . . .'

As the bleeding finally stopped, Celestia took a bottle from her topcoat and dipped her hand inside. She smeared the copper-coloured unguent it contained over the wound, then replaced the bandage with a clean one.

Cade looked at Tug, fascinated by his gentle strength as he maintained his grip on the length of twisted leather, while stroking the hammerhead's forehead with his thumb. Looking around, he saw the other injured warriors, dozens of them, bearing the scars of battle in this third age – the age of phraxmuskets and cannon.

He felt a nudge at his side and, turning, he saw that Rumblix had followed him. Celestia had risen to her feet and had seen him too.

'Rumblix, boy!' she said, and Cade saw her smile for the first time since his arrival. She reached out and squeezed Cade's hand. 'We'll catch up, I promise,' she said. 'But first I must get fresh bandages from the cabin.'

She brushed past him, and was gone.

Cade wanted to go with her, but he suddenly felt utterly weary, and the thought of seeing the brave disappointment on his friends' faces again was almost too much for him to bear. He slumped to the floor, and felt Tug's arm round his shoulder on one side, while Rumblix nuzzled against him on the other.

For the first time since leaving Hive, Cade felt himself relax – warm and comforted, hidden out here in the depths of the Western Woods. He closed his eyes. His head began to nod . . .

The explosion was loud and close by. Cade's ears were still ringing when there was another explosion, and then another. Then sporadic bursts of phraxmusket-fire. Cade's hand felt round automatically for the phraxmusket on his back.

From outside the hive-tower, someone shouted a warning.

Suddenly everyone inside was leaving. The fire

was doused. Young'uns were shepherded by matrons. Warriors seized weapons and helped the wounded. It all took moments, as was the hammerhead way.

Cade was on his feet, Tug and Rumblix beside him. The hive-tower was empty. The three of them ran outside, the sound of phraxmusket-fire growing louder. In the clearing, hammerheads from the other clans were pouring out of their hive-towers and silently streaming into the forest. Cade glanced up at the hanging-cabin, and his jaw dropped.

It was on fire.

Flames flickered in patches on the roof, in one of the upper windows, on the under-balcony. Four phraxsloops, each one piloted by a hulking mire-pearler in patchwork rodent-skin longcoats, heavy boots and crushed funnel hats, were hovering over the cabin, while the rest of their crew slid down ropes and entered the top storey.

Cade stumbled backwards in confusion as, from inside the cabin, there came stuttering flashes of phraxmusket-fire.

'Come,' said a voice at Cade's side, and he turned to see Chert, chief of the Shadow Clan, standing beside him. 'We must seek the safety of the forest.'

'But the others!' Cade protested.

As he spoke, he saw first Blatch, then Thorne, Gart, Phineal and the webfoots, together with the clan chief, Baahl, being led out onto the cabin roof at musket-point. Celestia came last, her face ashen white, but defiant. He felt Chert's hand on his shoulder pulling him away.

The mire-pearlers bundled their captives on board the waiting phraxsloops that now hovered beside the balcony, then flew up into the air as the flames took hold of the cabin.

Below, the clearing was deserted. The clans had slipped away unseen. Only Cade, Tug and Rumblix stood rooted to the spot, shocked and trembling, as the magnificent hanging-cabin turned into a buoyant ball of flame before their eyes. It broke the chains and soared up into the night sky, taking all their hopes and dreams with it.

Cade pulled his phraxmusket from his shoulder and pointed it at the last of the departing phraxsloops – only for the clan chief to step out of the shadows, grab him roughly by the arm and yank him back.

'Don't be a fool,' Chert growled. 'You won't be any use to your friends if you're dead.'

· CHAPTER THIRTY-FOUR ·

Cade looked around warily as Chert led him, Tug and Rumblix deep into the trees. It was dark, yet no lamps had been lit. The only light came from the full moon overhead, which penetrated the leafy canopy and dappled the forest floor with pools of silver.

Cade looked at Chert miserably. 'Baahl mentioned a plan,' he said. 'Something to do with . . . with the old ways; with the dark savagery of the forests . . .' He shook his head. 'What did he mean?'

'We must use the power of the Western Woods against the skyfarers,' said Chert curtly. He paused, and his eyes narrowed as he listened intently to the sounds of the forest.

Cade heard the hoots and shrieks of night creatures: the low sonorous booms of tree fromps, a lemkin's staccato calls, the chatter of quarms. Chert's ears twitched, then the hammerhead abruptly turned and strode off down a rock-strewn slope. Cade followed and, a few moments later, caught signs of movement in among the trees. Suddenly he found himself in the midst of hammerheads from all four clans, who silently emerged from the shadows around him.

They were standing in a small glade beside a hollow. Cade heard the sound of flowing water and, looking across the clearing, saw a stream running down through the trees and gathering in a dark, shimmering pool. The wounded had been carried to the broad hollow beside it. They lay on makeshift mattresses of scythed-down weeds and grass, nursed by goblin matrons, and Cade was struck by the fact that the hammerheads barely made a sound, despite their obviously painful injuries.

Further along the bank, a band of young'uns were clustered around the pool, plunging their hands into the white silt at the bottom and smearing it over themselves till they were covered from head to toe. They looked like pale spectres. Then, gathering still more of the mud and dolloping it into buckets, they returned to the matrons, who began smearing it over both themselves and their patients.

Suddenly, out of the darkness on the far side of the stream, two dozen or so hammerheads emerged. Like the young'uns and the matrons, their bodies were completely covered with the white silt. On their shoulders, they were carrying four heavy poles between them, from which were strung the bodies of three-horned tilder.

The clan chief turned to the approaching warriors,

his hands gesticulating silent commands.

Without saying a word, the hammerheads nodded, then crossed to a vast spreading lufwood tree, where they dropped the tilder to the ground. Cade was intrigued. As he watched, they tied ropes to the ankles of the four tilder and slung them from the branches, before cutting their throats and collecting the blood in the buckets the young'uns brought over from the pool.

Rumblix yelped. The smell of the warm blood was making him quiver with hunger. As Cade took a hold of his reins he realized that his hands were shaking.

These must be *the old ways* that Baahl had spoken about. They certainly were savage – though what use this bloody sacrifice might be when the mire-pearlers attacked, Cade could not imagine.

He turned to the clan chief, who had taken off his hammelhorn waistcoat, and was smearing himself with the white mud from head to toe. It had a deep loamy smell, like old leaf-fall and decaying logs.

'The skyfarers have defeated us with their phrax-cannon,' Chert said. 'Now they will want to enslave what is left of the clans. We will offer ourselves up to them.'

Cade swallowed. 'But why?' he asked.

'To take their eyes away from you, Cade Quarter, and your nameless one. We will lure the skyfarers from their ship, using their greed for slaves, while you strike.' The clan chief stared at Cade intently. 'Gart Ironside and Blatch Helmstoft were going to prevent the detonation of the mines which would block the cavern mouths, while

the fisher goblin was going to lead you and Helmstoft's daughter in an attack on the *Doombringer* to silence the mighty cannon . . . Now both tasks fall to you.'

Even as the clan chief spoke, Cade realized how hopeless it sounded. But what choice did they have, with the others held captive? He remembered the look of defiance on Celestia's face as she had been jostled onto the mirepearlers' phraxsloop.

'Rumblix and I will head for the Five Falls,' he said resolutely. 'Tug will board the *Doombringer* . . .'

'And we will provide the diversion,' said Chert. Then,

holding Cade's gaze, he picked up the hammelhorn-fleece waistcoat and gave it to him. 'We go to different fates, you and I,' the clan chief said solemnly. 'My warriors and I in plain sight; you in stealth. May the spirit of the great curling-horn watch over you, Cade Quarter.'

· CHAPTER THIRTY-FIVE ·

As dawn broke, Cade urged Rumblix on, the pedigree grey galloping over the treetops of the Western Woods towards the Five Falls. Glancing over his shoulder, he saw Tug on the edge of the forest behind him, heading off in the opposite direction round the lake. His great misshapen head was bowed low as he lumbered forward purposefully, as fast as he could, his great swinging arms propelling him on.

The fur of the hammelhornskin waistcoat Cade was wearing bristled as if sensing the danger that he and Rumblix were galloping towards. Cade pulled the collar tight around his neck as the *Doombringer*, moored at Gart's sky-platform, came into view in the distance. He thought of his friends held captive on board, and of the brave hammerhead warriors about to do battle.

'Earth and Sky protect us all,' he breathed.

Reaching the bottom of the Five Falls bluff, they

began to climb, Rumblix
expertly judging his
leaps up from outcrop
to rocky outcrop. When
they got to the top, Cade
dismounted.

'Good boy,' he said,
stroking the prowlgrin's
soft grey fur. He knelt
down beside him. 'Home,
Rumblix,' he whispered
urgently. 'To the cabin.
You'll be safe there.
Off you go.'

Rumblix licked Cade's
hand, then turned and
bounded away.

Cade watched him for
a moment, then, crouch-
ing down, he inched
forward as quietly as
he could until he was
able to peer over the
edge of the cliff. Below
him was the first of the
mighty cavern entrances,
out of which a great
torrent of water was
pouring.

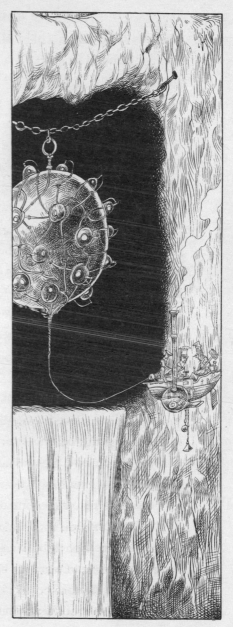

A series of rock-picks had been hammered into the cavern walls, and a chain strung across the entrance. And suspended from the chain was a large black globe, studded with glowing phraxchambers, each one set with a spring-loaded trigger mechanism. A network of cables covered the black globe in a silver tracery, linking the triggers to an evil-looking spike at the bottom of the globe. From the tip of this spike, a single glistening cable led out from the cavern and into the sky, where a phraxs-loop hovered.

There were three figures on board. Dressed in a filthy rodent-skin jacket, festooned with tiny quarm skulls and fromp-tail talismans, one was obviously a seasoned mire-pearler. He held a rock-pick in one hand and a hammer in the other; his funnel hat was pulled down low, almost covering his eyes. The other two wore robes that Cade recognized at once as those of academics from the Great Glade Academy of Flight.

'Three days of hauling all this gear up here, and hammering it into place,' the mire-pearler snarled. 'Not to mention beating off the attacks of the natives of these parts. All you two have to do is rig up a wire! What's taking you so long?'

'I could give you a lecture on the finer points of phrax-engineering, my dear Crote,' said one of the academics, who was checking the cable's connection to a small box with a crank mechanism in its side, 'but I fear it would go over your head.'

'Which is what I'll do with this hammer, smash it over

your head, if you don't hurry up,' snarled Crote.

'We need to be three hundred strides away for safety when she blows,' said the second academic. 'So I'd concentrate on your flight levers if I were you, Crote, and leave the detonation to us.'

'Don't care how you do it, as long as you get this lake drained so we can reach those clam beds – and get out of here.' Crote the mire-pearler shuddered as he glanced back into the inky blackness of the cavern. 'This place gives me the creeps.'

The fur of Cade's hammelhorn waistcoat bristled as he quietly unsheathed the knife at his belt.

Just then, across the Farrow Lake from the direction of the Levels, there came a long, low, mournful sound – the sound of a hammerhead war-horn.

Chert, chief of the Shadow Clan of the High Valley Nation, raised the great curling tilderhorn to his lips and blew once more. Stepping out from the cover of the trees, he began a slow, deliberate march across the marshy expanse of the Levels.

Around him, the warriors of the Shadow Clan marched, holding jag-blade spears, copperwood broadswords and long-handled axes of burnished ironwood. To their left were the warriors of the Bone Clan, walking proud and erect despite the grievous losses they had suffered leading the last attack. The warriors carried thorn-pikes and broad shields of tilderleather inlaid with hammelhorn ivory, their bone breast-plates

rattling as they strode
forward. To the right
strode the clans of the
Low Valley Nation; the
River Clan warriors
swinging their weighted
nets in arcs out in front
of them, while the Stone
Clan whirled flint-
loaded slingshots over
their heads.

All of them were cov-
ered in a thin film of
white, the slimy silt dried
hard now to form a
flaky armour. It helped
to camouflage them in
the bleached marshland
– not that the warriors
seemed to be making
any attempt to conceal
themselves.

Following the war-
riors out across the open
marsh came the shamans
– hammerhead goblins
from all four clans,
in heavy hammel-
horn fleeces, the spiky

fur twisted and braided with totems and charms; skulls of quarms, bones of rotsuckers, carved wooden amulets and painted clay discs. As they walked, the shamans left behind them a strange stain on the marshy ground, pungent and blood red in the early morning light.

The clans advanced, beating their weapons against shields or breast-plates, and giving the barking guttural war cry of the hammerhead goblins.

Tethered by the long chain to the sky-platform, the brooding black skyship juddered into life. Its mighty phraxchamber began to thrum and steam belched from its funnel. It turned in the air and began to move slowly over the lake towards the western shore until, midway, it reached the end of its tethering chain.

The phraxcannon at the *Doombringer*'s prow cranked down as it took aim at the ranks of warriors standing defiantly out in the open of the Levels. The figure of Merton Hoist appeared at the prow and turned to address the forty or so mire-pearlers who had mustered on the upper deck.

'They're making it easy for us,' he sneered, gesturing at the goblins. 'But this,' he said, tapping the barrel of the phraxcannon, 'is a last resort.' He smiled unpleasantly. 'Hammerheads make such excellent slaves – once they've been broken.'

He turned to the phraxsloops tethered to the sides of the *Doombringer*.

'Launch the sloops!' he barked.

With a triumphant roar, the mire-pearlers leaped to it, leaving the deck and taking their places on board the phraxsloops. Armed with phraxmuskets, phraxpistols, phraxgrenades, slave nets and shackles, they were ready for anything the hammerheads might throw at them.

As the phraxsloops set off from the skyship, Merton Hoist's voice boomed out from the prow of the ship after them.

'Take them alive, boys. Every single one . . .'

The seven phraxsloops steamed out over the Farrow Lake, streams of vapour from their funnels trailing back across the dawn sky. Cade crept forward. He climbed over the cliff edge and down the rock face to the arch of the cavern entrance.

Glancing up, he saw that the phraxsloop with the mire-pearler and two phraxengineers was halfway towards the *Doombringer*, trailing the fuse cord behind it. Cade looked at the spike that protruded from the bottom of the black globe. If he could just reach it, he'd be able to swing the globe towards him and cut the fuse cord attached to it. But he'd have to be quick. Setting the bulky hammel-horn waistcoat aside, he clambered down the side of the cavern opening. Then, with a shaking hand, he reached out towards the spike and . . .

'What the . . . !' The mire-pearler's indignant voice sounded from the phraxsloop.

'It's one of the Farrow Lakers!' shouted a phraxengineer. 'Stop him, Crote!'

Behind him, Cade heard the thrum of the sloop's phraxchamber grow louder as he reached out and made a grab for the spike. He missed. Gritting his teeth, he tried again.

'Get away from there!' Crote's voice sounded, blustering and angry. 'Or I'll shoot!'

But Cade knew Crote was bluffing. The phraxsloop was too close. He wouldn't dare fire a phraxmusket, for fear of setting off the explosive globe and blowing them all up. Cade reached out again, and this time his hand closed round the cold, shiny surface of the spike. He yanked the globe towards him and heard the chains rattle as it shifted.

Looking up, he saw that the phraxsloop was rapidly approaching. Crote was standing at the bow, while one of the phraxengineers steered. Tottering on the spur of rock in the mouth of the cavern, Cade held onto the spike to balance himself and raised the knife in his other hand.

With a roar, Crote leaped from the bow of the phraxsloop and onto the black globe, knocking Cade aside.

Cade fell, landing on the lip of rock beside the thundering torrent of water that spewed from the depths of the cavern. The wind was knocked out of him, and his knife tumbled from his grasp.

Crote looked down from the swaying globe and smiled triumphantly as he raised a phraxpistol and levelled it at Cade's head.

'Say goodbye to the Farrow Lake, boy,' he sneered. 'It belongs to us now . . .'

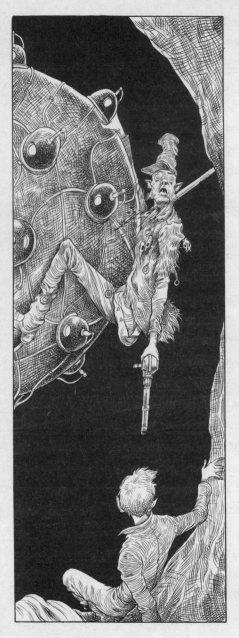

Suddenly Crote's eyes bulged and his mouth fell open as he made a strange gurgling sound. Cade saw the shard of crystal embedded in the mire-pearler's neck.

There was a flash of white, and out of the blackness of the cavern mouth two gigantic spiders emerged, white trogs on their backs. They leaped into the void and landed on the hovering phraxsloop. The trogs skewered the terrified phraxengineers on the ends of their crystal lances and tossed them overboard. Then, turning, they spurred their spiders on, leaping back to the cavern mouth. With a small cry, Crote slipped, toppled from the black globe, and was washed away by the falls.

Cade climbed slowly to his feet. Towering over him was the extraordinary figure of the queen of the white trogs, standing at the entrance to her realm.

Her jagged necklace and crystal crown sparkled in the early morning sun; her bleached snailskin cloak fluttered in the wind, the clusters of snail shells that festooned it emitting their strange flute-like sounds. On her arm was the scrawny cave-bat, while at her sides were half a dozen of her white trog guards, some on foot, some on spiderback. All of them had their long crystal lances pointed at Cade.

'I . . . I was trying to stop them,' he muttered hurriedly. 'The mire-pearlers. We tried to warn you, your majesty. You remember? Thorne and Blatch and me . . . I'm Cade . . . We—'

'I know who you are,' the white trog queen broke in evenly, her painted eyelids flashing like blood as she blinked into the dazzling sunlight. 'And I recall our meeting. I told you that if these mire-pearlers did not enter our caverns, we would ignore them.' Stroking the cave-bat on her arm, she nodded towards the black globe. 'But they *did* enter our caverns . . .' Her eyes blazed. 'And they have paid the price.'

'Thank you,' Cade called back, as he turned away and jumped onto the hovering phraxsloop, 'but the Farrow Lake is still far from safe.' He turned the vessel round and set it steaming towards the stern of the great black skyship in the distance. 'My friends are prisoners,' he called back, 'and I will do anything to save them . . .'

The phraxsloops from the *Doombringer* came in low across the water, the mire-pearlers crowding forward, trailing nets and ropes in anticipation of easy pickings. Their loaded broad-barrel phraxmuskets were levelled at the ranks of the primitive hammerheads, who were standing out in the open, brandishing their own puny weapons: the heavy arms of the Third Age of Flight against the Deepwoods' tribes of the First Age.

It was no contest.

The mire-pearlers were exultant. Here for the taking were more slaves to help dig the pearl-laden clams out of the claggy mud of a drained Farrow Lake. They brought the phraxsloop down lower, until they were skimming over the marshy ground.

All at once, like glade barley cut by an invisible scythe, the ranks of hammerhead warriors fell face-down into the mud. And in the treeline behind the prostrate goblins, following the strange blood-red streaks the shamans had left, a rolling, writhing mass emerged from the depths of the forest.

Logworms. Roused from the depths of the Western Woods.

Pressed flat in the mud, the hammerheads held their breath as the ravenous creatures tumbled out of the shadows and glided over them. Silt-covered, their odour was masked. And so long as they didn't move, they were invisible.

Homing in on the phraxsloops, the logworms abruptly reared up, the jets of air from their under-ducts hissing

as trunk-like bodies writhed and thrashed. One of them slammed into the side of a phrax-sloop, which spun and keeled and tossed its crew high up into the air. A dozen or more log-worms lunged, sucking the hapless mire-pearlers inside their great gaping mouths before they could hit the ground, and devoured them whole.

Phraxfire erupted as the mire-pearlers struggled to defend themselves. But it was hopeless. And in the rising confusion, two of the vessels collided with one another and crashed to the ground. The logworms were on them in an instant, plucking the mire-pearlers from the stricken vessels with a vicious delicacy, like birds picking berries from a branch.

Meanwhile, another of the massive creatures swallowed an entire phraxsloop in one great gulp, stern first. It swelled and convulsed, then, with one rippling spasm, spat out the unappetizing lump of wood and metal, now stripped of its tasty titbits.

Other logworms were less dainty. Frenzy-driven now, and reluctant to expel the two phraxsloops they had swallowed while any delicious morsels might still remain, they constricted their muscles and crushed the vessels, tighter and tighter – until all at once, one, then the other, exploded as the phraxchambers were breached. Scraps of metal and tatters of flesh rained down from the air.

Finally, there was only one of the phraxsloops remaining. The pilot tried desperately to boost the thrust, to gain altitude, to escape the squirming horror of the ravenous creatures – and he might have made it if he'd managed to pass between the two ironwood pines in front of him. Instead, the phraxship became wedged. Screaming with terror, the mire-pearlers leaped from the deck in all directions – and straight into the waiting mouths of the logworms that had swooped in and clustered around the stranded vessel.

Sated, the logworms drifted back into the forest. And then there was silence.

Cade docked the phraxsloop to the *Doombringer*, using a tether ring at the stern of the great black skyship, and climbed a rope ladder up to the deck. Out across the

Levels, the writhing mass of logworms was dispersing. It was the second logworm cascade he had witnessed – this one even more horrific that the first. He could only wonder at the bravery of the hammerheads, who had kept their nerve when the ravenous creatures had erupted from the forest.

So this was the deep dark savagery of the forests that Baahl and Chert had spoken of.

Cade made his way over the deck, past shuttered hatches, towards the prow. He climbed the steps to the phraxcannon-platform, then stopped and gripped the rails for support. The long mooring chain rippled from the sky-platform, sending a tiny tremor through the black skyship. In front of him, a dark shape, stark against the bright dawn sky, turned.

Cade stared at the tall, heavily built figure in the crushed quarm-fur hat and moss-green cloak, which flapped in the wind. Merton Hoist's face was set hard, the grime etched into the lines that crossed his brow and clustered round the corners of his eyes accentuating his grim expression. His deep-set eyes glinted, and his dark beard parted as he smiled, to reveal the chipped brown teeth that looked too small for his mouth.

Around his neck he wore a medallion from the Academy of Flight bearing the likeness of Quove Lentis, the High Professor of Flight himself. The mossy cloak parted, and Cade saw desiccated crests cut from the heads of Four Lake webfoot goblins strung from his waistcoat. Phraxpistols with mire-pearl handles nestled in a broad belt, while a row of leather pouches hung below, containing the spoils of countless other regions this mire-pearler and his gang had despoiled.

Hoist's eyes narrowed, and his smile turned to a sneer. 'You win some, you lose some,' he said. 'A crew can easily be replaced. But your hammerhead friends will pay for their defiance with their lives. My phraxcannon will see to that. But first, I'll take great pleasure in personally skinning you alive, boy, and wearing your pelt as a neckscarf . . .'

Cade boiled with anger. His fists clenched and unclenched as he stared at Merton Hoist's taunting face. And suddenly, he was running, head down and howling with rage. He threw himself at the hulking great mire-pearler. He wanted to hurt him, to *kill* him; to wipe that smug expression from his face once and for all . . .

The blow slammed into the side of Cade's head as, with a dismissive sweep of his arm, Merton Hoist struck him with his pearl-handled phraxpistol. Cade crumpled to the deck. Stars twinkled in spinning circles before his eyes. He looked up to see the mire-pearler towering over him, a filthy ham of a hand rubbing his bearded jaw thoughtfully. In the other hand was the phraxpistol. It was aimed at his head.

'Your lake is mine, boy,' Merton Hoist snarled. 'This is the Third Age, and you and your friends are history . . .'

Suddenly, a great muscular arm slammed down over the mire-pearler's shoulder, followed by another, pinning Merton Hoist's own arms to his side.

His face turned red as he bellowed and squirmed, but the arms around him did not slacken their hold. Instead, their grip tightened, and Cade saw the muscles ripple and go taut with a savage, primordial power.

Cade gasped. 'Tug,' he murmured. 'Tug, you made it! All the way up the mooring chain.'

But Tug did not acknowledge him.

'You made Tug go to sleep,' he growled softly in Merton Hoist's ear. Hoist's eyes bulged in their sockets. 'Now Tug make *you* go to sleep.'

There came the muffled sound of splintering bones. Hoist's face registered a moment of surprise – then went slack. His eyes rolled back in his head. With a soft grunt, Tug relaxed his grip and, almost tenderly, turned and allowed the lifeless body to fall from the skyship, down to the forest below.

'Tug,' said Cade, placing a hand on his friend's great shoulder. 'It's all right, Tug. It's over.'

Tug turned. He was shaking uncontrollably, and Cade saw that there were tears streaming down his cheeks.

· CHAPTER THIRTY-SIX ·

'Hey, Cade! Pass me up that bucket of nails!'

Thorne was at the top of the half-completed stilt-house, tiling the roof. He was kneeling on a crossbeam, a small ball-peen hammer in one hand and a leadwood shingle in the other. Beside him was Tak-Tak, silent for once, gnawing contentedly on a woodapple.

Cade had spent the previous day extracting the nails from the hull timbers of the great black skyship, which lay on its side by the lakeshore now, like some beached monster from the deep. Slowly but steadily, the Farrow Lakers were dismantling the mighty vessel and putting its parts to good use. They had dug a saw-pit in the ground the previous week and, bit by bit, were cutting the huge timbers from the *Doombringer* down to size, creating manageable planks, beams, pillars and joists for the rebuilding of Fifth Lake Village.

It was hard work, particularly with the sun at its

highest, beating down. But everyone pitched in with an energy borne of relief that the battle was over, and a determination that the terrible skyship would never fly again.

Cade grabbed the bucket of nails. Then, using his free hand to hold the side of the ladder, climbed the rungs, past three storeys of unfinished windows, and onto the rooftop. Thorne was halfway up the pitched roof, stripped to the waist, his skin slick with sweat. Wrapped around his head was an improvised sun hat, fashioned from a length of snailskin that dangled down at the back, casting a shadow over his neck. He was whistling to himself. With a soft grunt, Cade hoicked the heavy bucket up and placed it beside him – and hearing the nails chink, the fisher goblin turned.

A broad grin spread across his weathered features. 'Thanks, lad,' he said. 'If you could just get them up here . . .'

With one arm outstretched, Cade picked his way over the beams – taking care not to fall into the gaps between. He set the bucket down and passed a couple of nails to Thorne, who hammered the shingle into place. Cade watched his friend wielding the hammer for a moment, envious of his easy skill, then scrambled up the tiles that Thorne had already fixed, and sat at the top, his legs straddling the top ridge.

The view from the top of the stilthouse was magnificent. And up so high, Cade was cooled by the gentle breeze blowing in off the lake.

Six weeks had passed since the battle for Farrow Lake. The hive-towers that had housed the wounded were empty now, and Celestia and Tug had been able to put away their medicines. The land, though, would take longer to recover.

Behind Cade, the scars of battle were all too visible. It would be years before trees filled the phraxshell craters that pockmarked the forest. Before him, however, the Five Falls looked untouched.

'Thank Earth and Sky,' Cade muttered to himself.

The mines and cables had been removed from the cavern entrances, and the torrents of water splashed down into the lake below as they always had, white against the turquoise water. To their side were the Needles and High Farrow, glinting in the sun. Beyond them the beautiful tree-clad ridges, stretching off as far as Cade could see. While on the far shore was his own cabin, nestling safe and secure in the verdant meadowlands. The lakefowl and wild hammelhorn that had abandoned the Farrow Lake when the shells had started to fall were back now. Their calls, honking and booming in the air once more, mingled with the sounds of sawing and hammering.

Twenty strides or so to Cade's right, a mobgnome, a hammerhead and a woodtroll were plunging long-handled brushes into a tub of slaked lime one after the other, then slopping it on the walls of a newly constructed stilthouse, turning the sinister black timbers of the dismantled skyship bright white. Some way beyond them, half a dozen webfoots were busy securing a platform to the top of newly sunk stilt pillars, one plank after the other.

Phineal was with Firth and the hefty white webfoot, Phelff his name. Of the original party that had arrived on their skycraft, they were the sole survivors. The other three webfoots working on the platform had been slaves, imprisoned in the bowels of the *Doombringer*. One of them was the first slave Cade had freed when, following Merton Hoist's death, he'd hurried down to the cavernous hold, unchained the door and thrown it open.

Cade had been right; there *had* been hundreds of slaves on board the *Doombringer*. They'd been taken from all parts of the Deepwoods, and each had their own tale to tell of the destruction and terror brought to their communities by the mire-pearlers. Thorne, Blatch, Phineal, Baahl the clan chief, and Celestia were all unharmed.

Thorne had turned to the frightened faces staring up at him from the depths of the hold and smiled. 'You are all welcome to make a new home for yourselves,' he'd announced, 'here at Farrow Lake.'

And they had.

Eighteen freed webfoots in all had joined Phineal and his brothers at Fifth Lake Village to help tend and protect the Great Blueshell Clam that lived at the bottom of the lake of this, their new home. A dozen woodtrolls had set to work building a small settlement at the edge of the Western Woods, the round cabins they'd constructed now clinging to the sides of the lufwoods and ironwood pines like woodwasp nests, while an extended family

of cloddertrogs had taken to the caves of High Farrow.
And the rest – a collection of mobgnomes, gabtrolls,
slaughterers, fourthlings, hairy-backed quarry trogs from
the Northern Reaches, as well as goblins of every shape
and size – had begun building their own distinctive
dwellings beside the stilthouses of Fifth Lake Village.
Sunken pit-lodges, stone cairn-huts and long thatched
clan-halls now clustered along the shoreline.

Fifth Lake Village was turning into a town . . .

'I've been giving some more thought to your father's
barkscrolls.' Thorne's voice broke into Cade's thoughts.
'Those blueprints . . .'

Cade turned. His friend was looking at him, his hammer poised above a nail that had been half knocked in.

'That phraxchamber I constructed,' he said. 'The one
with the spheres . . .'

Cade nodded.

'Well, it's still going,' he said. 'That one tiny speck
of phrax crystal that I took from my old militia phraxmusket has been enough to power the phrax force for
. . . what? – nine . . . ten weeks now . . .' He shook his
head. 'Remarkable,' he breathed. 'And I've been working
on the second barkscroll which, if your father's calcu
lations are right – and I've no reason to think that they
aren't – will increase the efficiency of the phraxchamber
fourfold.'

Thorne straightened up and glanced over at the skel-
etal remains of the *Doombringer*. Blatch Helmstoft, pencil
and notebook in hand, was busy directing two burly

hammerheads, who were taking the vessel's phrax-chamber apart.

'I've discussed it with Blatch,' Thorne went on, 'and we reckon that we can use the *Doombringer*'s phraxchamber to build dozens of phrax-force engines, enough to power stiltshops, factories and foundries to provide work and livelihoods for everyone here at Farrow Lake . . .' He paused. 'If,' he said, 'that's the way we want to go . . .'

He turned away, and knocked the nail in flush against the shingle with three short sharp blows from the hammer.

'*Is* it the way we want to go, Cade?' He picked up another shingle tile, another nail. 'After all, we live in the Third Age of Flight. The age of phrax,' he mused. 'We can't *un*learn the advances that have already been made, however much we'd like to. But we can control how they are used.'

'Use my father's invention for good, you mean?' said Cade.

Thorne nodded. 'Just like that accursed skyship,' he said, his eyes glowing with a sudden intensity. 'Think about it, Cade. Instead of destruction, we can build something sustainable – a haven of peace and prosperity, at one with these beautiful surroundings . . .'

'Thorne! Cade!'

The two of them straightened up and turned, to see Celestia and Burrlix, her black prowlgrin, approaching from the forest. Beside them, Rumblix galloped, whinnying and purring with excitement and happiness.

'Fed and watered,' Celestia said with a grin. 'Not to mention well exercised, both of them.' She reached over and patted the pedigree grey prowlgrin. 'Only the best for a champion of the Hive Falls high-jump!' She sprang down from Burrlix's saddle. 'So what have you two been talking about so intently?'

Cade descended the ladder and joined her on the ground. 'The future,' he said.

As if in answer to his words, the sound of a steam klaxon echoed across the sky.

The sawing and hammering stopped as all eyes turned to the horizon. And there, looming into view, was the vast steam-belching skytavern, the *Xanth Filatine*, on its long, meandering return voyage to Great Glade from Hive.

Cade shrank back. So much had happened since the last time the skytavern had visited. Its appearance now took him by surprise. Along with Celestia and the others, he watched as it came down and hovered above Gart Ironside's sky-platform.

Gart was there to meet it, standing by his newly repaired water tank, crates of merchandise and supplies at his feet. The skytavern lowered a pipe from a hatch in the midships and began pumping up water, while Gart sent up crates in the nets that had been lowered. It all took a matter of minutes, while above, leaning on the balustrades and peering out of portholes, the passengers stared down at the bustling new settlement that had seemingly sprung up out of nowhere in this forgotten corner of the wild and savage Deepwoods.

One passenger was taking a particularly close interest in Farrow Lake. When he'd looked out of the porthole in the lower decks, he'd recognized the place at once. This was the sky-platform where it had all gone wrong for him. The place where that stowaway he'd got his hooks into had leaped to what Drax had fondly believed was his death.

His white hair fashioned carefully into spikes and his large pale eyes shielded from the sunlight by tinted eyeglasses, Drax Adereth slowly shook his head. His lip curled.

Because of the stowaway, Drax had spent three months in a cell in Hive. Three months before his master, Quove Lentis, High Professor of Flight, had seen fit to bribe the guards to release him. Three months in which he had nursed his hatred for the young stowaway, whose mentor, Tillman Spoke, had had him arrested.

And now, there he was, plain as day, standing by this miserable excuse for a lake. What was the place called? Ah, yes.

'Farrow Lake.' Drax Adereth spat the words out.

Free at last, he had to report back to Quove Lentis in Great Glade; explain how he'd been careless enough to get arrested in the first place. But after that he would return to this backwater – and when he did, Cade Quarter would not escape . . .

Gart Ironside steered his new phraxsloop across the Farrow Lake, a fluffy line of steam, silver in the moonlight, trailing behind it. The mire-pearlers had shamefully neglected its phraxchamber and flight weights, but Gart had made repairs and managed to get the little vessel skyworthy once more. Now, the *New Hoverworm* flew fast and straight, and with a low, pleasing thrum to its phraxchamber.

As he approached Cade's cabin on the far side of the lake, Gart's expert fingers played over the flight levers, and the phraxsloop came down lower in the sky. He brought it to a steady hover just above the stone jetty, to allow his passenger – a fourthling from the skytavern – to step down.

She was blonde, her thick hair piled up on her head, gathered together and secured with a silver clasp. She was wearing a dark cape made of a heavy material that shimmered in the light of the moon. And as she plucked up the hem and stepped down, Gart noticed that the boots beneath were weathered and worn from long journeying.

'Cade, lad,' Gart called out as Cade emerged from the cabin and descended the steps from the veranda. 'You've got a visitor from . . .' He paused, turned. 'Where did you say you were from?'

The woman approached Cade, treading lightly over the stone jetty. She smiled, her eyes bright and tear-filled as she uttered a single word.

'Sanctaphrax.'

ABOUT THE AUTHORS

STEWART & RIDDELL are the co-creators of the bestselling *Edge Chronicles*, which now boasts sales of over three million books and has been published in over thirty languages around the world. They also created the award-winning series *Far Flung Adventures*, and the fantastic *Barnaby Grimes*.

PAUL STEWART is a highly regarded and award-winning author of books for young readers – everything from picture books to football stories, fantasy and horror. Before turning his hand to writing for children, he worked as an English teacher in Germany and Sri Lanka. He met Chris Riddell when their children attended the same nursery school.

CHRIS RIDDELL is an accomplished graphic artist and author. He has illustrated many books for children including *Coraline* by Neil Gaiman and Russell Brand's retelling of *The Pied Piper of Hamelin* and writes and illustrates the *Ottoline and Goth Girl* series. He has twice won the Kate Greenaway Medal and his book *Goth Girl and the Ghost of a Mouse* won the Costa children's book award.